Prepare yourself for a journey, ~~~~~~ ~~~~~ ~~~~ɔ ᴄxacuy wnat *Three Gates to Hell* will take you on. Unlike many other authors in this genre, Randall breathes authenticity into every page of this story. Even when exploring complex themes like faith and redemption, this story never sacrifices realism or turns a blind eye from difficult subject matter. Protagonist Bob Richards is likely to stay with readers after "the end," as will engaging settings like The Arena. Randall is an author who is going places, and it's a journey readers will want to join him on.

—Vincent Davis
Amazon best-selling author of *The Man with Two Faces*

Three Gates to Hell by B. F. Randall is amazing. I worked in law enforcement for 27 years, and this book gives insight into a life and career that hits close to home. This book realistically peels back the layers of Officer Richards and allows the reader to experience his daily trials and tribulations involving life, family, and career. But at the same time, it shows how God is working each and every day. The more I read, the more I wanted.

—Steven Lambeth
Department of Homeland Security Investigations
Senior Special Agent (Ret.)

B. F. Randall masterfully shares the story of Officer B. Richards and his career. He writes with passion and humor and with the experience of someone who's seen and experienced plenty. He brings it all to life in *Three Gates to Hell*. From the very beginning, this book grabs you and doesn't let go. B. F. Randall gives you a realistic look into the life and career of Officer Richards, and it isn't long before you feel as if you are there with him, experiencing everything he sees, hears, feels, and thinks. If there is one thing B. F. Randall knows, it's how to keep you wanting more.

—Gregory S. Agresta
Martinez Police Department (CA); Chief of Police (Ret.)

In *Three Gates to Hell*, writer B. F. Randall walks you through the journey of Officer Richards and his relationship with God. This book gives you some insight of the daily struggles of our law enforcement officers and how God's hand is at play in even the darkest of times. B. F. Randall writes this story in a way that leaves you eager for more of Officer Richards's story as well as God's story in our own lives. B. F. Randall shows us in this story that sometimes God walks us through dark times in order to bring us closer to him and bring us to a greater purpose in life.

—James Strasser
FCC Coleman, US Penitentiary (FL), Lieutenant

A sustained glimpse into some of the struggles and shortfalls of the modern justice system, *Three Gates to Hell* addresses aspects of law enforcement that many will never see or refuse to acknowledge. This book portrays Officer Richards, a police officer and combat veteran who struggles with the hardships of his past experiences and a challenging career as he fights against evils that exist in our broken world. Through the use of comedy and suspenseful and detailed storytelling, B. F. Randall navigates the true meaning of Ephesians 6:12.

—Travis Whitley
Leesburg Police Department (FL), Lieutenant

Have you ever wondered what it's like to be a prison inmate or to be on the other side of the bars working to protect the public and ultimately incarcerating those who prey on weaker people? Here is a book that opens the door on some of the most misunderstood aspects of society, while showing how God's hand is at work, making a difference in some of the most desperate of situations. B. F. Randall masterfully spins the tales that open your eyes to what takes place daily in communities across America. The impacts of domestic violence, gangs, substance abuse, and crime in general are laid bare, exposing the life-altering effects on all involved in the drama. This isn't just a book about crime and justice; more importantly, it is a book about God's work through people as they grow and age, gain experience and wisdom, and maybe most importantly, learn that God is still in charge. I found this to be a compelling read and hard to put down.

—Jan Makowski
Vacaville Police Department (CA), Lieutenant (Ret.)

Joy, frustration, anger, fear, hate, love, peace, and redemption—these are mirror words describing human emotions. But when woven carefully through a story they become the sinew that binds you to the very body of it. B. F. Randall is able to extract these emotions from the reader as he pulls you right into the situation as experienced by the characters. It grabs you from the beginning and never lets go. So, strap in for a great read! You won't be disappointed.

—Brad M. Maty, SMSgt, USAF (Ret.)

THREE GATES TO HELL

Hell's Detours Can Lead to Heavenly Destinations

Nancy + Aaron
Bless ya,

B. F. RANDALL

B F Randall

Ps 121:7-8

IRON STREAM FICTION

An Imprint of Iron Stream Media
Birmingham, Alabama

Three Gates to Hell

Iron Stream Fiction
An imprint of Iron Stream Media
100 Missionary Ridge
Birmingham, AL 35242
IronStreamMedia.com

Library of Congress Control Number: 2023938137

Cover design by Hannah Linder Designs

ISBN: 978-1-56309-644-0 paperback
ISBN: 978-1-56309-645-7 eBook

1 2 3 4 5—28 27 26 25 24

To Roberta, my editor, muse, best friend, and so much more.

To those who must stand blameless in the throes of adversity, who are the first we call, and the last we thank. To the men and women who, each day, face what most will never experience in a lifetime and are the first to run toward what the rest of us will run from. Thank you!

CHAPTER ONE

Refreshed from a moment of reflection, watching the sun set on San Francisco Bay, I ascended the wraparound steps on Arsenal Tower and was met by a young trainee on the upper landing. His spit-shined boots and immaculately tailored uniform spoke volumes of his expectations and lack of experience.

"Chaplain Richards? Chaplain Bob Richards?"

"That's me." I smiled.

"I'm Cadet James Kilpatrick. I have a message for you from Assistant Warden Halbrook." He handed me a sealed envelope.

He stood for a moment as if I was to either thank him or tip him, then turned quickly, "Have a good evening, sir," and disappeared through a large wooden door with a sign over it that read: "Office of Warden Earl Kilpatrick."

If nepotism stays in vogue, I had a feeling I may have just met the young man who would one day be my boss.

Running a bit late, I tucked the envelope into my coat pocket and crossed over to the upper landing that led to the main entrance. That first glimpse of "the Arena"—a name the inmates had given to San Quentin State Prison—always made me shudder. The hundred-and-sixty-year-old block and stone walls gave it the appearance of a medieval castle that reminded me that I was about to be transported into a different world.

Within these walls is a world where tomorrow holds little hope, and where routine seamlessly blends days, months, and years into one another. Those who reside here measure the passing of time only by the aging of their own reflection.

I have been working here as a chaplain's assistant for nearly four years, and nothing, as of yet, has become routine for me. Each time I enter this mausoleum of the living dead, I encounter a new face with a tragic past, and an even less promising future. My job is to meet the "new fish," those entering the state penal system for the first time, and introduce them to the services of the chaplaincy.

Clipping my ID onto the leather lanyard my wife, Rosie, made for me for our anniversary, I greeted the guard at the entrance and walked into the general office building that consisted of a maze of long hallways and countless wooden doors in desperate need of fresh paint. At the end of a narrow corridor, two huge metal green doors opened into what was once a gymnasium, but now was adorned with wood and glass partitions. It provided workspace along the walls for middle management with a clustering of clerical cubicles in the center.

Senior Chaplain Howard Hays greeted me warmly by name, and I returned the same greeting to him.

Standing, I thumbed through the notes and letters on the top of my desk. I shared the desk, two filing cabinets, and a pole lamp Thomas Edison used, with two other chaplains in a ten-by-ten glass work booth. We were all volunteers and worked on different days and at different times, so the space was more than adequate.

"Have you read the note from the warden's office?"

"No, sir, not yet."

"Let me suggest you take the time to do that," Chaplain Hays said, more as a directive than a suggestion.

"Yes, sir." I dropped the mail on the desk and removed the envelope from my pocket.

I read it. And a second time, slowly, taking in each word. A feeling of wonder mixed with dread swept over me. It has been more than fifteen years, yet the ghosts of my past continued to haunt me.

I stammered, "Sir, I can't do this."

Hays stood silent, his steel gray eyes performing laser surgery on the inner recesses of my heart. "Why?"

"Well, for one thing, I'm not cleared to enter the Adjustment Center."

Following the California Supreme Court's decision in 1978 to reinstate the death penalty, and the fact that San Quentin was the only prison where executions took place in the state, the "row" had experienced a population explosion. What had been a single block of cells reserved for inmates on death row, was now three separate sections, each with its own designation—"North-Seg," or "the North Segregation Unit," the least populated section; East Block, with the largest number of prisoners; and "the Adjustment Center," better known as "the Hole." Here condemned inmates were held in isolation, behind solid steel doors because of their volatile and violent behavior. Under the attentive eyes of the guard towers, prisoners in the Hole were allowed only a limited amount of time outdoors to exercise in individual eight-by-ten-foot chain-link cages.

"Bob, I spoke with Assistant Warden Halbrook about this, and he has given you clearance to enter the AC." Hays crossed his arms and smiled.

I shook my head. Great, it appears God wanted me to have an adjustment of my own.

"Sir, I'm sorry. I don't want to do this, and you know why."

"I understand, but this may be why you're even here." Hays stepped around the desk and placed a hand on my shoulder. "I want you to take the next couple of days off and go away, spend some quiet time with God, and work this out in your heart. Finish your rounds and go home." He nodded toward the door. "I'll see you Thursday."

"Yes, sir."

I glanced at the window behind Hays. The evening sky had taken on a golden glow with the sun drifting below the horizon. Although I stood in the center of some of the most hostile real estate in the country, the scattering of the sun's rays created an atmosphere that was warm and inviting. It was nice, but it wouldn't last. Clearing the steel door into South Block, the usual mayhem vented from cells on every tier dispelling the pleasant yet fleeting ambiance.

I ascended the narrow metal stairwell to the third floor and was granted access to the tier by a sour overweight guard whose crumpled uniform shirt was partially untucked. Some of the guards are antagonistic toward the chaplaincy; they see it as codling the inmates, and a nuisance to deal with.

Most of the prisoners accept us. For some, though, we're a tool to manipulate. The Bibles and reading material we

4

provide are used for cigarette paper, chapel services are just another way to get out of their cells, and a profession of faith in God looks good to the parole board.

But some lives have been radically changed, and those new believers work to help improve the lives of those around them. This was not the case for the man I was about to meet, Big Jim Perez.

Jim was a lifer whose death sentence was commuted in 1972 when the Supreme Court temporarily ruled that capital punishment was unconstitutional. He had been convicted in Los Angeles and sentenced to death in 1965 for the beating deaths of four rival gang members. Among his victims were a woman and a boy of sixteen. After being transferred from death row to the main population, he spent his first five years in solitary confinement for assaulting two guards, one of which he put in the hospital. Since moving back into general population, Perez had made few friends because almost everyone feared him, including guards. Today, I came to tell him that his mother—the only one who visited him, called him, or sent him mail—had died.

I walked along the tier past sixty-five four-by-eight-foot cells to Perez's cell, the last on the row. Above the windows opposite the row, two guards—one armed with a 12-gauge shotgun, loaded with 7.5 buckshot, and the other with a 9mm carbine rifle—walk back and forth with a clear view of every cell.

When I neared his cell, he stuck a mirror between the bars to see who approached.

"I need to talk to you."

"Yeah." Jim grunted and turned away from the bars.

"I don't know how to break this to you. I have some very sad news." I stopped outside his cell and leaned against the rail, trying to judge if I was out of Jim's reach and glancing around for an escape route.

"I know . . . I know what it is." He looked back at me.

I expected to see fire in his eyes, but instead I saw tears. Dropping onto his bunk, he put his face in his hands, and his body convulsed. I wanted to say something that would bring some peace, but nothing could be said. This wasn't a time for words.

After several minutes he took a deep breath and leaned back against the wall. In front of him, taped to a cardboard box on a shelf, was a photo of an elderly woman with a pink crown and a broad smile sitting at a table behind a candle-covered birthday cake.

"Is she in your heaven?" Jim asked.

"From what you have told me about her faith in God, I can guarantee it."

"Will I ever see her again?"

"I think that's really up to you."

"I've done some bad stuff, some really bad stuff." Perez racked his hands over his face. "I don't think your God can forgive me."

"He's not just my God. He is everyone's God. His love for you is bigger than what you have done." I pushed off the rail, took a step toward the cell door, and glanced over my shoulder at the guards. "The question isn't if God can forgive you, it's can you forgive yourself and accept the love and forgiveness God has for you? He sent His son to die for . . ."

"Yeah, I know. I've heard it all my life. My mother preached it at me every day. That's one of the reasons I hit the streets at fourteen. I didn't need it then, and I don't need it now."

"Okay." I stepped back. "Is there anything I can do for you, maybe contact your family?"

"No. I haven't heard from them in twenty years. They stopped talking to me when I got arrested."

I placed a small devotional that had been written by another inmate housed on death row, along with a copy of the book of John, on the bars. "I'm here if you want to talk."

I waited a couple minutes, and with no response, I knew it was time to leave. On my way out, I stopped to talk to a few others and looked back in time to see Big Jim's bear-like paws take the books.

Walking back through the Upper Yard, I went around the North Block toward the chapel. The bright wash of the security lights amplified the presence of the Adjustment Center, bringing me back to the note I had received from Assistant Warden Halbrook.

Chaplain Hays said I needed to work it out in my heart. Really? Why?

Telling me that the contents of the note may be the very reason God put me here could be true, but it could also just be a way to spiritually strong-arm me. I wonder if Hays would think differently if he had traveled the same road I had, one filled with potholes, detours, and dead ends.

I sat on a bench that faced the AC, with no one around and only the muffled sound of a chorus of voices emanating from the blocks. Landscapers had placed rolled turf, planter boxes, an assortment of small trees, and a fire pit that had never been lit. A comforting sight for those who needed some relief, like me at the moment. I held Warden

Halbrook's envelope out in front of me and looked up. "Is this your idea? Is this some kind of test?" Crushing it tightly in my fist, I closed my eyes and prayed, "Lord, if this is part of your plan, you're going to have to show me."

In the moonless night the rhythmic pounding of the waves could be heard in the distance as the wind increased off the Bay, bringing with it a light mist of brine leaving its smell and salty taste in the air.

"Lord, help me . . ." I whispered and let my mind drift into the recesses of the past, like an abandoned ship adrift in a sea of reflection.

CHAPTER TWO

The darkness engulfed me like a warm blanket as my glasses fogged over from the damp morning air. I tilted my head out the window and listened intently into the night for any sound of movement, a car, voices, a dog in the distance, anything. There was nothing, not a bird, not even a breeze. The silence felt tangible. I was alone, totally alone, parked snugly behind the right rear corner of Dee's Country Store, Tow, and Flying 'A' Station.

Dee was a sweet old lady who took over the store when her parents died in a traffic accident. She was just seventeen. There was nothing out here then, just a long strip of dirt road. When I first met her, the county was preparing to pave the road. She told me that when they finished the project, the peace and quiet would soon be gone. She was right.

Twenty years ago, her sons convinced her to add the service station, which they would run and manage, and recently her grandsons added the tow service. It was a good move to diversify because the area had built up quickly. Across the street a new Safeway Store with a full-service deli opened and a 7-Eleven was being built next to it. It was understood by all who worked on the southside, that whenever possible, get your coffee and gas fill-up at Dee's.

Pulling down the flex light on the dash, I shuffled through my briefcase for an incident report and an arrest report. Securing each to a clipboard, I began to write the ongoing saga of Marylou Carmichael and her ever abusive husband, Carl. It was a weekly ritual that played like a bad B movie. Every Friday Carl would get paid, spend four or five hours at a local pub, go home, and take the week's frustrations out on Marylou. This time, however, Carl forgot to put the bottle down before he demonstrated his male superiority over Marylou's towering five-foot-one physique.

She was safe now in her own bed at Montgomery General, and he was safe also in his own bed in Alameda County's lockup. I had lost count of the Friday nights I had been called to their home, only to find Marylou in tears with a swollen eye or bloodied lip. Each time I booked Carl into county jail, he would be back on the street the next morning. Marylou just couldn't bring herself to press charges. Hopefully this time would be different.

A quiet night like this was a good time to catch up on some work and make up a couple of incident and arrest reports for the next few Friday night visits to the Carmichael household. As I began to pen a few words, I heard a strange sound in the distance. It sounded like hammering. Who would be hammering at four in the morning?

I shut off the dash light and sat listening to the rhythmic pounding coming from across the street. Holding the door with my right hand and pulling on the latch with the other, I pushed the door open slowly, swinging my legs out. Stepping clear I let the door gently close and moved along the dark side of Dee's store to get a clear view of the construction site across the street. The pounding continued, but

I didn't detect any movement. Nothing seemed to be out of place.

I turned back toward the car when my brain whispered, "Did you see it?" Yes, I did.

With my back against the wall and staying in the shadows, I moved slowly toward the street to get a better view. Removing my glasses, I peered into the darkness. There, on the roof of the Safeway, silhouetted by the city's horizon lights, were two figures bent over what appeared to be a box. Within a minute both figures disappeared.

Returning to the car, I picked up the mic and turned down the volume on the Motorola. "Xray-12 to Dispatch."

X, or Xray, is the designation for the graveyard shift. A, or Alpha, was dayshift, 8:00 a.m. to 4:00 p.m., and B, or Bravo, was swing shift, 4:00 p.m. to midnight. There were other designations for Administration, Investigation, and so on, but A, B, and X are the worker bees of the department. The number that followed references the specific beat area that unit was responsible for. The city was broken up into three districts, each having twelve beats, and the size of each was determined by population and crime rate.

"Go ahead, Xray-12," came the response.

"I may have a four-five-nine in progress," I said. "Check the emergency call sheet for the Safeway on Alhambra Avenue, and call and ask if they have anyone doing work there this morning."

"Ten-four, Xray-12. Need cover?"

"Negative." I didn't want the whole Southside to roll in. "Xray-7, you awake?"

"Wide awake, what do ya got?" came the gravel voice of Alford Jackson, better known as A. J., who remembered when this area was nothing but fruit trees and dirt roads. He was the oldest of us working the Southside graveyard shift, and we were all glad to have him. There were very few like A. J., having the knowledge, experience, and ability to handle just about any situation, and still willing to work graveyard. He could have retired anytime in the last five years, or by seniority chosen a day shift position with weekends off, but not A. J.

"I may have a couple guys shopping at the Safeway Store. It looks like they may have decided to go through the roof instead of the front door. I'm behind Dee's. Come in off the old Ranch Road."

"On my way, be there in five." He grumbled.

"Xray-12." The Motorola popped. "Contacted the manager, says there's no maintenance or work being done, and no one is supposed to be there until 6:00 a.m. He's en route with a key. Said he would meet you in the field behind the store."

"Ten-four." I sighed. "Is there still a K9 unit on shift?"

"Xray-12, I'm en route. ETA about ten," said Gary Alison, one of the best K9 handlers in the county. "Meet ya behind Dee's."

I confirmed by keying the mic twice, then retrieved the compact binoculars from the glove compartment. I went back into the dark side of Dee's and scanned the roofline, building, and parking lot of the Safeway. There was no movement, but there was an old Chevy pickup parked on the left side of the building, facing out toward the street. A slight puff of smoke formed around the back of the truck. It was running. After several minutes I heard the crunch of gravel under car tires and saw A. J. followed by a K9 unit, all with lights out.

"What's up?" asked A. J.

"I counted two on the roof. I think they dropped down inside. There's a pickup on the left side, running. I can't tell if there's anyone in the driver's seat."

Standing in the shadow I pointed out the truck, "A. J., can you take care of the truck and come up on that side?"

"Affirmative."

"I've been through the store before when their alarm system was acting up. I saw the two disappear in the area over the office. There's a safe in there. I'll work my way around to the right side. Gary, hustle over to Beasley Avenue. It runs along behind the store. The manager will meet you there. Get the key, and drive across the field. We'll let you know when we've cleared the truck and sides of the building. Then let Turk in the back to do his job."

Without a word, Gary returned to his K9 unit and disappeared along Ranch Road. A. J. just disappeared. I didn't even see him leave. Removing the 12 gauge from the dash mount, I secured my car and began to run silently along the drainage ditch that ran parallel to the street. When I knew I couldn't be seen from the store, I crossed over the street and worked my way through the trees and underbrush until I was looking at the side of the Safeway. Scanning the roof and seeing no movement, I stepped out of the tree line and moved first to the side of the building, checking the doors. All were locked.

When Gary arrived at the rear of the building, I returned to the front corner. A low gravely whisper cracked over my portable radio, "Xray-7, I have one WFA in custody." A. J.

referred to the occupant of the truck as a white female adult. "Gary, is your unit in the back."

"Affirmative," Gary replied quietly.

"Good. I have some company for Turk." After a couple of minutes A. J. said, "Back in position. Gary, let Turk go to work, then park against the rear door so they can't get out."

"Ten-four."

Within moments Turk could be heard barking, followed by two high-pitched screams. Moving up enough to peek through the corner of the front window, I saw two bodies dashing haphazardly across isles and over counters. One vanished among display cases, and the other leaped behind a checkout counter.

With a growl Turk jumped onto the top of the counter and stood motionless like the statue of an old Civil War general. His teeth were bared and eyes intently focused as he snarled at a whimpering figure drawn up tightly in the fetal position on the floor.

My peripheral vision caught movement along the inside wall just below the window where I was standing. Stepping back slowly into the darkness, I watched as a lone figure crawled to the door. Remaining as low as he could, he reached up and unlocked the door. Pushing it open, he crept out on his belly, looking over his shoulder to see if the beast that cornered his partner was on his trail.

Just as he cleared the door, he began to rise to his feet, when I stepped from the shadows and racked a round into the shotgun. "Freeze." And freeze he did, all but his bladder.

"I'm coming around, Bob. Doing some late-night shopping are ya? Stay on your knees. Hands on your head." Bending over he pulled the suspect's hands behind him, cuffed him, and began patting him down. "The woman in the truck said there were just two guys in the store."

Looking up at me with a wide-eyed expression, A. J. gripped the collar of our shopper's shirt and lowered him face down onto the concrete. Reaching up under the hem of his shirt he withdrew a loaded .45-caliber Colt, Model 1911, and an additional clip from his back pocket.

"Gary, standby," I said into my portable radio. "We have one in custody outside, he's packing. The other may be armed too. A. J.'s coming in from the front to assist."

"Ten-four. Turk's keeping the other one company, and from the look of him, he isn't planning on moving anytime soon." Came the response.

A. J. brought out the other suspect and put him on the ground with his partner, while Gary let Turk clear the rest of the building.

"Xray-12 to Dispatch, we need transportation for two WMA and one WFA, in custody at the Safeway on Alhambra."

"Ten-four, Xray-12, en route," was the response.

Within ten minutes our guests were on their way to their new lodging, and we were surveying the damage they left behind. Except for some pry marks on the safe, a broken skylight, and a couple rows of chips and cookies scattered about, it was in good shape. The only real loss was a two-pound filet that found its way into the back of the K9 wagon. The store manager said it seemed like a fitting reward, as he handed the package of prime to Gary.

We gathered in the front parking lot and filled in the responding crime scene tech. It was determined that each of us would get a collar and write our own arrest report. Since

I originated the call, I would be responsible for the burglary report. It was going to be a long morning.

"I saw Dee's Pinto station wagon out front. She usually isn't open yet, but maybe we can grab some coffee."

The aroma of sweet rolls and coffee welcomed us warmly into Dee's little store. "Good morning, boys," Dee called from the back room. "I saw all the commotion across the street, so I figured I'd be seeing you early this morning. Lock the front door and have a seat. I'll have your coffee and rolls up in a bit." Within a few minutes we were tasting a bit of heaven and sharing the events of the morning with a wide-eyed, petite lady who was as sweet as her rolls.

CHAPTER THREE

The dayshift briefing was short and routine while we sat in the squad room. Sergeant Tom Alan went over what took place the night before but for some reason left out the Safeway burglary. As he concluded handing out warrant packets and addressing the various things to be on the alert for, he stepped away from the podium as Lieutenant Steven Miller, shift commander, walked in from the side door.

"Good morning." Alan smiled. "An excellent job was done this morning by three of our officers. Officers Bob Richards, Alford Jackson, and Gary Alison. They observed and arrested three professional burglars making a rooftop entrance to the Safeway Store on Alhambra."

He pointed at me. "Good job." Several officers turned and gave me a thumbs-up.

"Those arrested were Willy Johnson, his wife, Carol Johnson, and Curtis Mitcham. The Johnsons are three-time losers who got hooked up with Mitcham because Carol worked at the Safeway Store and knew the layout. She and her old man aren't going anywhere. They don't have the connections or resources to bail out."

The lieutenant put a booking photo up on the screen. I recognized one of the people as the fellow who had a bladder problem earlier today. "Mitcham, on the other hand, is a different story. He's part of the Savages motorcycle club and is being looked at as the primary suspect in the assassination of two rival gang members in Phoenix. Intelligence Division says he's a big moneymaker and enforcer for the club."

"Good to have him off the street," one of the officers said.

"That's the problem." Miller frowned. "He's being discharged right now." A collective groan resonated through the room. "His attorney was at the gate before his booking was done with a release order from a federal court judge. Seems he's working with the Feds on some interstate thing. I called Phoenix PD to see if they could put a hold on him for their case, but they don't have enough yet."

"Any time line on when Phoenix may go to warrant?" I asked.

"No, Bob, but they assured me that they would notify me personally." After a long pause he said, "There's something else. While he was in lockup, he was going off about taking care of the one who brought the cops down on him. He was making all kinds of threats."

"Threats are a norm in lockup, LT. If he feels froggy, let him jump. Then maybe we can put him away for good."

"This guy is dangerous. Don't underestimate him, or those he hangs with. Truth is, I have no problem with him facing up to any one of you, but his threats weren't aimed at you. When they were taking him away at the scene, he saw the old lady who owns Dee's store standing out front and one of our police cars at the back corner. He thinks she called us."

Turning to Sargent Alan, "I want extra patrols around the clock on that little store. I've called Concord PD about keeping an eye on her house." Tapping the screen for emphasis, Miller said, "Don't forget that face. You're dismissed."

On the way home I made a slight detour to stop by Dee's old store. Pulling my canary yellow, 1972 Dodge Charger R/T up to the gas pump, I could almost hear every one of the 440 cubic inches say, "I'm thirsty." This chunk of metal eats and drinks more than all three of my sons put together.

"Sweet ride, Officer," came a voice from the garage. "When are you going to let me tweak it up a bit?" John Steller, Dee's eldest son, walked over and reached for the pump lever. He was a good man and a good mechanic, and if I really needed work done, he would be the one to do it.

"Not now, John, but I'll keep ya in mind."

"I assume you don't put anything but High Test in this buggy."

"You got it. Last month I was choking on thirty-nine cents a gallon, but this recent spike to fifty-five cents is killing me. If I didn't know better, I'd think there was a hole in the tank."

He held the pump nozzle in the air like a handgun. "There is, it's called a four-barrel carburetor. I hear it could be as much as seventy-five cents by this time next year." With a big smile he pointed the nozzle at his mother's Pinto. "You might want to trade this guzzler in for something else."

"Don't tempt me, John. Listen, I was out here early this morning, over at the Safeway Store. We arrested a couple bad guys, and well, this area hasn't built up that much yet so be careful out here, okay?"

"Sure will. That will be $7.70."

Handing him the cash, I got behind the wheel and started the engine. Leaning into the open driver's window, John looked me in the eye. "Is there something you're not telling me, Officer?"

"Those are some really bad guys we took down this morning. They're making all kinds of threats to anyone and everyone, including those around here. Just be careful and call us if you see anything that concerns you. Okay?"

"You bet. Thanks." Stepping back, John smiled and gave me a salute.

I slowly rolled out onto the hot pavement of the Alhambra and could see John in my rearview mirror watching me. I had to make an impression. Dropping it into low, I punched it. The roar was sweet as all three hundred and seventy horses under the hood pushed me back into the seat like a rocket. The rear of the car got squirrely, as a high-pitched shriek resonated off the tires, and a thick cloud of rubber filled the air. Within seconds I was doing sixty and searching the rearview and side mirrors for any sign of red and blue flashing lights appearing through the thick smoke. Pleased with the results, I slowed down and settled in for the ride home.

Approaching the house, I turned the corner and parked at the curb just out of sight. In the front yard were three little ragamuffins, each just a few inches taller than the other. Striking across the lawn, they had a clear objective in mind. In the center of the yard was a large pile of autumn leaves I had taken an hour to rake up, but it was about to be scattered like snowflakes. With shouts and squeals they dove into the leafy mountain, redistributing fall's foliage in every direction.

It was worth the work, I thought as I pulled into the driveway. The first head to pop up through the leaves was Joseph, named after his grandfather. From the moment he was born, the two were inseparable. "Little Joe" is my oldest. He has a heart as big as his mother's. Even at the age of seven he was always looking out for his brothers.

The next head to come up for air was my second boy, Stefan. His mother would sing him to sleep every night, "Climb upon my knee, Sonny Boy, though you're only three, Sonny Boy, you've no way of knowing, there's no way of showing, what you mean to me, Sonny Boy." The name stuck. Sonny is our artist. He draws on everything.

One head didn't make a showing, my youngest Casey, or Critter as we call him. When his mother washes his clothes, she doesn't reach in and turn out the pockets to empty them of rocks, marbles, and the like. With Critter's britches, she drops them on the floor and stomps on them a few times. Because of several unique finds, Casey had earned the handle "Critter."

Standing at the front door, like a centurion at the gate, was the feared fixer of fabric, the daring defender of dinner, the controlling Commander in Chief of the Republic of Richards. In her hand glistening in the noonday sun, was her weapon of choice. Slowly she raised it toward the helpless children and, with a Cheshire-cat smile, looked at me as if to dare me to make a move.

"Watch out!" I shouted just as she opened fire. A long stream of water shot from the nozzle as the boys began to squeal with laughter.

Breaking into a dead run, I zig-zagged across the lawn, scooping up Little Joe and Sonny in my arms, holding them in front of me as a shield. I felt a tug and found Critter clinging to my pant leg. Squirming and giggling I moved toward the adversary as she took aim and drenched us unmercifully.

Putting them down I shouted, "Let's get her."

With eyes as wide as her smile, Rosie dropped the hose, turned, and ran back into the house. Just before the boys reached the door, I leaped over three steps, spun around, and stretched out my arms, stopping their attack on the porch. "Hold it guys. We can't go inside all wet. I'll get some towels, and after we're dry, we'll go get mom."

Returning with the towels, I stopped dead in the hallway. Stepping back, I turned to the bedroom and said in a loud whisper, "Baby, get out here, quick."

Stepping into the hall she looked to the open front door, and there stood three naked little troopers, with their clothes in a pile at their feet. It took everything we had to keep from laughing.

"Well, go give them a towel before the neighbors call the cops."

My life was on track. I had a beautiful wife, three great kids, and a job I loved. We just moved into our first home, and the future was looking bright. Watching little bundles of energy fidget and fuss as their mom wiped faces and ruffled hair, I wondered what I had done to deserve all this.

A decade earlier I was cutting a firebase for the 101st Airborne in the Central Highlands of Vietnam. I spent my first week in Camp Alpha, Saigon, waiting to be assigned to the 1st Cavalry Division where I would man a 106 recoilless rifle, a direct fire cannon mounted on a jeep. After three days I explored the camp and found three pieces of heavy engineering equipment: two International Harvester TD-24 bulldozers and a field stripped John Deere road grader.

Climbing onto one of the dozers, I sat back in the seat, put my feet up on the hood, and took a nap in the warm afternoon sun. I don't know how long I slept, but I was jarred awake by Master Sergeant Buck Bennett.

"Wake up, Private! Where the hell do you think you are?"

Rolling my legs off the hood, I missed the floor plate and dropped onto the tracks. From there it was a gymnast's nightmare, as I landed face down at Bennett's feet. I lifted my head slowly and looked into eyes that had seen things I didn't want to imagine.

"On your feet, Private," he barked.

I jumped to my feet and stood as ridged as I could, although I was shaking like a leaf on the inside.

"This is not your home, boy. This is a war zone, and that's not your cradle; it's military equipment. Do you understand me, Private."

"Yes, Master Sergeant."

"You operate that dozer?"

"No, Master Sergeant. I'm eleven-bravo. Infantry. Waiting for orders to the 1st Cavalry."

"Okay." He looked down at my nametag. "Stay put, Richards. I'll be right back." He turned toward the command tent, then looking over his shoulder, "Don't go to sleep again, boy. The next voice you hear may be Charlie's."

I waited for over an hour and was tempted to just go back to my bunk when Bennett appeared from a row of tents with another soldier.

"Richards, this is Specialist Kippell. Just call him Kip. He will be showing you how to use that dozer. You have three, maybe four days. Use them well. You're now twelve-bravo, Combat Engineer. Stay alive, boy." And with that he turned and disappeared out of my life forever. I went from Infantryman to Engineer in less than an hour.

Later I learned that the two guys I bunked with, and who would have been part of my crew manning the 106 recoilless, were hit just two weeks after joining the 1st Cavalry. Only one survived. He sustained serious injuries and was sent home. Why them and not me? Would I ever really know the answer to this question that would interrupt countless nights of sleep?

A tear ran down my cheek as I watched three naked little dudes hug their mom and scamper off down the hall to their rooms. What had I done to deserve a life like this? Why me?

CHAPTER FOUR

Like every rookie, once I completed the academy, my first patrol assignment was the graveyard shift, midnight to 8:00 a.m. The first six months would be spent riding with a training officer, or TO. If you make the cut, you spend the balance of your one-year probation period in your own patrol car shadowing and covering your TO. You patrol your TO's beat area and monitor his calls for service, but you only respond as backup. However, with this assignment also comes the laborious responsibility of writing all your TO's reports. I was fortunate to get one of the best TOs in the department, Alford Jackson, A. J., who would become a very good friend.

Rolling into the City Corporation Yard that first night, A. J. cut the lights and pulled up to the gas pumps. The refueling island was in an open area in the back of the yard. Over the pumps hung a high-pressure sodium streetlight, the kind most cities use because they're inexpensive and almost maintenance free. That's almost . . .

"I don't know why they keep trying to set us up like sitting ducks." A. J. pointed up at the streetlight. "Never put yourself in a position to be the only lit candle on the cake."

Getting out of the car, he said, "Grab your flashlight and fill it up. Make sure you answer the call and tell them we're Code-4."

"What call?" I asked.

Walking up to the streetlight, he removed his service revolver from its holster, took aim, and pulled the trigger. The light exploded, leaving an empty shell and us in total darkness. Heading toward the mechanic's shed he shouted over his shoulder, "Shots fired in the Corp Yard of course. I have to take a leak."

The call came within moments, "Xray-7, we have a report of shots fired at the end of Marina Boulevard near the Corp Yard." After a long pause, "Xray-7, are you at the Corp Yard?"

Though I watched him do it, the gunshot shook me up. Taking the mic, I did everything I could to keep my voice from quivering. "That's affirmative, . . . uh, we're Code-4."

"Of course you are." Came the sarcastic response. It was clear, this wasn't the first time the light had gone out.

After filling the car, I returned to the passenger seat and waited attentively for my handler like an obedient puppy. Leaning on the armrest in the dark, I was going over what I would have to write in the report about the "shots fired" call, when the door flew open so abruptly, I almost fell out. "Wake-up, rookie, and take the wheel, you're driving."

Climbing into the driver's seat, I felt like a kid with a new toy. Rookies usually aren't given the opportunity to drive by their TO. The only time I was behind the wheel was during driver training in the academy. This isn't practice; this is the real thing. This was great, and on my first night on patrol too. Only with a TO like A. J. would this be possible.

Starting the car I asked, "A. J., what am I supposed to write in the incident report about the shots fired?"

"Don't worry about it, I'll take care of it. They know how I feel about that light. My patrol car is usually full when I pick it up. Someone overlooked it last night. Must have been another rookie."

"What do you have against that light?"

"Bob, don't you know that this is the generation of love?" he said. "The world is clad in polyester bell-bottoms and platform shoes, with long hair and multicolored sunglasses. Underneath those flowing tie-dyed robes, covered in peace signs, are M-14s and pipe bombs, and you, my friend, are the target."

Pushing the seat back as far as it could go, A. J. stretched out his six-foot-two frame. "We got the Weathermen, SDS, Panthers, and now the Symbionese Liberation Army to contend with. What we don't need is to have a spotlight put on us as we hover over gas pumps in the dark."

"Got it." I pulled out onto the street and headed downtown. If I brought anything home from my tour in Vietnam, it was to listen to experience. It has saved me a lot of pain, and even my life.

Our beat was an urban area made up of older residential apartments and a dilapidated commercial district with many of the once-prosperous stores and shops boarded up. What remained were secured by heavy metal roll-down doors or retractable security gates. During the graveyard shift, with no one on the streets, the colorless, nondescript architecture felt like I had driven into the gray gloom of a prison block.

With the windows down, the cool early morning air washed through the cab with a refreshing scent of fall, contrary to the odor I knew hung over the grimy streets of South Central. We'd been on duty for over an hour, and except for loud music radiating from some of the dives that dotted every corner, it had been quiet. Stopping at the end of a cul-de-sac, I couldn't help but notice that A. J. had fallen asleep. It wasn't his eyes being closed, or the unusual, cocked position of his head that gave it away; it was the volume of his snoring. I was tempted to roll up the windows when he jerked up and looked around.

"What's up?" He looked up quickly. "What's going on?"

"Nothing. I just wanted to clear the neighborhood before you woke them all up."

The feeling of regret struck me as I looked over at him and waited to catch his wrath for my disrespect and insubordination. A. J. turned and looked at me with fire in his eyes. "It was that bad?"

"Uh, yes, sir."

"Yeah, okay. Thanks. I've been known to break glass and knock birds out of trees. Head over to the Pancake House. Let's get some coffee."

As I turned around in the cul-de-sac, my headlights picked up movement in the overgrowth next to a run-down duplex. Hitting the breaks, I pointed. "Look, I think I saw something over there."

The door to the duplex on the left opened, and a large belly attached to an even larger frame stepped through the opening. He blocked most the light from inside, but enough showed around his massive physique to give him the appearance of the Stay-Puft Marshmallow Man in *Ghostbusters*.

"What do you cops want?" he growled.

Before I could put the car in park, A. J. was out and crossing over the lawn. "We thought we saw someone trying to peek in your window, sir. Investigating some suspicious activity. Just want to make sure you and your family are safe."

"There ain't no one out here. Go do your investigate'n some wheres else," the big man said, just as a boy of about fourteen stepped out of the bushes. The man reached for him, but the boy stepped back quickly. "Get your butt in the house," the man shouted. "Now."

Walking up behind A. J., I could see that the boy was bleeding from his nose and mouth, and he was holding his left arm with his right hand in a sling position. A. J. turned to the boy. "Come here, son." He hesitated, looking at the big man, then approached A. J. slowly. There were signs of swelling and blacking around both of his eyes, and his arm had taken on an unnatural form.

Placing his hand on the boy's shoulder, A. J. turned to me. "Put him in the car. We have to get him to the hospital."

His voice raising to a high pitch, the man said, "Where you taking my son? You can't just come here and take our kids. Who do you think you are?"

"Sir, calm down." A. J. raised his hands in the air as a peaceful gesture. "It's clear your son has had an accident. All we wish to do is get him patched up. If you have a few minutes I need to get a little information from you, then I can get him to the doctor, and I won't bother you any longer."

"Yeah, yeah. He must have had an accident. You going to bring him back or do I have to go get him? I got to work in the morning, so I need to get to bed."

"Sure, no problem. Just a few questions and you can hit the sack."

A. J. turned to me and nodded toward the car, "Get the info on the boy. I'll be back in a minute."

Putting the boy in the backseat, I tried to make him as comfortable as possible. Climbing behind the wheel, I could see A. J. standing just inside the door. Looking out he gave me the thumbs-up with a smile, then closed the door. I tried to get some answers, and even make small talk with the teenager, but he remained silent, his swollen eyes fixed on the battered front door of his house.

After close to ten minutes had passed, I was becoming concerned. Unhooking my seat belt, I told the boy to sit tight and assured him we would be on our way soon. When I reached halfway across the yard, the door opened and A. J. appeared with a small, middle-aged woman dressed in a torn nightgown and a threadbare robe.

"There's two boxes just inside the door. Get them, put them in the trunk, and shut the door." A. J. escorted the woman to the car.

Stepping inside, I looked around for the big man, but there was no sign of him. Empty beer bottles and overflowing ashtrays covered the end tables. In spite of that and the well-worn furniture, it looked to be clean and well cared for.

While heading to the hospital, A. J. told me to take a bit longer route along MacArthur Boulevard. About midway he had me pull into the Motel 8. He retrieved the boxes from the trunk and went into the office. Returning to the car he handed a key to the woman and told her that she was paid up for a week, and that when she leaves the hospital, she would find her stuff in the room.

As I drove, A. J. asked questions and took notes. After leaving the motel, the boy was more than willing to talk. The woman was his mother, but the man was not his father, just someone his mother had met who was willing to provide a place for them to stay. Things had gone badly right from the start, and both had the bruises and broken bones to prove it.

After depositing mom and her son at Montgomery General, we finally got our long-awaited coffee and parked in a secluded spot. A. J. gave me the reports that needed to be completed and dictated the narrative.

"What about the old man? What's going to happen to him?"

"Our report will first go to the DA's office where a criminal complaint will be filed and an arrest warrant issued. I'll request the warrant to come back to us rather than to Wants and Warrants for service. That way we have the pleasure of scooping him up and booking him."

"When you went into the house, what did he have to say about all this?" I asked.

"Oh, he didn't have much to say at all." A. J. snickered.

I had a sneaking suspicion that a little cowboy justice had been dispensed, but it was never discussed again. I remember the last thing he said to me that night: "Do you believe in God?"

The question threw me a bit; it was out of sync with everything else that had happened. I told him I didn't know, that it wasn't something I'd put much thought to. He didn't say another word about it, just left it hanging in the air, like an unfinished song.

CHAPTER FIVE

I woke up to the sound of loud little voices in the backyard just below my window. It wasn't their voices that woke me, but Rosie's, as she shouted over their squeals, "Boys you need to be quiet if you're going to play out here. Daddy is sleeping."

"Well, not anymore." I mumbled, pulling the pillow over my head. I've developed a real personal relationship with these blankets, and if I got up and just left, they could develop trust issues. Lying there I realized that my argument wasn't valid because blankets are fickle and will bed down with anyone who'll tuck them in.

Today is Friday, November 24, 1972, also known as Black Friday, just one month till Christmas. It is the day the Richards family takes their annual pilgrimage to the mall to get lost in a sea of human chaos. It's also when I get dirty looks and nasty comments from a host of judgmental moms. Why? Because I know my boys, and I know that within moments of our arrival they would disappear in the high tide of crazed shoppers. So what do I do? I have them leashed. That's right, just like shaved, untrained puppies, and so far, I haven't lost one.

Rosie took Critter in the stroller and faded into the bedlam toward women's fashions. I leashed Little Joe to my belt loop and hoisted Sonny into my arms. "Okay guys, where do you want to go first?"

"Toys," they chimed.

"Great." I chuckled. "Kings Sporting Goods it is," and off we went into the swirling pool of humanity. The boys knew we would hook up with Mom and Critter, get a Happy Meal, and end our day in the toy department. It was our routine every year.

As we approached the main entrance, we were confronted by two large, uniformed security guards. Both had a scowl on their face that indicated there might be a problem. The biggest one on the left bent down and put his face within inches of Little Joe's. The other stepped in front of Sonny. "You boys looking for trouble?"

"You wouldn't be that bad guy named Little Joe, would ya?" The big man swooped him up in his arms, and his partner grabbed Sonny out of mine.

Snickers and squeals could be heard over the clamor of crazed consumers, drawing the attention of a number of Kings customers. Charles, the big fella, and Scott are good friends and fellow Oakland PD officers. This was their day off, so they were doing a little side work to pick up some extra Christmas cash. Soon we would join them and their families for the annual department Christmas party, where Charles would make his appearance in a decorated police car as Santa. He got the job, not because he was big enough to fill the position, but because his jolly disposition was as real as he was.

Whenever we were in Kings, Little Joe would make a bee-line for the fish and tackle department. Ever since his grandpa took him out fly fishing he couldn't get enough of the sport. Now with his grandpa's assistance, he even tied his own flies. Sonny, on the other hand, headed to the trophy section where the US Fish and Wildlife Service posted beautiful photos and guest artists set up their easels. If they ever got loose from me, I knew where I could find them. Getting them to leave, however, was like getting a T-bone from a pit bull.

Taking both Little Joe's leash, and the collar of Sonny's hoody in one hand, I grabbed our bag of acquired treasures and maneuvered through the crowd to a series of glass display counters, arranged end-to-end forming a large square. This was known as Gun Island. Each counter exhibited an extensive assortment of handguns, from small-caliber automatics that would fit into a purse, to handheld cannons big enough to stop a Mack Truck. In the center, surrounded by the counters, several salesmen worked, answering questions, and removing firearms from the glass displays for customers to inspect.

Moving slowly around the island, I looked down and noticed that the boys had their faces pasted against the glass. As they moved, they left a smeared streak on the clean glass panel. I was about to laugh when I caught the eye of an unhappy and seriously stressed clerk.

I put on a serious expression. "Amazing, isn't it, how creative we've become in devising such lethal tools." It didn't go over, so I just moved on, leaving behind a trail that Hansel and Gretel could have used to find their way home.

In the last counter near the corner was a Smith & Wesson .357 Magnum, six-inch Police Special. I had been carrying a department issue .38-caliber Colt for two years and it was time to graduate.

Drawing the boys close to my right side, I released my grip and leaned down. "You two stay right here at my side, and don't move." Placing the bag on the counter, I was handed the revolver. The weight felt good as did the squared end grips.

"That's a nice gun there," another shopper said.

"Yes, it is." I looked up and saw a tall, scruffy man in a black sweatshirt and knit cap. It took a second but then it registered, as Lieutenant Miller's words rang in my head. *This guy is dangerous. Don't underestimate him, or those he hangs with. Don't forget that face.*

As I stared into Curtis Mitcham's eyes, a variety of scenarios were going through my head. My first move was to get my boys out of harm's way.

I put the revolver on the counter and leaned down. "Joseph, I want you to take your brother's hand and go find big Charles. He's over by the door. Okay. Go on now." Little Joe knew when I called him Joseph, I was serious.

Taking his little brother's hand, he said, "Come on, Sonny," and disappeared toward the entrance.

"Those are fine looking boys you've got there, Officer Richards."

I didn't respond, but the heat in my head jumped to a boil. The only weapon I had available was sitting on the counter with a price tag looped through the trigger. He was standing at the counter that ran vertically from mine just around the Gun Island's corner. He wasn't within reach, but he was close enough to create real damage.

No words were spoken, just stares as shoppers milled around us. His right hand was in his sweatshirt pocket, and his left rested on the counter. After several long tense moments, he was joined by three ratty, leather-covered bikers. He pointed at me. "That's the pig who harassed me the other night."

I noticed that it got strangely quiet around Gun Island as people were slowly stepping away. I wondered if it felt like this at the O.K. Corral, then something struck me and I couldn't help but say it, "You tell your friends about how you wet yourself when we last met?"

Rage flashed across his face, "You son of a—"

"Is there a problem here?" came the voice of Santa, as Charles and Scott stepped to my side. "Local law enforcement will be here in a moment, and we can work it out then. Unless you boys want to work it out now."

"No, there's no problem here. We just came to do some Christmas shopping and ran into an old friend." Curtis withdrew his hand from his pocket and stepped away from the counter. He walked away and looked over his shoulder. "You take care of those little guys of yours, Officer Richards."

"Where's my kids?" I asked, with a bit of panic in my voice.

"They're fine." Scott pointed to the manager's office. "The bookkeeper's got them drawing and playing games."

"Great. Is it okay if they stay there for a few minutes? I need to find my wife."

"Sure," Charles said. "Want one of us to go with ya?"

"No, but do you have a backup I can borrow for a few?"

"Sure. Come with me." Charles led me to the office. There he lifted his pant leg and withdrew a small revolver and handed it to me.

"Thanks. I'll be right back."

First stop, ladies' fashion. It didn't take long to find Rosie and Critter. She was trying on jumpsuits while the boy was playing in a fully enclosed inflatable bounce house filled with soft rubber balls.

"Baby, I don't want to cut your time short, but we need to go. We can stop and get the Happy Meals on the way home. I'll explain it all to ya later. Okay?"

She studied what was going on behind my eyes. "Are the boys okay?"

"They're fine. I left them at Kings with Charles Williams and Scott Johnson. Charles and Scott are working a side security job at Kings for Christmas money."

Rosie took one more look at me. "Fine. Let's go." Returning to the dressing room she retrieved her clothes and purse while I went to snag Critter. She knew that there were times to just follow the directions and get the answers later, and this was one of those times.

Walking over to the bounce house I scanned the inside as my heart began to pound. There was no sign of him. "Critter, where are you?" There were no kids in the bounce house or on any of the other pieces of play equipment. "Casey!" I shouted. "Casey!" Looking around the area I spotted a large woman seated in a chair by the small gate that entered the play area.

"Where's my son?" I demanded. "Did you see someone take a child from here?"

"No, sir, no one took any children from here, except their parents. They would have to come by me, and they would have to have the child's ID tag, or they wouldn't be taking anyone anywhere. Now I don't know who you are so I'm going to ask you to leave, or I'll call security."

I could feel the sweat begin to form on my face as I planned my next move. "Call security. Great idea. Get them down here now. I need to call the police. Where's the closest phone?"

She pointed down the mall's main corridor just as Rosie came out of the dressing room and walked over to the bounce house. Moving to her side, I was about to break the news when she said, "Casey, get your butt out here."

In an explosion of giggles, the towheaded little gremlin jumped up from the center of a mountain of multi-colored plastic spheres. My heart skipped a beat as I dropped my head and whispered, "Thank you, God. Thank you."

On the way home I explained what had taken place, and although the bad guys may have left, I couldn't take a chance. I promised them all that I would take them back to that mall or another to finish our Christmas shopping.

After the boys were put down for the night, Rosie and I set a plan to make sure everyone was going to be safe. I assured her that Curtis Mitcham wasn't stupid enough to really do something, and I believed the mall encounter was just a chance meeting he took advantage of.

Rosie put her head on my shoulder. "I thank God you and our boys are safe. I don't know what I would do without you." I could feel her shaking as tears began to soak my shirt. "Bobby, would you pray with me? I think we should pray, and thank God, and ask Him to protect our boys."

"Sure, baby."

We prayed for the first time in our ten years of marriage.

CHAPTER SIX

Awakened by a kiss on the cheek and the smell of hot coffee, I opened my eyes just enough to see the red letters on the clock radio. Three o'clock—p.m., early enough to take Little Joe and Sonny to the movies before work. It was another lame, second-rate science-fiction flick about Martians and outer space stuff. I think the title is "Star" something or other. It's worth sitting through because the boys love them, and it gives us a chance to have a "guy's night out." We always get there early so we can get the three center seats, four rows from the front.

I sit in the middle so if it gets scary, they can dig in and hide their eyes under my arms. I stuff them with popcorn, get them hyper on sodas and candy, then when we get home, I watch them bounce off the walls like helium balloons.

That's usually when I get the look because Mama knows I'm about to go to work, leaving her with the task of trying to get those frenzied inflatables tucked in. This evening I had to go in early to finish my reports, so I kissed Rosie goodbye and looked over her shoulder at two warring storm troopers dueling to the death with their lightsabers.

"Hey guys, how about a kiss?" Dropping their taped-together toilet paper tubes, they ran and jumped into my arms, gave me a sloppy smooch and a hug, then returned to the battle at hand. I had a sneaking suspicion that being policemen or firemen when they grew up had just been kicked to the curb.

Sitting at one of the empty desks in the detective division, I reviewed a report of an arrest that I had made over a year ago and that was going to trial in the morning.

"Bob, you have a call on line three," one of the detectives said over the partition.

"Thanks." Punching the flashing button, "Officer Richards."

"Officer, this is John Steller, over here at Dee's Country Store. I know you're not on duty yet, but when you are, could you come out here? I want to show you something."

"Sure, John. Is everything okay?"

"Yeah, yeah, we're okay. But if you could come out to the store, I would appreciate it."

"No problem. I'm about to go into briefing, so unless something urgent pops up, I'll be out there within a half hour."

Pulling up to the old gas pumps, I saw John, clad in coveralls and straw hat, standing at the rollup door of the garage. Illuminated under an old rusted goose-necked light fixture, he looked like a Norman Rockwell painting.

"John, what's up?"

"Thanks for coming out. I really don't mean to bother you with this, but do you remember a while back telling me that threats had been made toward us folks around here."

"Yeah, I remember."

John turned and walked toward the right corner of the building, "Come on back here."

On the garage side, away from the store, there was a small, detached building that housed two public restrooms. Just above the doors was another old goose-necked light fixture. Under the light someone had nailed the body of a dead cat with a note attached to a string around its neck.

Scrawled in red crayon, "Tell the old lady I'm coming for her."

"Have you touched any of this John?"

"No."

"Good. I'll be right back." I went to my car and retrieved gloves and a plastic baggy from my briefcase. I took the note off the cat and put it in the baggy. "John, this may just be kids but be careful anyway. I'll see if we can get anything off the note."

"Officer, I wouldn't have bothered you with this, but this isn't the first one."

Going over to the storefront he opened the door and motioned me to come in. In a small office in the back, just large enough to hold a desk, a chair, and a filing cabinet, he handed me a cardboard box. Inside the box was a stack of notes, all written in different color crayon, each a different threat.

"We get a note hung around a dead animal just about every week. Cats, dogs, squirrels, ducks, birds, you name it. I've stayed here overnight a lot to catch this SOB, who or whatever he is." Taking a deep breath, "This note is the first one to threaten someone in particular. My mother."

"Okay, John, I want to keep this box. We'll process them for prints. Are you the only one to touch them?"

"Yes. Neither my mom nor my boys know about them. I get here before anyone else and have been coming back at night to check things out. When I find this stuff, I clean it up. I'd appreciate it if you didn't tell Mom, at least not yet."

"No problem, this will be between us for now. I need you to stop by the police department to be fingerprinted. We will need to eliminate your prints from what we get. Can you do that sometime today?"

"Sure."

"Good. I'll let them know you're coming in, and John, be careful. It may be nothing, but let's not take a chance."

I located Chester Duncan, one of the best crime scene analysts in the state, in the department's forensic lab, what we have affectionately nicknamed "Duncan's Dungeon." He was bent over a microscope examining what looked like leftovers out of my fridge.

"Chester, I know you're up to your knickers thumbing through something disgusting, but is there any way I can get these notes printed. I really need them ASAP."

With an annoyed look that answered the question, Chester returned to his work, then mumbled, "Check your watch, Bob. It's the wee hours of the morning. You may enjoy the vampire shift, but I should be home in bed."

"You're right. Sorry, Chester."

Just as I reached the door I heard, "Package them, write it up, and dump them in the processing box. I'll get to them when I can."

"Okay, thanks."

I requested the records division to send Chester the print card for Curtis Mitcham and any known member of the Savages motorcycle club. To justify the work that needed to be done, I explained that it was more than cruelty to the animal kingdom; if we found Mitcham's prints on those notes, it was witness tampering. An added felony to the Safeway burglary charge.

The night ticked by quietly with little activity. With my reports done and a thorough examination of my beat area, I felt it was a good time to invest in an intellectual pursuit. The elevated lot of Grace Lutheran Church was in the center of my beat area and overlooked most of the streets. I parked my car facing out at the entrance in case I needed a quick exit. From my briefcase, I removed a classic piece of law enforcement literature, Joseph Aloysius Wambaugh's, *The Choirboys*. Settling in, I turned to page 1 and began to read.

A rhythmic tapping sound drew my attention to the driver's window. Looking up, I found myself sitting in bright sunlight and staring into the eyes of a smiling gentleman, wearing all black and a clerical collar.

"Yes, yes, sir." I rolled down the window. "How can I help you?"

"Are you alright, Officer?"

"Yes, yes, of course. I was, I was a . . ."

"Thank you for providing our little church with some special attention. Being up here we are a bit vulnerable."

"Of course. That's what I'm here for." Clearing my throat, "What time are your services?" I asked with as much interest as I could muster.

"We have just one service at eight. You're most welcome to come in." Looking down at his watch, "We begin in about fifteen minutes."

"Fifteen minutes!" my brain screamed.

"I would love to. Unfortunately, I'm still on duty. Maybe next week." *If I have a next week*, I thought.

Looking around I could see the entire parking lot was full. Each and every carload of smiling churchgoers had driven right past me, as I snoozed away peacefully. The last time I felt like this was when I failed a job interview, shook everyone's hand, and walked into the coat closet.

"Well, Pastor, er Father, I mean Reverend, I have to get back to the police department. I'm running late. You have a wonderful church time, sir. And God bless ya."

"We will," he said with a Cheshire-cat smile. "And thank you again for taking good care of our church."

I began to pull away as he stepped back, revealing a group of children who had gathered with their teacher to see the nice policeman. If I couldn't drive out of there, I was ready to crawl out.

With briefcase in hand, I slid slothfully into the squad room just as Sergeant Alan was about to dismiss the shift.

"Office Richards, welcome." Alan smiled. "I'm glad you could make it."

I froze in place, waiting for the question about where I had been, followed by an embarrassing public reprimand. Gremlins began racing around in my head trying to come up with a plausible answer, but none materialized.

"Bob, come on up here."

Setting my case on a table near the wall, I nervously walked up to the podium.

With a hand on my shoulder, Sergeant Alan said, "I got a call just before briefing from Pastor William Henderson at Grace Lutheran Church."

Those Gremlins in my head were back at work trying to devise a way of how I can explain to Rosie why I'm no longer employed with OPD.

"Bob took the last few minutes of his shift to develop good community relations. He stopped by Grace Lutheran and greeted the congregation as they arrived for services, and let the children look at his cruiser. Well done, Bob, great initiative. Okay, gentlemen, let's hit the street. Be alert and be careful. Dismissed."

On the way home I honestly thought about dropping into Grace Lutheran for their service but quickly dismissed the idea, besides it was probably too late.

From the driveway I could see movement in the kitchen as Rosie prepared breakfast for the troupe. In the living room I found the storm troopers repairing their paper lightsabers, getting ready to join the Jedi in fending off Darth Vader. Around them Casey ran in small circles, squeaking, peeping, and making noises I'd never heard him make before.

"Rosie, what's with Critter? He looks crazed and sounds like he's possessed. Do we need to call a doctor or a priest?"

"He doesn't need healing or an exorcism. His brothers made him their robot. They have spent most of the morning teaching him how robots talk. Our youngest is now bilingual."

"That's a relief. I was afraid our new carpet was about to be christened with pea soup."

After breakfast, I told Rosie about falling asleep in an empty church parking lot and waking up to a full house. The pastor had to wake me up, and yet he still called to thank us for greeting his congregation as they came to church.

"We should go to his church some Sunday. It would be good for the boys."

"We don't have boys anymore, we have storm troopers. Besides, I'm not ready to be a churchgoer. Maybe after I retire, you know, when I'm closer to meeting my maker."

"Sweetheart, I grew up in the church and I understand your reluctance, but the church could be good for our whole family. They're fine people, with big hearts, and the message is simple." It was clear she was about to apply a bit too much pressure. "When you're ready, sweetheart, when you're ready."

CHAPTER SEVEN

I arrived at work a little early and sat in an empty squad room organizing the various code books and forms in my briefcase. Rosie's request about church this morning kept running through my head. Why would she bring that up? She knows how I feel. Besides, the last time we went to church, other than our wedding, things didn't go so well.

I had recently returned from Vietnam with six months remaining of active duty before I would be discharged. Rosie and I were introduced by mutual friends and were about to have our first date. I showed up at her home in my dress greens because other than my fatigues, there was nothing else in my closet. The last two months were spent in Letterman General Hospital, at the Presidio, San Francisco, and now I resided in the outpatient billets located near the base of the Golden Gate Bridge.

I saw Rosie's smile peek from an upstairs window as I walked along the cobblestone path that snaked around flower beds leading to a large, beveled glass door. Within moments the door swung open, and there stood a girl who would become the mother of my children and the love of my life. Taking my hand, she led me into the kitchen and introduced me to her mother, Alberta, and to one of the kindest and wisest men I would ever know, Joe Hensley.

After several awkward minutes of small talk with her father, as her mother sat silent at the kitchen table, he said, "I understand you have been in the hospital as the result of injuries you received in Vietnam?"

"Yes, sir."

"Thank you for your service to our country. We are blessed you are home, and honored you are in ours."

"Thank you, sir."

"Is there anything you need? Anything we might be able to provide you?"

"No, sir, but thank you." I said, while my brain shouted, "Yes! I need that little girl standing next to you."

Getting up from the table, Mrs. Hensley walked over to a cabinet, removed a cup, turned, and looked at me sternly, "If you wish to see our daughter there is one thing you must do."

"Yes, ma'am." I began to feel like I was back in boot camp about to be dressed down by a drill sergeant.

"You must attend church with us this Sunday. Are you available?"

Church? Sure, I can do church. The way she looked at me I thought she was going to ask for a kidney. "Yes, ma'am. I'll be there."

"Good. I'll write down the time and address for you. Would you mind wearing your uniform? You look very nice."

Sure, I thought, besides, it's all I have.

The church was an old but well-cared-for building with a tall steeple, two large wooden doors, and a fresh coat of white paint. Inside, the walls were dotted with stained glass windows, and there were rows of straight-backed pews. On a raised platform was a large ornately carved podium, and behind it hung a massive cross that rose from the floor to the ceiling.

Mrs. Hensley took the lead as we entered, greeting people, shaking hands, getting hugs, and introducing both Mr. Hensley and myself. Must be his first time too. Everyone was pleasant and acted as though they were truly pleased that we were there, with one exception. A well-dressed, middle-aged man in a black suit and tie approached Mr. Hensley and me and shook our hands. "Welcome. It is good to see you in the house of the Lord."

Although the greeting was hospitable, I got the feeling Mr. Hensley and I were trespassing.

With the tenacity of Moses at the Red Sea, Alberta Hensley divided the gathering crowd apart and led us to our seats in the front row. After several songs were sung from a dog-eared hymnal, the man in black approached the podium, opened the biggest Bible I had ever seen, and read several verses. Closing the Bible with a dramatic thud, he stepped around the podium and stood surveying his flock. I was seated on the center aisle, placing me in a position close enough to note that he used a little too much Old Spice.

"Jesus tells us we are to love our enemies, to turn the other cheek, and to care for those in need." He dropped his head and shook it as he moved to the left side of the podium, directly in front of me. "Then why are we killing women and children in Vietnam?"

I flinched, like I had been slapped across the face. His voice began to raise as he continued to rant about the horrors of war, and those responsible for promoting and prolonging it. It was clear by the images and metaphors he used that he had never been to Vietnam or been in the military, let alone combat.

I did the best I could to sit there, but after close to twenty minutes, I had enough. Standing, I turned to Mrs. Hensley, "I'm sorry, ma'am, but I have to leave." Then turning to Rosie, "I will pick you up tomorrow at seven."

"Wait just a second," Mr. Hensley said, "I'm coming with you."

As we walked down the aisle, I noticed several families, and a number of men leaving their seats and following us out. I turned to see the good pastor standing speechless, and I wanted badly to toss a hand gesture his way but thought better of it. Next stop for me and Mr. Hensley: Denny's.

Church? No thanks. Didn't need it then, don't need it now. As the memories faded, I was jarred back to the present by a familiar growl.

"What are you doing here," A. J. said from behind me.

"I couldn't sleep. Rosie took the kids to her folks. It was just too quiet, so I thought I'd come in and clean out my locker. You're working overtime?"

"Yeah, I'm a catcher today."

There were two catchers on each shift, in each district. They were not assigned a beat area to be responsible for but floated throughout the district, backing up the beat officers and catching calls for service that the beat officers couldn't respond to.

"Do you remember that kid and his mom we took out of an abusive situation and put them up in the Motel 8. It's been a while, more than three years. You were in training."

"Yeah, I remember them."

"The kid called the PD and said he wanted to talk to me. Said it was really important and I was the only one he would talk to." From his notepad A. J. wrote the time and date next to the name Jimmy Hall.

"We were waiting for a warrant for the old man who beat them up, but it never came. I really wanted to arrest that SOB, but he turned himself in, pled out, and served six months in the bucket." A. J. dialed the number.

"Jimmy, this is Officer Alford Jackson. Yes, I'm the one who took you and your mom to the hospital. What? Slow down. Where? Hold on I need to write that down."

Signaling me to grab the pen, A. J. tossed me his pad. "Go ahead. Highway 13 south, okay. Take the Carson Street exit and head into Reinhardt Redwood Regional Park, okay. What do you mean about two miles? I need something more specific. That's a forest, I could get lost out there. Take the logger trail on the left when I see a large rock with red graffiti on it." Shaking his head, A. J. looked at me with wide eyes, "Did you get all that?"

"Yes, I got it."

"Okay, Jimmy, you need to come in here so we can talk. I know, I know, but that's the only way . . . hello, hello. Jimmy." The phone went dead.

"What's up?" I tossed his pad back to him.

"He said there's a dead guy in a chair in the Redwood Regional Park."

"Well, he may not be dead, he may just be taking a nap. People do that sometimes in the park you know."

A strange look spread across A. J.'s face. "No, I don't think so."

"Why?"

"Because Jimmy said he was the one who killed him."

"Let's check with the Watch commander and see if you can check it out." I stood. "I want to go along with ya. Is that okay?"

"Sure."

We headed to the park, turning onto an old logger trail partially covered with branches. We spotted at the end of the trail a dilapidated lounge chair about twenty yards off the path on the right. To avoid damaging any evidence we stopped well short of being parallel to the chair and walked around, coming in from the back side. The pungent odor of decay filled the air, and in the chair was the decomposing body of a large man.

"Well, there's nothing we can do for him," A. J. said. "I'll go back to the car and call in for a crime scene unit and an investigative team. You go back to the entrance of the logger trail and direct them in when they arrive."

"Know where the boy is?"

"Not a clue."

Back at the PD, we completed our reports, and I called Rosie telling her where I was and why. She said her parents asked if she and the boys could spend the night. They were going to watch a movie on TV and make s'mores on the fire pit in the backyard. I said I loved her, to kiss the boys for me, and to make me a s'more. Then I headed to the records division to find A. J.

"Rosie and the kids are at her parents for the night. I've got nothing to do but hang out with you. Got any ideas where we might begin to find Jimmy?"

"Yes." He pointed to an attractive brunette, sorting through a filing cabinet. "Shirley did a reverse directory search of the phone number I had for him and came up with an address. It's the desk clerk's phone at the old Travelers Hotel. I'm heading over there now. You ready to go?"

"Want additional cover? I can stop by dispatch on the way out and get a couple units to meet us there. He is a suspect in a homicide."

"No. I don't think he'll do anything stupid. Besides I want to talk to him while he's alive. I don't want a trigger-happy rookie limiting my chances to do that."

We parked in the alleyway behind the hotel, a five-story brick building constructed in the twenties. In its day it was known for its decor, now just for its drunks. The desk clerk sat in a tattered swivel chair with his feet on the desk. Next to him was a pile of discarded wrappers, empty soda cans, and old Playboy magazines.

"Good afternoon," A. J. said in his usual gruff baritone. "What room is Jimmy Hall in."

Without turning around, he said, "He's in room A22 on the third floor."

"Okay. Is there anyone else in that room?" A. J. reached through the opening in the clerk's security cage, took the phone, and disconnected it from the wall plug. "This is evidence."

The clerk spun around, "Hey, what do you think you're . . ." He stopped suddenly when he saw the badge on A. J.'s chest, "No, there's no one else."

"You'll get it back when we're done. I don't want any unnecessary calls being made."

"Is anyone in the rooms on either side of A22?" I asked.

"No. It's at the end of the hall, and no one is in A21."

"Good, give us the key to both A21 and A22."

It was common knowledge that the elevator in the Travelers hadn't worked since the fifties, and the stairs were narrow and rickety. Every step creaked loud enough to wake the dead, so a surprise entrance was impossible. A. J. took a position at the door of Room A22 as I went into room A21. Each room had a small wrought-iron balcony with a one-foot space between it and the balcony of the room next door.

I climbed over the railing onto the balcony of room A22. Through the old French doors, I could see a light on in the bathroom. On the bed was an open backpack with a military issue Colt 45 lying next to it. Sliding the blade of my pocketknife between the weather stripping, I flipped the latch up and unlocked the doors, then A. J. knocked loudly.

A young man, clad in boxers, stepped from the bathroom, turned, and headed for the bed. I threw open the French doors just as A. J. cleared the front, and we both tackled him at the same time. The .45 remained untouched.

"Calm down, Jimmy." A. J. handcuffed him. "I'm Officer Alford Jackson, and this is Officer Bob Richards. We're not going to hurt you, so calm down."

Lifting him up, we placed him in an old wicker chair opposite the bed. Putting on a pair of latex gloves from a pouch on his utility belt, A. J. removed the clip and cleared the chamber of the Colt 45.

"That's the gun I used to kill that SOB," Jimmy said. "I should have done it a long time ago."

"Okay, Jimmy, shut up. Don't say another word. We're going to the police department, where you can give us your statement."

We made a cursory search of the room and packed up what little the boy had in his suitcase. With the exception of a pair of jeans, two T-shirts, and an old jacket, all he had was what he was wearing and a Colt 45.

In Interview Room A, I carefully advised Jimmy of his rights, emphasizing the main points and assuring that he understood them.

"I know my rights, and I know I shot the SOB. That's all there is to it."

"Why?" I asked.

"My mom and I moved to Reno right after he went to jail for beating her up. When he got out, he came up there with a lot of promises and she let him move back in. It started all over again and last year he beat her to death. He went to court, but the cops did something wrong, and they let him go. I came back here to stay with my uncle, and he showed up. Said I owed him money that my mother had and if I didn't pay up, he'd kill me too. My mother didn't have any money. He took everything she had. She didn't have a dime."

A. J. leaned across the table and took his hand, "Jimmy, I want you to listen to me. Listen carefully to every word. You're eighteen now. That makes you an adult. We have to book you in County Jail for murder. Do not talk to anyone, not in jail or anywhere else. A lawyer will be coming to the jail to see you. You can trust him. He is the only one you talk to. Do you understand?"

"Yeah, I understand, but I can't afford no lawyer."

"Don't worry about it. Just don't talk to anyone but him and do whatever he tells you to do."

Out in front of the jail my curiosity got the best of me. "A. J., what's with the lawyer you promised him? Were you talking about someone from the public defender's office?"

"No. Jack Cinto. I have a call into him. He owes me one."

"Even with a favor, Cinto could be expensive."

"Have you ever wondered why our lives are so good, why we weren't born in Zimbabwe or Niger or some other godforsaken hole? Why we weren't raised in a home like Jimmy's? There's an awful lot of kids who are."

He was somber, almost melancholy when he reached the bottom of the steps, turned, and tossed me the keys, "Bob, you take the car back to the PD, I'm going to walk."

"You sure?"

"Yeah, I'm sure. Me and God are going to grab some coffee."

CHAPTER EIGHT

"Rosie, would you come in here, please."

I was facing a problem that attacked me emotionally in ways that few things have. I controlled the level of my voice the best I could because I couldn't expect my wife to understand what I was dealing with. "Rosie, please come in here."

"What is it? I'm trying to get ready for work and get the kids ready for school."

"If God wanted me to wear a tie, I would have been born with one. Can you make this thing look presentable? I have to be in court in an hour."

Slapping my hands away she tucked, flipped, and twisted, then backed up to admire her work. Kissing me on the nose, she turned and headed to the sound of squalls and giggles emitting from our storm troopers.

Badge clipped on my belt, Smith & Wesson model 39 holstered, and my coat under my arm, I hit the road. Today Curtis Mitcham goes on trial for the Safeway burglary and witness tampering.

Mitcham's cozy relationship with the Feds turned sour when he refused to hand over information that would have implicated one of his biker buddies. The FBI pulled his free pass and contacted the district attorney's office so they could refile the complaint before the statute of limitations ran out. His prints were all over the threating notes left at Dee's store, so an additional felony charge was added.

I stood before a Romanesque three-story building with massive pillars and a manicured lawn. This is where justice is served. Chiseled into a block over the entrance were the words: *With Rule There Is Order—With Order There Is Peace.*

Inside the lobby the thick tiled floors, light-colored marble walls, and double-height ceiling created the sense that you had entered a cathedral. Opposite the main entrance, just past the security perimeter, was the information desk. On the wall above it, in old English print was the Ten Commandments. I heard on the news that someone was offended by it and they were trying to get it removed. That would be a cold day. They would have better luck removing the moon.

Showing my badge and identification I asked the clerk in which courtroom the Mitcham trial was being held.

The young lady behind the desk thumbed through several pages in a leather binder, "That would be Judge Fairland's court, Courtroom Five, on the second floor."

"All right, thank you." I headed for one of the two exposed marble stairways on either side of the lobby.

Behind me came a familiar voice, "Officer Richards."

Stopping on the first step I turned to be greeted by the sardonic grin of Curtis Mitcham, dressed in a suit and tie, and his hair pulled back in a ponytail. On either side were four scruffy leather-covered members of the Savages motorcycle club.

"Well, good morning, Curtis, don't you look human this morning."

"When this is all over, we'll have an opportunity to talk, real personal like."

Looking over his head and around the room, "I don't see your friends from your other club. You know, the FBI."

He sneered. "I don't see yours either, Officer Richards. You know, those little boys of yours. I look forward to seeing them again."

My heart began to pound like a base drum and my gut tightened as he turned away.

"Hey, Curtis." I came down off the step. I lowered my voice so only he and his friends could hear. "That's a nice suit. Be careful, you don't want to piss yourself in those pants."

The anger in his face intensified, as he stepped toward me. One of his entourage took hold of his shoulder, pulled him back, and whispered in his ear.

"Yeah, yeah, you're right. Another day, another time." His demented smile reappeared. "We'll play this out another day, Richards."

On the second floor I found A. J. sitting on a wooden bench in the hall outside Courtroom Five, going over the report.

"Good morning, A. J. Have you checked in yet?"

"No."

"Let's get it done so we can go grab a cup of coffee."

In the courtroom, the judge's bench was empty. Above it hung the county's jurisdictional seal. Adjacent to the bench was the witness stand and desks occupied by the court clerk and court reporter. Twenty-five feet away sat the counsel tables with chairs facing the bench. The prosecution on the left and defense on the right from the judge's perspective. Off to one side of the bench was a door leading into the judge's chambers. In front of the door stood the bailiff, an armed, uniformed officer.

At the prosecution table sat a pair of very thick glasses on a young, well-dressed man, not much older than twenty-five. He sat looking over papers placed in neat stacks on the table in front of him.

"Sir," I said, "excuse me, are you the DA handling the Mitcham case?"

As he looked up from his papers I almost giggled. He looked like a guppy peering out from its fish tank. "I'm Officer Richards, and this is Officer Jackson. We were the arresting officers."

Extending a strong, callused hand, "Good to meet you both. I'm Daniel Martinez. Just call me Dan, no more 'sirs,' okay?"

"Yes, sir, I mean, Dan."

"We have a strong case thanks to your work. I will be calling you first, Office Richards, to lay out the narrative in chronological order, then you, Officer Jackson. Is Officer Gary Alison here yet?"

"We haven't seen him," A. J. said, "but he should be here soon."

"That's okay, I won't be calling him until this afternoon, after lunch."

"Do we have time to grab a cup of coffee?"

"Sure. I got a note that Mitcham's attorney wants to meet me for a pretrial conference."

In the coffee shop Gary joined us as we sipped hot coffee, munched glazed donuts, and exchanged dirty looks with the Mitcham crew across the room.

Returning to the courtroom we were told to meet DA Martinez in the DA's conference room on the third floor. There we were informed that the defense asked for a delay so they could look into the statements of the other witnesses, and it was granted.

"What other witnesses? Us and the bad guys were the only ones there." Gary huffed. "I can bring Turk in if they want. My puppy would love to have a conversation with them."

"I understand," Martinez said, "that there may have been some people at a gas station across the street that witnessed something."

"The only thing at that station was my car." I glanced around. "They're just trying to drag this thing out."

"I agree, but it's a done deal. We have a good case. When it hits the docket, it'll be a slam dunk. Go on home and enjoy your day."

"I'm looking forward to seeing if Richards can tie that tie again," Gary said.

"It'll look good. It's Rosie that ties it for him," A. J. chuckled.

I got home, changed clothes, and joined Rosie writing Christmas cards. She insisted that each one must be unique and specific to the one receiving it. From a distance I could hear the pipes of a motorcycle gradually getting louder. Going to the window I searched the street as the sound faded away.

"What's with you?" Rosie asked. "You seem jumpy. Is everything all right?"

"Yeah, I'm okay."

After scrolling out a half dozen cards, I caught the sound of another motorcycle heading our way. Lifting the blinds, I checked the street but saw nothing.

"You're as nervous as a cat. What's going on? Every time you hear a motorcycle, you're at the window." Putting her hand on my arm, "We have two motorcyclists on our block, and they have their friends who come from time to time. Relax, baby."

"Yeah, you're right, I'm sorry."

Little Joe rushed through the door from the garage. "Daddy, daddy, look. Look at what the man gave me." Clutched tightly between his chubby fingers was a live jacketed .380-caliber bullet. "He said he had some for you."

Snatching it from his hand I pushed him into his mother's arms. "Get the boys and keep them here."

I ran down the hall to our bedroom. Retrieving my .357 from the gun cabinet, I raced out the front door and combed the street for three blocks. Walking back into the house I was confronted by our resident mama bear. "What the hell is going on, and don't give me a line of bull."

After spending some time with Little Joe about talking to strangers, and getting a pretty accurate description, I turned my attention to Rosie. When I was done telling of the events in court earlier, I suggested that maybe it would be good if she and the boys stayed with her folks for a few days. Just until things calmed down. She reluctantly agreed just so long as she could come back to make me breakfast and dinner.

Together we packed the boys' clothes and the essential toys, and Rosie called her parents who were delighted at having them come for a while. Her mother wanted to know if Rosie was finally leaving me. She sounded disappointed that it was only a safety measure but cheered up when she heard it was because of threats I had received. Oh, how I love that lady.

With kisses all around, I sent them on their way. Once out of sight, I went in, secured every window, and put a glass filled with marbles on every sill. At each door I hung tin cans strung together around the doorknob. From the gun cabinet I took out my small arsenal and loaded them along with additional clips. I put the 12-gauge shotgun on the bed, and the Browning High Power on the nightstand. In the hall leading to the front door was a large-leaf philodendron in a porcelain pot. At its base, under the leaves, was a snub-nosed Smith & Wesson .38.

I called the Watch commander and relayed what had happened both in court and at the house and asked for extra patrol around my home. Then another call to the records division requesting photos of the known associates of Curtis Mitcham and local members of the Savages motorcycle club.

The next couple days were quiet, and it was nice to have some romantic dinners with my bride without the chaos three little storm troopers can make. As much as I missed those guys, I didn't realize how much I missed those intimate evenings without interruption.

It was the end of my shift, and I sat in the back of the squad room, debating if I should bring my family back home, when Sergeant Alan put his hand on my shoulder.

"Bob, how are things around your place?"

"Fine. It's been quiet."

"Don't get comfortable. Mitcham is a snake, I've dealt with him before. Keep your guard up. Deputy Chief Woodard has informed the DA of what's happened and asked if he could expedite Mitcham's trial. If we get him off the street and send him to prison, he'll have no reason to continue the threats and intimidation."

"I hope you're right, and thanks for the extra patrols." Looking at the other officers around the room, "If you guys come by, bang on the door. Coffee's always hot. I've been working graveyard so long I'm never asleep."

"I have a stack of pictures for ya from Records." Alan tossed me a large manila envelope. Inside I found fifty mugshots of various creatures, a few looked like Sasquatch.

At the Hensley's household I got attacked by a miniature Darth Vader, a storm trooper, and a deranged R2D2. It was a battle I lost willingly. When dinner was done, Little Joe, his grandpa, and I sat at the kitchen table and looked at the pictures. After looking at each one, my little man looked up at me with a sparkle in his baby blues. "Daddy, both those men's pictures are here."

"Both? I thought there was only one."

"No, there were two."

"But you only told me what one man looked like."

"I know. You asked me what the man that gave me the bullet looked like, and I told you."

I had to laugh, "You're right, son, I only asked you what the man with the bullet looked like. Show me their pictures, will you?"

Pushing the pictures back he began to sort through them, pulling two from the pile. "This is the man that gave me the bullet, and this is the other man."

"Rosko Tanner and Curtis Mitcham. Got ya, you . . ." I cut myself off. "Son, you did good, now go play with your brothers. I think Grandma has a cookie for you."

"Did he pick out the pictures?" Rosie asked from the door.

"Sure did."

"He doesn't have to go to court, does he? I don't want him to have to sit there in front of those men."

"No. Handing a little boy a bullet is stupid, but not illegal. Knowing who they are will let us go to the judge and ask for a speedier trial. It will also come in handy during sentencing."

"Can we come home now?" Then she turned to her father and put her arms around him, "I love you, Daddy, but I miss the other man in my life."

"I understand, little girl," Joe said.

"Baby, can we wait just another day or two? I want to see what happens after the DA hears about this. Okay, baby?"

Joe put his hand on hers, "I agree, sweetheart, another day or two won't hurt. It will also give you two a couple more romantic evenings."

Patting his head, "Daddy, you weren't supposed to say anything."

"I didn't tell your mother." He smiled. "Bob, would you mind if I prayed for you two and our boys?"

"No, sir, I would appreciate it."

Lowering his head, he grasped Rosie's hand and reached across the table for mine.

"Heavenly Father, I place these children in your hand. Protect them, keep them safe, let no harm come to them. For those who bring fear and pain, I ask for justice and retribution in whatever manner you choose. We trust you, Lord. Amen."

CHAPTER NINE

On the door of each officer's locker hangs a wall-mounted file holder where messages, reports, and other communiques are left for the officer's review. Protruding from the top of mine was a yellow "Smiley Face" sticker, the well-known moniker of Rachell DeLand, Lieutenant Steven Miller's secretary. The last time I got one of Rachell's smiley faces, the lieutenant was congratulating me on the birth of my youngest.

On a sheet of white, lined binder paper, Lt. Miller wrote, "Bob, I have some good news. I received word that the Mitcham case has been moved up and should go to trial by the end of the month. Judge Fairland went ballistic when he heard about your son and the bullet. You did a great job, Bob. Thank you for making us all look good."

"Good news or bad?" asked Officer Scott Johnson.

"Good. Do you remember that slug and his biker friends at the mall? It was when you and Charles Williams were working security?"

"Yeah, I remember that."

"His name is Curtis Mitcham. A. J. and I busted him pulling a burglary. It's been a quagmire of legal delays, but we're finally getting a court date. All good news."

"That's great, man. How are Rosie and the boys?"

"They're good, and Charlotte, how is she doing?"

Scott dropped his head and went silent.

"What's the matter, Scott?"

"We're having some problems. Can we meet for coffee someplace?"

"Sure, I'll give you a call after bar dump." I headed for my cruiser.

Coffee breaks on graveyard never happen before three in the morning. There's a lot of activity from midnight to what we call bar dump, or two in the morning. That's when the bars dump their drunks out onto the street. If trouble is going to come, either on the street or at home, it's usually between two and three.

It was a nice night, but the streets were eerily quiet without the slightest hint of movement. I pulled to the curb, rolled down all the windows, shut the engine off, and listened. It was unusual for this area to be muzzled this way. Then it occurred to me why I was getting the silent treatment. Two of the pubs that provide most of the inebriated rowdies along Mackinlay and Canal had been shut down by the narcotics division.

The Matador Lounge and the Beer Garden were known as "speed labs," producing injectable amphetamines. The drug was big in the sixties, but due to increased public awareness of its dangers and a crackdown on San Francisco pharmacies, its production had to go underground. The amphetamine trade is now dominated by outlaw motorcycle gangs, and guess what club is in deep. The Savages.

"Xray-12, we have a report of a 415 in progress at Dee's Country Store. Xray-9, respond for cover."

"Xray-12 en route from Mackinlay and Canal."

Within four minutes I was cresting the rise on Alhambra where I could see Dee's store a half mile away. "Dispatch, we need fire and a bus. Dee's place is on fire."

"Ten-four, Xray-12."

I slid to a stop short of the south side of the store, away from the gas pumps. On the ground lay John Steller, badly beaten and unconscious.

"Dispatch, I have one WMA down, expedite the bus."

"Done, Xray-12."

"Xray-9, come to the south side away from the pumps. I'm going in to see if there is anyone else."

Stealthily I moved through the aisles, around the counters, and into the storage room in the back. The door to a small loading ramp stood open, wedged by a five-gallon gas can. Stacked on a pallet against the inner wall were newspapers and cardboard boxes reeking of gasoline. Confident that there was no one else in the store, I took hold of the pallet and dragged it and the gas-soaked papers out, down the ramp, and onto the gravel parking lot. Taking the fire extinguisher from the storeroom I made a feeble attempt at controlling the flames that had engulfed the side wall of the garage. The fire department arrived and quickly went to work extinguishing the blaze, limiting what could have been extensive damage.

In front of the store, members of the emergency medical team were working feverishly on John, preparing him for transport.

"How's he doing?" I asked.

"Hard to tell," one of the attendants said. "He's been beaten up pretty bad. He could have some serious internal injuries."

"Can I talk to him?"

"Not yet, we got to get him to the hospital quick. Check with the medical staff there."

I got out of their way and let them do their job. Pushing your way past these guys, and making demands is only done in the movies.

"Scott, did John say anything to you about what happened?" I asked Officer Jackson.

"No. He opened his eyes a few times, but he couldn't talk. Bob, he wasn't in a fight, he was attacked. I've never seen anyone beaten like that."

Behind us a lime green Pinto station wagon pulled onto the gravel and a petite woman stepped out and began to run toward the ambulance. Bending down over her son, Dee took his hand and began to cry.

"Ma'am, we have to go. We're taking him to Montgomery General. You can follow us, but we have to go now." The attendant lifted the gurney and rolled it into the ambulance.

"Dee." I put a hand gently on her shoulder.

She looked up into my eyes, wrapped her tiny arms around me, and buried her face into my chest.

When her tears began to subside, I said, "Dee, John is in good hands. Let's go into the store and sit down for a few minutes."

I took a couple folding chairs from a sales rack and set them in front of the counter. "Scott, would you get us a couple bottles of water, please?"

With her hands in mine, "Dee, I know you want to get to the hospital, and I promise this won't take long, but I need to ask you a few questions." Handing her a bottle of water, "Dee, do you know who may have done this?"

The reflection in her eyes changed from grief to rage. "Yes. We've been getting threats, you know about some of them, the cats and all, but it's been getting worse. Last week a bunch of motorcycles pulled in and used just one pump to fill up all the bikes. There were about seven of them. Then they dropped the spigot on the ground letting gas run and took off. One of them yelled at John that he needs be careful, he might have a fire."

Taking a sip of water, she went on, "Two days ago, a rough-looking guy wearing a leather vest with one of those patches on the back bought a six-pack and on his way out he said, 'You better not do no testifying in court lady.' Then he pushed over one of the displays. I didn't know what he meant. He must have me confused with someone else."

Dropping her head she took a deep breath, "I got a call an hour ago and a man said he drove by the store and saw a small fire on the side of the building, then hung up. I called John and he went to check it." Dee began to sob, "It's my fault. I should have called the police."

"Dee, it is not your fault. You did what needed to be done." Patting her hand, "I will need to talk with you and John again, but we'll do it later. For now, you need to get to the hospital. Are you okay to drive?"

"Yes."

"I'm going to have Officer Jackson follow you to make sure you get there okay."

"Scott, I'll have dispatch call out a detective and the fire inspector and wrap things up here. When I'm done, we'll get that coffee and compare notes."

"Sounds good."

When the detective and fire inspector arrived, I filled them in and showed them where things had been moved or disturbed. After answering their questions, I went to the 7-Eleven and retrieved two well-deserved cups of coffee. At the counter I looked up and saw a surveillance camera.

"Is that thing working?" The clerk nodded. "Is there one outside?" Another nod. "Is it hooked up to one of those VHS recorders?"

"Sure, the manager doesn't trust any of his employees, so he records us. The VHS is locked up in his desk so we can't turn it off."

I stepped around the counter to a door next to a freezer and tried the knob—locked.

"Do you have a key?"

"Are you kidding? In the morning he comes in, checks the receipts, and counts the beers. He don't trust nobody."

Keying my portable radio, "Delta-4, this is Xray-12."

"Go ahead, Xray-12."

"I'm across the street at the 7-Eleven. They have cameras both inside and out that may have recorded everything on a VHS."

"That's great. Get the tape."

"That's a problem. It's locked up in the manager's desk, and his office is also locked."

"Okay, I'll have another Delta unit get ahold of the manager, thanks."

Back in the car, "Xray-9, you ready for that ninety-eight at the end of Arch Street?"

"Affirmative."

Sitting in the dark, with dash lights on, driver's door to driver's door, I passed Scott's coffee to him, and we went over the events at Dee's. John was rushed into surgery, and according to what Scott heard from one of the doctors, plastic surgery may be required. I knew who was responsible, and I intended to do whatever I could to put him away.

"Bob," Scott said, "I need some advice."

"About what?"

"Charlotte and I have been married for almost fourteen years. We have two beautiful kids, a nice home, and good jobs. We get along great with each other's families, don't have money trouble, and we don't fight with each other."

"Sounds to me like you should be giving me advice."

"This is just between us, right?"

"Of course."

"I've been sleeping with Vicky Harper, the parking enforcement officer in District Ten. I was going to break it off, but she told me last week that she might be pregnant. I don't want to lose Charlotte, and if it gets out, I could also lose my job."

I was stunned. I didn't know what to say. We sat quietly in the dark for several minutes.

"Might be pregnant? Has she taken a test?"

"I don't know."

"Wow. You do have some stuff going on. I think you need to know fully what you're dealing with first. Is she pregnant or not? And whether she is or not, you're still going to have to make some serious decisions and take some action."

"I don't know where to begin."

"I would think breaking it off is the first step. Then find out if you're going to be a father or not. At some point, Charlotte's going to have to be brought into the loop."

"Oh, I don't want to do that. She'll leave me."

"If the girl is pregnant, you're not going to have much of a choice."

"Yeah, I know."

Then I opened my mouth and what came out surprised me almost as much as Scott's dilemma, "Do you and Charlotte attend church? That might be a good place to seek council. A lot of people have found the answers they needed there."

Scott stiffened up, "Church? Are you serious? Why would I go to a place built upon condemnation? All they'll do there is tell me what a sinner I am. I don't need confirmation on what I already know. I need help. I've got enough guilt in my life. Why would I go looking for more?"

"You're right. It was just a thought."

"Xray-12, John Steller is out of surgery and has asked to speak with you. Delta-4 will meet you there."

"Ten-four, en route."

"Scott, I got to go. Whatever you find out let me know. I don't know what you should do. I don't know what I would do, but I have your back. I'm here for you, buddy."

At the hospital, I met Detective Wilson in the ICU wing, in front of John's room.

"Bob, the doctor said he's awake but heavily medicated. He's with his wife and mother and asked to talk to you. Introduce me, then I'll back out and listen."

"You got it. Were we able to get anything from those cameras?"

"They're real grainy and hard to make out faces in the dim light over the station. What is clear is John was jumped by three guys wearing the same kind of vests, with the same type of patch on the back. Unfortunately, the patch isn't clear enough to determine what it says. A fourth guy got a gas can from somewhere and went around the back of the store. All four rode up on motorcycles."

I greeted Dee and John's wife, Lorie, introducing them to Detective Wilson and explaining that he will be following up on any leads in the case. In the bed lay a mound of gauze, bandages, compresses, tubes, wires, and blood transfusion bags, with a man lost somewhere in the midst of it. A hand slipped slowly from under the sheets and the fingers beckoned me to come closer.

I moved to the side of his bed and leaned close, staring into the one blacked, swollen eye that was not bandaged, "I'm here, John."

Through a jaw wired shut on both sides, John formed words slowly and distinctly, "It—it—was—the—Savages."

"We're going to get them, and we're going to put them away, I promise."

"If—the—gar—garage—is—is—ga—gone—I—can—wo—work—your—car—in—mine." And with some effort a small grin appeared on one side of his face.

"You got it, John. It needs a tune-up when you're ready."

Dee kissed me on the cheek and, to my surprise, so did Lorie. I wished them the best and left with Detective Wilson.

Outside I asked the detective if he would keep me in the loop about how the case is progressing, and I wanted to be in on any arrests that were made. He agreed and we parted ways.

The sun had risen above the horizon as I headed home. Taking the long way, I went by Dee's Country Store to see the extent of the damage, and was pleased that the fire department, who was still on scene, had saved everything but one exterior wall. Just above the store a solitary white cloud drifted overhead. Looking into the sea of blue that surrounded it, I imagined angels perched on that fluffy ball of mist, protecting that sweet lady's heritage.

CHAPTER TEN

On the lawn in front of the Hensley home, my father-in-law stood like General Westmoreland examining the troops, as ten pint-sized combatants faced off in neighborhood combat. The battlefield is four yellow bases about forty feet apart. The weapons of choice, a soft foam baseball perched on a waist high stand and a green plastic bat. The uniform varied, half in red T-shirts, half in blue T-shirts, and each sporting miniature, multi colored catcher's mitts. All thanks to Papa Joe, who has a plan for helmets and jerseys in the fall.

Stopping the car short of the outfield, I watched as Sonny came up to bat. With a little coaching from his grandpa, he swung with all his might, missing the ball, but hitting the ball stand. The ball dropped like a rock and Sonny took off like a rocket. I joined in the cheers as he rounded each base and headed home. Every little soldier, even the opposing team, got excited and cheered him on. The ball? The ball was in Grandpa's pocket. That's what happened when every player came to bat. Home runs were part of the game at this stage.

Sonny never made it to home base. He heard my shouts, veered off track, and jumped into my arms, "Daddy, did you see, did you see?"

"I sure did, little dude, that was great. You're almost ready for the big leagues." Putting him down, I patted his bottom as he headed back to the game.

On the porch Rosie stood with Critter at her side, cheering every player as they went to bat. I sure love that woman.

Rosie and I took our favorite spot on the porch swing and watched the most adorable baseball game in history. Between innings when the ice cream man came around, or a Kool-Aid break was needed, I filled Rosie in about what went down at Dee's store. Then with as much diplomacy as I could muster, I told her that I felt it would be best if she and the boys stayed a while longer with her parents. To my surprise, I didn't get any push back.

"Bob, I got a job." Rosie bounced on her feet. "Walsh, Harper & Smith, the big real estate firm in that new glass high-rise downtown, hired me as an assistant bookkeeper. Isn't that great?"

"Yeah it is, but what about the boys? You don't have to work you know?"

"It's only part time. The full-time bookkeeper is going to be off for maternity leave, and when she comes back, she'll be part-time until the baby can be left with a sitter. It's not permanent, but it will give us a little extra money. We've been wanting to take the boys to Disneyland."

"You're right. When do you start?"

"Monday. Mom and Dad love having the kids with them, so it will work out well."

Her understanding and willingness to stay brought a huge relief. It meant I wouldn't have to worry about them until the trial is over and Mitcham is put away.

After the big game Papa Joe guided all the players and their cheerleaders to the New Life Presbyterian Church, three blocks away. The men's group was putting on a barbecue with all the fixins to raise funds for a family who lost everything in a house fire.

While the boys played and made new friends, Joe grabbed two burgers and motioned me over to an empty picnic table under a large shade tree. "How are you doing, son?"

"We're doing good, but I have a favor to ask."

"Whatever you need."

"Would you and Alberta mind if Rosie and the boys stayed with you a while longer?"

"Of course not, we love to have them here." Then with that inquisitive eyebrow raised, he asked, "Now fill me in, what's going on?"

I told him about the fire at Dee's, her son John's beating, and the upcoming trial. That my primary concern was making sure my family was safe until we get Mitcham locked up. He assured me that he would do everything he could to protect them and suggested we not let on to Alberta about the threat. He felt it would only create tension. I readily agreed.

With Critter asleep on my shoulder, Little Joe and Sonny running ahead with their grandpa, and Rosie's hand in mine, we took a leisurely stroll back to the Hensley plantation. There I kissed my boys and Rosie goodbye and headed home to snag some sleep before going back to work.

I drove past our house and parked in the driveway three houses down, opened the garage door, and pulled in. My garage is full so Stan Foster, a good neighbor, offered his while he and his family were away. With Mitcham and his crew causing mayhem, I didn't want to expose the Charger to potential damage.

The clock on the nightstand read two-thirty when my head hit the pillow. I was good for a snooze until nine tonight. With the windows blacked out, and no squeals or shrieks from the backyard, I was out like a light in seconds.

Standing motionless in the Safeway parking lot I looked across Alhambra Avenue and watched as Dee's Country Store was engulfed in flames. Running toward the blaze was a petite elderly lady, dressed only in nightclothes and a robe, and behind her a tall young man, wrapped in bandages. I knew who they were, and I desperately wanted to warn them, to tell them to stop, but nothing came out. My mouth opened and I screamed, but there wasn't a sound. I tried to run, but my legs were frozen, my feet glued to the ground. I couldn't move. All I could do was watch as the gas pumps ignited and they disappeared in the flames.

Dropping to my knees I began to weep. Looking up I saw the small billowing cloud that I had seen before hanging over Dee's store, and on it were two figures looking down at the inferno with smiles on their faces. When the bells started to ring, I recognized who they were. Curtis Mitcham and Rosko Tanner.

The bells didn't stop. They kept ringing and ringing, and that's when I realized it was just a dream so I answered the phone.

"Bob," A. J. said, "you there, Bob?"

"Yeah, yeah, I'm here."

"My neighbor just called me, said he saw two guys walking around my house. When I turned on the outside lights and went out, I saw two guys running around the corner, then I heard a couple bikes taking off. Be careful, man. We go to court tomorrow."

"I will. Thanks for the call, I almost overslept."

"Just be careful, we don't know how far these punks want to take this."

"Got it. I'll see ya at the Cop Shop."

A few hours later I passed by the courthouse and smiled. Before this day was over, the trial would be done, and Mitcham would be out of my hair.

I stopped at the intersection of Court and Pine streets on a green light, as a Nash Rambler coasted through the red light at about five miles an hour. In slow motion it swerved slightly and struck the light pole on the opposite corner, coming to a stop.

"Dispatch, this is Xray-12. I have a DUI at the intersection of Court and Pine streets."

"Ten-four, Xray-12, a DUI at Court and Pine. Unit to cover."

"Xray-7 en route."

I moved to the vehicle's right rear and examined the interior for passengers. Empty except for the driver. Opening the driver's door, I was met by the strong odor of alcohol and a man in his mid-sixties holding his chest and grimacing in pain.

"Dispatch I need a bus, possible cardiac arrest."

"Bus and EMTs en route."

With my hands under his arms, I lifted him out of the car and laid him on the ground. Folding up a coat I found on the seat, I tucked it under his head and felt for a pulse. I was about to begin CPR when A. J. pulled up. "Wait."

Standing over the man, A. J. keyed his portable radio, "Dispatch, cancel the bus and EMT. We're code-four." He looked down at the man. "Let him die."

"What?" Frowning, I looked up. "Let him die?"

"Sure. Look at him. He isn't worth the trouble of all those reports or wasting the EMT's time. The ambulance could be used for somebody important, not this loser."

I couldn't believe my ears. "A. J., have you lost your mind?"

"Let's leave him here and grab some coffee. With any luck a garbage truck will come by, run over him, then pick him up and haul him off."

Our heart attack victim's eyes popped open, "What the hell do you mean? Are you just going to leave me here?"

"Yep." A. J. smirked. "Looks like a miraculous recovery. Praise the Lord." Reaching out his hand, "On your feet, Edgar. If there is any damage to that light pole, you're going to jail."

"You know this guy?" I asked.

"This is Edgar Dollar. Edgar, this is Officer Richards. You run into him again and you won't get any breaks, got it?"

"Yes, Officer Jackson."

"Edgar pulls this heart attack routine with officers he doesn't know when he's about to get busted on a DUI. He lies in an emergency room wired up for an EKG and sleeps it off. When they find nothing wrong with him, he's released. He catches a cab, gets his car, and goes home to the little lady, sober as a judge. It's worked a lot for you, hasn't it, Edgar?"

"Yes, Officer Jackson."

We examined the light pole and found that there was no damage, not even a scratch. Edgar had gone over the curb but stopped just inches from the pole. A. J. backed his Nash off the curb and parked it under a sign that read, "No Parking Between 8:00 a.m. and 5:00 p.m."

A. J. put Edgar in the back of his police car. "I'm taking you home. Make sure you get back by eight or your car gets towed."

"Are you just going to take him home? He's clearly drunk, and I saw him driving. Shouldn't we book him?" I asked.

"How about next time, Bob, if there is a next time. Edgar is about to be in big trouble. I'm taking him home and handing him and his keys over to his wife. The woman is a battleship on legs with an attitude of a Brahma bull. We've been called there a few times in the past when Edgar came home drunk. Seems the little lady don't care if he's out all night, but when he shows up drunk, she sees red, and things get ugly."

Sliding behind the wheel, "Okay, Edgar, let's go see the little lady."

From the backseat came a high-pitched voice, "Wait. Wait, the other officer arrested me. He has to take me to jail. Wait, I have to go to jail."

I waved goodbye to Edgar as a look of absolute desperation stared back at me through the rear window.

In the squad room, A. J. let the oncoming shift know that he had dropped off Edgar Dollar, limp as a hand towel, a cork high and a bottle deep, at home and that Mrs. Dollar was as wound-up as an Oklahoma tornado. There was a strong likelihood that they would be getting a disturbance call, if not a possible homicide.

I had to be in court in two hours, so I went straight home to change, and missed seeing the boys. From the house I called, talked to each one, and told them that I loved them and would see them later today.

In the marbled hall outside Judge Fairland's court, I met A. J., and together we checked in with Deputy DA Martinez. He informed us that the calendar was full and that the judge would be hearing arraignments first. If we wanted to go to the cafeteria for breakfast, he would call down there when we were about to start.

"Another stinking delay," A. J. groaned. "I'll bet you we don't get started until this afternoon."

"I'll bet you both a buck we don't get started today at all."

"We'll get started today." Martinez glanced around. "The judge is really unhappy about the harassment everybody is getting from Mitcham and his gang."

In the cafeteria we ordered a light breakfast, scoured the *Chronicle* for some good news, and got as comfortable as possible.

"It stinks a lot like pig in here." Came the gravel voice of Curtis Mitcham.

I folded down the paper and smiled. "Well, it sure beats the smell of urine."

He took one step our way. "Yours is coming real soon. Count on it, pig. Your time is coming."

Angered, A. J. began to stand. "Hold up, A. J." I put my hand on his arm. "Someone must be getting pretty nervous. You don't want to go over there." Pointing toward Mitcham, "Smell that? Smells like someone may have dumped in their denims."

A uniformed officer stepped through the door. "Is everything okay in here?" He stepped between us.

After a long dramatic pause Mitcham and his boyfriends backed out of the door and disappeared up the steps.

"Gentlemen, you're wanted in Courtroom Five on the second floor."

"Thank you, officer, your coffee is on me." I dropped a five-dollar bill on the counter.

In the courtroom DA Martinez waved us over and handed me a dollar bill. "You called it. The defense has asked for a postponement until Wednesday. It has something to do with an FBI case that Mitcham is involved with. I don't have access to any information because it doesn't have anything to do with our case. Sorry, gentlemen."

Walking out of the courtroom, A. J. spewed a few expletives and handed me a dollar bill.

I stopped by the Hensley homestead and checked in on the boys. Rosie was working late so I left her a note, hugged Grandpa and Grandma, kissed my troops, and dragged my behind home.

As I was lying in bed it occurred to me that I hadn't seen Rosie in three days. That is the longest we've been apart since we've been married. Then the phone rang, "Hello—Hi, sweetheart . . ."

CHAPTER ELEVEN

The sound of breaking glass and marbles bouncing off the floor brought me to that threshold of consciousness that teeters between deep sleep and fully awake. The boys must have broken a glass, and in a moment, I'll hear one of them calling for mom, and blaming the other for the breakage. I pulled the blanket up over my shoulder and pushed deep into the pillow, with the full expectation of returning to dreamland. Boys will be boys.

My eyes shot open when my brain received a cold frightening message: the boys aren't here.

From Little Joe's room I heard someone whisper, "What the hell was that?"

"Some kid's toy. Don't worry about it," came a second voice.

"Are you sure he's gone?"

"Yeah, he's at work. You didn't see no yellow Charger out front, did ya?"

"What about the family?"

"They're holed up somewhere. Curtis knows where. Now shut up and let's get to work."

I carefully rolled off the bed on the side away from the door taking the shotgun with me. Rotating so I could see from under the bed if feet were at the door, I gripped the slide and made ready to rack in a round.

"Let's start down there." One intruder said, as footsteps could be heard going down the hall.

I set the shotgun down and took the phone from the nightstand.

"OPD, is this an emergency?" The police dispatcher answered.

"This is Bob Richards, two men have . . ." I was interrupted.

"I'm sorry, sir, I can barely hear you. Please speak up."

"This is Bob Richards." I said a little louder, "Two men broke into my home. I think they're armed."

"What's your address?"

"207 Laurel . . ."

The noise in the kitchen went silent. "Did you hear that? There's someone here."

"They're coming." I leapt across the bed, hit the button on the clock radio, and scrambled back to the side of the bed.

"Sir, sir. Don't hang up. Sir."

I tucked the phone receiver under the mattress to muffle the sound, ducked back under the bed, and put my finger on the trigger.

Four feet appeared at the door and stopped just as music began to play on the clock radio.

"It's a damn radio. There's nobody here," one said and turned away. "Let's go, we don't have all night for this."

Within minutes, that seemed like hours, I heard car doors being slammed and commands being given outside in front of the house.

"It's the cops," came a shout from the kitchen. "Come on, we'll go out the back," as the bad guys headed my way.

Just as they cleared the bedroom door, I rose up from behind the bed, racked in a round, and said loud enough for the neighbors to hear, "You move, you die." Stunned, both stopped.

I knew one of them, Rosko Tanner, the human sludge that gave Little Joe the bullet.

"On your knees, lace your fingers over your head." Then I heard the cracking sound of my front door being kicked in. For some inexplicable reason all I could think of at that moment was how much it was going to cost to repair. Please don't let it be Charles Williams's size-fourteen foot at my door. He'd take out the door and the frame.

I rose to my feet, looking like hillbilly militia with my shotgun and boxers and waiting for the cavalry to arrive.

"Back here," I shouted, placing my gun on the bed. No need to get through this and then get shot by the good guys.

I could hear officers clearing each of the rooms as Officer Philip Mann stepped behind my unwelcome guests.

"Anyone else in the house."

"No, Phil. I think these are the only two."

"Their motorcycles were parked a couple doors down. Unfortunately, they were in the way of the SWAT wagon and got run over."

A groan came up from Rosko's gut.

"Yep, darn shame. Looked like nice bikes too."

After cuffing and searching them, Phil got them on their feet.

"Nice undies," he said through a toothy grin. Then dropping his head, "I'm sorry about the door, man."

"No problem, you're forgiven. Just don't bring up my boxers ever again."

In the kitchen one of the SWAT members opened a duffle bag that was on the counter and found four sticks of dynamite taped together with the blasting cap wired to a clock. The alarm was set for 8:00 a.m. on Wednesday, the time I would be getting ready for court.

"Hey, I remember one of these guys saying, 'Let's start in the kitchen.'" I began opening cabinets and drawers. Under the sink, pushed back in the corner, was another bomb, identical to the one in the duffle bag.

Calling his team together the SWAT commander ordered, "We have two bombs. We don't know if we have more. Split up and thoroughly search every room from top to bottom, and I mean everything. Try not to make too much of a mess but be thorough."

"I don't think they were here long enough to plant any more."

"Maybe not, but we're not going to take any chances. Where's your car?"

"It's in a neighbor's garage. I parked it there so it wouldn't get trashed."

"Okay. How about putting on some pants and going with one of my guys to check it out."

"No problem, but are the pants really necessary?"

"Trust me, with those legs, it's necessary. Mann, go with Richards to his car and check it out."

The cool evening air helped calm my nerves as the Charger got a thorough going over. Our pace going back to the house was a bit slower, allowing me to assemble my thoughts.

"That was a close one, Bob."

"Sure was, Phil." Then it struck me. "I have to call A. J. If they're coming after me, they'll be going after him."

Officer Mann keyed his portable, "Dispatch, this is SWAT-9, go to channel 6."

Channel 6 is an encrypted radio channel used to conceal what is being said from police scanners and others who monitor law enforcement frequencies.

"Go ahead, SWAT-9."

"Call Officer Alford Jackson's residence and send a unit there. He and Officer Richards have been working a case that may be connected to the bombs we discovered in Richards's residence. Tell Jackson to vacate the house. We will respond shortly."

"Got it. I'll advise you once I've made contact."

Back at the house I was given an all clear, and SWAT faded into the sunset toward A. J.'s.

Thanks to some of the finest neighbors on the planet, my front door was quickly boarded up and awaited a real carpenter to do his or her magic. I've always wanted a windowed door. This might be the excuse I needed to get one.

Showered, shaved, and uniformed, I backed out the Charger and headed for work, expecting to see A. J. safe and sound in the squad room.

Half a block down the street I slammed on the brakes and skidded to a stop. Words began to bounce around in my head, "If they're coming after me, they'll be going after him." Looking into the rearview mirror I could see my house. If they're coming after me, they'll be going after them.

Throwing it in reverse I raced backward to the house, jumped out, and ran to the back door. Fumbling with the keys I began to curse. "Breathe," I said to myself, "breathe." Once inside I dialed Joe's number.

"Hello," said an unfamiliar, friendly male voice, "the Hensley residence."

"Who is this?"

"Well, hello, Officer Richards, and how are you? Are you having a bang-up day? Get it, bang up?"

"Mitcham, if you have so much as touched any member of my family, I'll kill you."

"Now that's no way to talk. If you do what you're told, everyone will be just fine."

"I want to talk to my wife. If I don't talk to my wife, I don't do anything but track you down."

"Calm down, Bob, calm down. Here she is."

In a shaky but angered voice, Rosie said, "Bob."

"Is everyone okay there? Are the boys okay?"

"Yes. They're locked in the basement with Dad and Mom."

That was good news. When the boys were born, Joe turned the basement into a playroom for them. Each boy had their own treasure chest filled to the brim with games and toys. There were beanbag chairs, sofas with rollout beds, rubber mats on the floor, and two TVs with VHS players.

Every time a new movie for kids came out, Joe made sure it was on their shelf.

Rosie's tone was strong, a mixture of rage wrapped in fear, "What's going on? Who are these people?"

"Rosie, how many are there and are they armed?"

"There's four of . . ." she was instantly cut off.

Mitcham came back on, "Your family is okay for now, Richards, so long as you don't do something stupid."

"What do you want?"

"You, Bob, just you. This is all about us. You and me."

"Between us? You think this somehow is going to make the Safeway thing get any better?"

"No. I don't give a damn about that. I want to settle things up with you."

"Okay, name the time and place, and I'll be there."

"Right now, Bobby boy, and right here in your daddy's front yard. We're going to settle things right here in grandpa land. When I'm done with you, I'll hit the road and disappear."

"I'm on my way, but if you've harmed anyone . . ." the phone went dead.

That narcissistic SOB wasn't angry about getting busted for a botched burglary. He was angry because he lost respect when he lost control of his bladder. I guess he expected to save face by taking me out. He was a piece of human dung who was even willing to kill a whole family, including children, just to get even.

In the bedroom I stripped off my uniform and put on a T-shirt, jeans, and a light jacket. From the nightstand I slid the Browning High Power into a hip holster and retrieved the Smith & Wesson .38 from the planter in the hall. In the kitchen I took two rolls of quarters from Rosie's change jar, putting one in each coat pocket.

On the lid of the jar was engraved, "For where your treasure is, there your heart will be also." Matthew 6:21. I began to feel weak, my legs started to shake, and my heart felt like it was going to explode.

Leaning over the kitchen sink I began to cry. My treasure was locked up in a basement by people whose only joy in life was hurting others. Screaming so heaven would hear, "God, if you're up there, if you're somewhere, anywhere, then show yourself."

I wanted to fold up on the floor, close my eyes, and let this nightmare melt away, but that wasn't an option. "God," I whimpered, "protect my family. Please, God, don't let anyone get hurt."

With a deep breath I shook off the fear, straightened up, removed the Browning from its holster, and confirmed that a round was in the chamber. It was time to go to war.

In the street in front of the house where my family were imprisoned were four motorcycles. On the porch swing sat Curtis Mitcham, alone.

I scanned the sides, windows, and driveway—no one. Stepping from around the car I moved cautiously onto the lawn. "Where's your backup? You sure aren't going to do this alone, are ya?"

"I don't need anyone else to take care of a pig like you." Mitcham rocked in the swing.

Working the street had taught me that keeping a cool head gives me an edge. Anger only pushes you to do stupid things. So, I was going to get him angry.

"That's not like you, Curtis. You're the kind of coward who needs at least two more to blindside a guy and beat him half to death. Isn't that what you did to John Steller at Dee's the other night?"

"Yeah, but I don't need anyone for you." He stood and three leather-clad trolls appeared from the house.

"Uh-oh. Too late, Curtis. Looks like your boys are going to see you wet yourself again." I began to laugh.

His face flushed and neck swelled, and he bared his teeth like a mad dog. Enraged, Mitcham leapt from the porch and ran toward me cursing. I pulled my right hand from my pocket with a firm grip around a roll of Rosie's quarters and waited. My father taught me how to pitch the fastest baseball, throw the farthest football, and hit the longest golf drive. It was all a matter of timing and the shifting of your weight toward the target. Just as he was almost upon me, I stepped forward and swung with everything I had, throwing my weight behind it. My fist landed squarely between his nose and left eye, as quarters exploded into the air. Pain shot through my hand and up my arm, as his eyes rolled back, and blood poured from his nose. Like my dad used to say, he went down like a sack of potatoes.

I looked up to see that the trolls had come off the porch with a look that said I was in for a lot of pain. Behind them the screen door flew open, and Lieutenant Miller stepped out onto the porch, racking a round into his 12 gauge.

"That's far enough." the lieutenant motioned to the ground. "On your knees."

They stopped but hesitated, debating their next move.

From either side of the house appeared A. J., Scott Johnson, and Gary Alison with Turk, growling and biting at the air. He was hungry for a rare serving of bad guy.

"I don't mind cutting you in half, I just don't want to write the reports. So I'll say this just once more. On your knees, hands on your head." Each dropped obediently.

I stepped over Mitcham, who lay unconscious at my feet, and ran into the house. Unlocking the basement door, I hit the steps so fast I fell and slid down most of them.

"Daddy," yelled Little Joe when he jumped into my arms, followed by the other two ragamuffins. "We've been playing games and watching movies. Mommy is letting us stay up late."

"That's great." I reached out to Rosie.

After a couple dozen well-deserved hugs and kisses, even from Alberta, I went outside to meet my gang in blue.

"How did you guys know I needed ya? And how did you know I was here?"

"In nearly four years you've never been late, always early," Lieutenant Miller said. "Today you just weren't there. I got no answer at the house, so I had A. J. call over to where your family was staying. He said there was trouble, because some guy answered the phone and said that everyone was at the movies. Three little boys at the movies after midnight? Really?"

"We had an unmarked unit do a drive-by, and reported the motorcycles parked out front." A. J. frowned. "We were pulling in around the back when we saw you roll up. If we had gotten here any later it could have turned ugly. Any sooner and Mitcham may not have had his lights put out."

"Speaking of that," Miller said, pointing at the ground where Mitcham had landed, "that looks like about ten bucks in quarters. Any idea where they came from?"

"Yeah, my pocket," I smirked. "All's fair in love and war, right?"

The lieutenant smiled. "Charles Williams is covering your shift, so take a few hours and get things settled here. Then come in and make your reports."

"Yes, sir, and thank you, sir."

"By the way, we received a warrant for Mitcham and Rosko Tanner from Phoenix. After they face charges here for everything from kidnapping to jaywalking, they'll be going to Arizona on first-degree murder charges. They won't see the light of day until they're in their eighties."

From the porch Joe called out, "Bob, come on in, the boys want to say goodnight to their dad."

In the basement, Alberta had made up all the sofa beds. Each held a Richards storm trooper. In the corner Rosie sat with a broad smile on her face. "I was scared, Bob, but I knew you would come for us. I just knew it."

"Where else would I be?"

Standing over three of the most important little men in the world, I took a deep breath and thanked God for their protection. Wherever He is, He answered my prayer.

CHAPTER TWELVE

Lieutenant Miller told me to take the day off and stay with my family. It was a weekend so Mitcham and his crew wouldn't be arraigned until late Monday or Tuesday. This would give time for each of the officers involved to complete their reports.

Following Monday morning grave shift, I sat at the desk in the back of the squad room and assembled the various parts of my report. Along with my extensive narrative of the evening's events, I attached written statements from Joe, Alberta, and Rosie, along with the arrest reports, evidence logs, and transcribed accounts from A. J., Scott, Gary, and Lieutenant Miller. This report was sure to be a ten pounder.

Just about every officer reporting for duty that morning patted me on the back, gave me a high-five, or expressed kudos in some way as they arrived for briefing. I would have questioned how so many knew what had happened had I not known that the two places in the world where news travels fastest are ladies' hair salons and police locker rooms.

Sergeant Alan approached the podium, and the room went silent.

"I'm sure you have all heard that Curtis Mitcham and six members of the Savages motorcycle club are off the street in County on a variety of felony charges. The detectives are working on identifying those who attacked John Steller at Dee's store and set the store on fire. I have been told that numerous fingerprints have been removed from the explosive devices found in Bob Richards's home and the gas can from Dee's store. A search warrant is being served today on the bikers' clubhouse and on certain members of the club. We expect to receive arrest warrants for more members of Mitcham's knitting circle in the near future."

Following the briefing I filed my reports and headed for my car. All I wanted to do now was go home, get my family together, and move back into our own house where we all belong.

"Hey, Bob. You have a minute?" Scott Johnson called from across the parking lot.

"Sure, what's up?"

"Can we grab a cup of coffee?"

I hesitated, wanting to say no, that I had a family waiting for me. Then a little voice inside me somewhere said, *"Your family is at home. His might be coming apart."*

"Sure, meet you at Dee's. I need to pick up some of her sweet rolls for the boys."

In Dee's parking lot I was surprised to see that work had already begun repairing the fire damage to the garage. Workmen went about shoring up the roof and removing the burned-out wall on the east side of the building.

"Good morning, Officer Richards, make yourself comfortable. I'll be with you in just a minute," Dee said from the kitchen, peering through a small rectangular opening in the wall behind the counter.

"Take your time. I'm not in a rush."

The little bell that hung on the front door rang as Scott came in.

"Every time I come in here and smell Dee's sweet rolls, I gain a pound." Scott rubbed his stomach.

"They're worth the additional tonnage." I said when he pulled up a chair. Cutting through the small talk, I went right to the heart. "So, is she pregnant?"

"No. She went to her doctor and took a test. What a relief. I didn't know what I was going to do."

"Have you broken it off with her?"

"Not yet. I wanted to know about the pregnancy first. I'm meeting her tonight."

"You're meeting her? That's not a smart move. If you're going to end it, then end it. Call her, don't meet her. You can say what you need to say on the phone. Be honest, and make it brief."

Dee came to the table with coffee and two of her sweet rolls. "You boys doing okay?"

"Yes, ma'am. How's John doing?" I asked.

"We really don't know, but he takes after his father who was a tough old bird." The coffeepot in her hand began to shake and a tear ran down her cheek.

I pulled out a chair from the table and took the coffeepot from her hand. "Sit down, Dee. There's nobody here but us. Please sit down."

"They're doing a lot of tests and may have to put him into a medically induced coma to protect his brain from swelling.

His jaw, nose, and three ribs are broken." She began to cry. "They beat him real bad. Why would anyone do that? Why?"

The bell on the door rang as a tall young man came in.

Scott was on his feet, "Good morning, what do you need?"

"A large coffee and a sweet roll." He smiled.

Scott snatched a tall Styrofoam cup, filled it with coffee, wrapped a sweet roll in a napkin, and handed it to him. "There you go, it's on the house. Have a good day, goodbye." Looking puzzled but pleased, the young man said thanks and walked out. Scott put two dollars near the cash register and locked the front door.

I spent the next fifteen minutes explaining how the men who were arrested burglarizing the Safeway store mistook her as a witness and were trying to intimidate her into not testifying. It was a mistake on their part that led to the assault on John, the fire, and the threats.

"Last night we put in jail the men responsible for all this. They are being charged with a long list of crimes, as well as being wanted in Arizona. They won't be getting out to hurt anyone again for a very long time."

"That's good to know." She wiped the tears from her eyes with a napkin, "When John is better, would you go and see him? I know it would mean a lot. He really likes you. Talks about your car all the time. Says one day he'll have one."

"Sure." I handed her a business card. "Call me when he's up to it."

She stood, straightened her apron, and picked up the pot of coffee, "I'm going to lock up for today. You boys stick around awhile. I have a dozen rolls for each of you. I'll get you some more hot coffee too."

I was about to politely protest because I wanted to get home to my family when something told me she needed us to be here a little while longer. She just didn't want to be alone.

With a fresh cup of coffee and a warm sweet roll, we got back to the subject at hand. "Scott, there's one question I failed to ask. Does Vicky Harper have any other boyfriends?"

"No, she says she loves me." Rocking back in his chair, he looked up at the ceiling and sighed. "No boyfriends, she's married."

"Married?" I was floored. "Does her husband know about you?"

"No, he doesn't know anything. He's been away for almost a year, now."

"So, she and her husband are separated?"

"Yeah, in a manner of speaking."

I was getting frustrated with his word games. "What do you mean, in a manner of speaking? They're either together or they're not. Are they separated and getting a divorce?"

"He's some kind of Special Forces guy. He's over in Vietnam, been there over a year now, getting things ready for the big pullout Nixon has ordered. This is the second time he's been there."

I felt my blood begin to boil. I knew my face was flush. "You're sleeping with a married woman whose husband is in Vietnam?"

"Yeah. She doesn't know when he'll be back."

Dee set a bag of sweet rolls for each of us on the table and asked if we wanted more coffee. I politely declined, stood, said I needed to go, and added, "Scott will stay and keep you company. Won't you, Scott?"

I looked down at him as a mixture of emotions ran rampant through me, and in a voice as calm as I could muster said, "Her husband has her on his mind and in his heart right now as he works his way through jungles and hip deep in rice patties. He'll be coming home, maybe in a body bag, and here you are eating sweet rolls and sleeping with his wife."

I picked up my bag of rolls, dropped five bucks on the table, and walked toward the door.

"Don't talk to me again, Scott, till it's over," I snarled.

It was a Sunday morning and the traffic on the road home was light. I opened the windows to get some fresh air and cranked up the radio. Wolfman Jack's gravelly voice filled the car as he spun the latest hits. The first tune he introduced was "She'd Rather Be with Me" by the Turtles. How ironic. The title could not have fit Scott's situation better, and the song itself brought back memories I didn't need. Although my body was cruising down Highway 80, my mind was back in Southeast Asia.

At our base camp in Tuy Hoa, some new arrivals were listening to music on a portable tape recorder. I asked about the music and was told it was a group called the Turtles. We didn't believe it. It was bad enough to have "Beatles," now we had Turtles.

With no horizon lights to obscure the night sky, the nights there were spectacular. The stars were brilliant against a pitch-black firmament. It was almost like you could reach out and touch them.

I would walk outside between the tents at night and hear the muffled sound of music playing in the new recruits' tent.

When there was a full moon I would sit at the edge of our bivouac, look up, and imagine that only fourteen hours earlier that moon had been looking down on my fiancée, Pat. Then I would go back to my bunk, pull out her picture, and reread her letter that said how much she missed me.

The picture was getting ragged, and the letter had become like parchment, brittle and stained. I received Pat's letter when I was at the Oakland army terminal waiting for my transport to this cesspool of mosquitoes and bullets. I never got another.

I turned off the radio and finished my drive home in silence.

All the memories and emotions I had built up washed away when I saw Rosie's white 1970 Chevy Vega wagon parked in the driveway. My family was back. Walking toward the door, I counted one bike with training wheels and one without, a tricycle, a Stretch Armstrong, two rubber lightsabers, and a half dozen Hot Wheels. Inside I heard little Joe, "Daddy's home," and the door flew open. Despite the odds, three against one, I fought my way to the kitchen where I was met by the queen of the realm, who bestowed upon me the honor of a kiss. It almost felt like the last forty-eight hours had never happened.

"You're late. I expected you would be home by 9:00 a.m. I wanted to get to work early on my first day."

"I'm sorry, baby. What time do you have to be there?"

"Ten. I called and told them that my husband was a police officer and sometimes he's late getting home. They were very kind and said not to worry, but I could tell they were not happy. This is a horrible way to start a new job."

"Okay, we have thirty minutes to get you there. Get in the car. Boys, let's go, everyone in the car. Daddy's car, the Bumble Bee," the nickname for my yellow Charger R/T.

"Guys, buckle up." I backed out of the driveway. Usually at this point Rosie would grab my arm, give me that don't-do-something-stupid look, and say, "Take it slow, Robert." Instead, she checked the boys' seatbelts and latched hers. "Let's go, Bob."

When the big hand hit twelve and the little hand hit ten on the clock in front of the Walsh, Harper, & Smith building, the Bumble Bee slid to a stop. With kisses from all around Rosie was on her way to work. With a quick wave from the top of the steps, Mommy disappeared through the glass revolving door.

I dropped my three little cowboys off at the Hensley ranch and made a point of greeting Alberta and admiring her needlepoint. In the backyard, between the sandbox and the jungle gym, Joe was assembling a swing set. The way he treated his grandsons made me wonder how Rosie turned out so well. She should be the most self-absorbed brat on the planet.

My offer to help in the construction was kindly declined. This was a labor of love that required the skilled hands of a grandpa to complete, so I went home to get some sleep. At five, Rosie's four boys would pick her up and head out for a gourmet meal at McDonald's. At home there would be family time, followed by one hour of TV, then tucked into bed with a story read by Mom. The day would come to a close with kisses and prayer, followed by Mommy and Daddy stealing an hour to become reacquainted.

"Have I told you how much I appreciate you?" I said, "How much I love you?"

"Yes, by your words and by everything you do."

"I have made a lot of choices in my life, Rosie, but the best choice I've ever made was to do life with you. I love you, baby."

CHAPTER THIRTEEN

A. J. pranced into the squad room like a peacock in bloom. He had a smile that reached from ear to ear, and if his chest got any bigger, he'd pop all his buttons. Everyone noticed, but no one said a word. We all just watched him strut in and take his seat. The Cheshire-cat smile on his face never faded.

Sergeant Helmer stepped to the podium, looked around the room, and stopped at A. J. "Gentlemen, we have some very good news, the kind of news that can even change A. J.'s scowl to a grin. Senior Officer Alford Jackson has just become the grandpa of an eight-pound, six-ounce baby boy."

The room resonated with applause and a few shouts, as A. J. stood and waved his appreciation. "They're naming him Alford," A. J. said with a smile I had never seen on him before. "He's going to be a teacher like his dad." He was one proud papa.

"Congratulations, A. J. Okay, gentlemen, now down to business. The DA's office notified us that Curtis Mitcham has been placed on house arrest." A loud groan mixed with curses filled the room. "Once again he made some kind of deal with the Feds. Judge Fairland set a high bail and ordered that he must be in the company of a federal officer at all times. Whatever he is doing, it must be big."

"They're not going to drop any of the charges on him, are they?" I asked.

"No. Judge Fairland made a point to say that Mitcham's release is only temporary and that he will stand to answer every charge listed in the complaint. He has refused extradition to Phoenix on the murder charge, so that hearing will have to take place too. He and his lawyer know the system and they're using it. Okay, give Grandpa a pat on the back, pick up your warrant packets, stay alert and safe out there. Dismissed."

I covered the majority of my beat, then checked my digital watch, with its bright red numbers. It told me it was 1:45, time to saunter toward the bar district. There are three individual areas that have the highest concentration of bars and liquor stores, each with its own exclusive clientele. Along Pine Ridge, the drinks run twelve dollars, there's a cover charge, and the music is live. On South Main, the beer is cold, the booze is watered down, and the jukebox only plays country. At the intersection of Moyer and Grand, a bar is on each corner. This and three blocks in either direction is known as Skid Row. Around the front of each bar sit four or five aged rummies, staking out their territory as the kings of the corner. They will be there until five, then vaporize into one of the dilapidated hotels or vacant buildings or a makeshift mansion made from discarded boxes. Occasionally, curses and threats are tossed back and forth from one corner to another, but rarely does anyone venture away from their domain.

Passing Moyer Drive I continued onto Grand Avenue toward South Main. Seeing movement ahead I hit my high beams and illuminated a large hairy figure stepping off the curb into the street. Chewbacca, the Star Wars Wookiee warrior, stepped out into the street and stood in front of my car with a crazed look. Slowly he raised his hands, as if to surrender.

"Dispatch, this is Xray-12, I'm on Grand one block south of Moyer, with one WMA, I think. Request backup."

"Xray-7, roll to cover Xray-12 one block south of Moyer on Grand."

"Ten-four, en route."

I slipped out from behind the wheel, stood, and let the door close softly. "Good evening," I smiled. "A bit late to be out, isn't it?"

"I need you to come," the Wookiee said. "She needs you to come."

"Where am I supposed to go, and who is she?"

"Come." He turned and disappeared between two abandoned buildings.

"Wait."

The alleyway was shaded from the streetlights. I had to let my eyes adjust to the dark, and when they did, the Wookiee was gone. Mounds of trash lined the walls, and every fifteen to twenty feet a hut was constructed of scrap wood, taped cardboard, and blue plastic tarps. The flickering of small fires burning in fire-rings, and the occasional gas lantern cast a dim glow off the block and brick walls, creating an eerie, surreal environment. At each fire several people squatted and watched silently as I maneuvered around them.

I stopped at a fire with two adults and three children, "A big guy, long hair and beard, just ran through here. Where did he go?" Not a single response, just blank stares.

"He's not in any trouble. He said he wanted me to follow him. I think he needed help. I need to find him."

Sitting on his mommy's lap, a boy of about six pointed to the end of the ally. "He went down there." The little guy's help earned him a slap on the wrist from Mom.

I worked my way to the end of the alley and out onto the sidewalk on Pearl Drive, a street lined with abandoned office buildings. Across the street, Chewbacca stood in a doorway waving to me. Above his head were chiseled the words *Kessler Wealth Management.*

"Xray-7, I'm at the Kessler building on Pearl," I said into my portable radio.

"Be there in one," A. J. responded.

I hesitated for a minute and then crossed the street as my backup rolled to a stop at the curb a few yards short of the Wookiee. Together we followed him through dark hallways and up two flights of steps. On the third floor at the end of the hall stood a large, ornate wooden door. Carved on the door was *Herbert J. Kessler, President.*

Inside, several squatters had erected cardboard petitions, sectioning the empty office into three small but private dwellings. Each had several lamps lit that illuminated the entire room. One of the residents of this cardboard high-rise jumped to his feet when he saw us. Indignantly he shouted, "What are you doing here? We have a right to be here. You can't make us leave."

"Relax. We're not here to roust anyone," A. J. said. "We're here to help someone. So go back to whatever you were doing."

"You don't have a right to be here, so get out," the man continued as we followed Chewbacca to the back of the room. "I know the mayor, and if you don't get out of here now, I'll call him, and you will be fired."

A. J. stopped, turned slowly, and in a low, gravel tone said, "Go sit down and shut up, or I'm going to put you in another box. Then you and the mayor can talk during visiting hours."

The man hesitated for a moment, weighing out his options, but when he looked into A. J.'s eyes, he chose option A and returned quietly to his section of the world.

In the back, sectioned off by screens discarded from a clothing store, was the Wookiee's lair. Along one wall lay a mattress with two blankets, a pillow, and a nightstand with a kerosene lamp. On the back wall, on either side of the window, hung two large Raiders football posters. Under them were four plastic milk crates filled with books and two open ice chests. There was no sign of alcohol, drugs, or paraphernalia. Opposite the mattress on the other wall, tucked into a dilapidated La-Z-Boy, was a girl of about fifteen. Her legs were pulled up tight against her chest, and through a mop of dirty hair, she peered out at us with eyes filled with fear.

I moved past A. J. and whispered, "Call for a female officer and get our big friend's information. Find out what he knows about this young lady."

The closer I got the more terrified the girl appeared. I stopped about six feet from her, sat on the floor, took my hat off, and smiled. "Hi. My name is Bob. What's yours?"

She didn't make a sound, just stared at me with terror in her eyes. "I'm not going to hurt you, I promise. Do you live around here? Are your mother or father close by?" The mention of where she lived and her parents only caused her to tighten up even more. There was a problem at home, that was for sure.

I scooted over and leaned back against a crate of books, removed one, and thumbed through it. "I love to read. I read to my little boys every night before they go to bed." That initiated a response. She turned slightly, pulled her hair back from one eye, and looked at me. I could see under her hair that her left eye appeared swollen and dark.

"Do you like to read?" A small nod. "What's your favorite book?"

A long pensive stare, then slowly she sat back in the seat, "*Little Women.*"

"Really. That's my wife's favorite too. She must have read it a dozen times." I smiled. "She says she feels like Meg with our three boys."

Her legs no longer tight against her chest, and the fear fading from her eyes, she said softly, "I'm Beth. I don't go to school, but I want to be Amy."

"Do you want to go to school?"

Her voice broke as if she were about to cry, "Yes."

"We're here to help you. A friend of mine is coming. Her name is Chelsey, and she's a police officer too. She has two beautiful girls who go to school close to here. You may know them. I have asked her to come and help you. Is that okay?"

With a nod she cautiously stood and meticulously brushed out the wrinkles in her dress that was two sizes too big, dirty, and threadbare. Her eye was blackened and nearly swollen shut, and there were bruises on her face and arms. She had been beaten severely, but what caught my attention was that she was pregnant.

I didn't want to show my surprise, so I remained seated on the floor and smiled. "So you are Beth, but you want to be Amy. Is Beth or Amy your real name?"

A grin slowly appeared on her face as she sat back down on the chair. "My name is Zoey."

"Hello, Zoey. Would you mind if I asked you a few questions?"

"Okay."

"Do you live around here?"

"No."

"Do your mother or father live near here."

"No."

"Well, good early morning to you, and who do we have here?" Came the pleasant, cheerful voice of Officer Defo.

"This is Zoey. Her favorite book is *Little Women*, and she plans on being an artist like Amy. Right?" I smiled. "Zoey, this is Officer Chelsey. I have to go and talk with the other officer. Is it okay if I leave you with Chelsey?"

With a look of apprehension Zoey nodded her approval.

Chelsey didn't miss a beat, dropping the lid on one of the ice chests, pulling it over in front of Zoey, and sitting down. "When is your baby due, sweetheart?"

Outside A. J. waved me over and introduced me to Chewbacca. "Bob, underneath all that hair is Hilbert Hendrix, offensive lineman for the Oakland Raiders."

"Hilly. I have your jersey in my closet. My kids use it as a tent." I extended my hand.

Hilbert "Hilly" Hendrix was the most feared lineman in the NFL. Six-foot-six, three hundred and eighty pounds of solid muscle. Trying to push your way to the quarterback with Hilly in the way was like trying to push your way into the vault at Fort Knox. He had the world at his doorstep until a low blow rearranged his kneecaps. He finished out his contract on the bench, becoming addicted to the pain-killers the team doctors gave out like candy.

"If you don't mind," A. J. said, "tell Officer Richards what you told me."

"I was coming back from a recovery session when I heard crying in the tall grass outside the restrooms in Bellflower Park. The girl was hiding behind a dumpster. Someone beat her up real bad. I went to help her, but she pulled away and started screaming, so I backed off and left. About halfway home, I decided I just couldn't leave her, so I went back. I thought she was asleep, but I couldn't wake her, so I picked her up and brought her here. She woke up and rolled up into a ball in the chair, so I thought I'd go to the phone booth on Grand and call you guys. That's when I saw you."

"Thank you. Did you know she is pregnant?"

"No." His eyes watered. "I see a lot of kids around my neighborhood with extended tummies. Mom and Dad spend any money they get on crack or horse rather than food. Then they rely on a system that don't work for nobody."

"Okay. We're going to get her checked out by a doctor and we'll make sure she's looked after. If we need anything else, we know where we can find you. Thanks again, you may have saved her life."

At the door of the Kessler building, Chelsey was walking out with Zoey at her side. "We're going to see a doctor, get something to eat, and then we'll be back at the PD. Come by for info," Chelsey shouted.

"Will do. Thank you for all your help," I shouted back. Then seeing Chewbacca walking away, "Hilly, wait a minute."

"I would like to take you to a late dinner or early breakfast, but I have to get back to work." I shook his hand again and left a twenty-dollar bill in his palm. "I hope I can come back with my jersey for an autograph."

"Thank you, but that's not necessary. Any time on that autograph."

Maneuvering my way back through the occupied alleyway, the little boy on his mother's lap was standing in a makeshift doorway of two large refrigerator boxes nailed together and covered with tarps. He grabbed my pant leg as I walked by, looked up at me with the brightest blue eyes. "Did you find the big man? Did ya?"

"I sure did, thanks to you. You really helped me, and I was able to help him too." In my breast pocket I took out a Junior Police Badge business card and handed it to him. "You are now an official Junior Police friend." His blues eyes got even brighter, and over his shoulder I could see his mom sitting in her improvised residence with a smile on her face.

"I will pray for you, mister policeman." The little guy scampered off into his box.

I'm glad I kept a few cards with me. Most of the guys stopped carrying them because you don't run into too many kids on graveyard, especially ones who will pray for you.

CHAPTER FOURTEEN

In the hall outside the chief's conference room, I heard a sound I didn't expect: laughter. Gathered around Chelsey and a very pregnant Zoey were two dispatchers and two ladies from the secretarial pool. On the desk were several bags and an assortment of wrappers from Danny's All-Night Diner.

When she saw me at the door, Chelsey said, "Officer Richards, please join us. I called ahead and ordered us a little breakfast."

"Thanks, but I'm going to pass. I'll grab a cup of coffee from the squad room. When you get a minute, I'd like to talk with you."

"I have a minute right now, Officer Richards." Chelsey turned to the other women in the room, "Ladies, do you mind taking care of our guest for a little while?" By their response, you would have thought they were asked to take care of the Hope Diamond.

Once we were out of range of being heard, Chelsey said, "You're not going to believe what that little girl has gone through. I've contacted Protective Services and asked for Angela Doran, an agent I have worked with before.

Detective Carol Fielding has been assigned the case and will be here in an hour to follow up."

In the breakroom I poured each of us a cup of coffee and took a table in front of a large window overlooking the parking lot. From here we could watch the sun rise over the city. I could tell that Chelsey needed a little light in her day.

"It's nice to see a smile on that girl's face."

Withdrawing her notepad from her pocket, Chelsey sat back and filled me in on what she had learned. Her name was Zoey Carlson. She was fourteen, would be fifteen in two months, and was about to enter her third trimester. Raised in a hippie commune on Mount Tamalpais, she ran away when her father and another man raped her. She had just turned twelve.

After being arrested by Oakland PD for shoplifting, she was put into the system. Her father was arrested and tried for the rape and is serving time in Folsom. She moved back with her mother, but within a couple months she was abandoned when her mother ran off with her father's best friend.

Things started to look better when she was placed in the home of Fred and Brenda Walsh, pastors of the First Baptist Church in Auburn. She was happy, cared for, back in school, and although it was a bit rough at first, made some good friends in the church. She lived with the Walshes for a year and a half, when Fred, at the age of forty-four, had a heart attack and died. Brenda was not able to continue as a foster parent, so Zoey was moved to a new home in central Contra Costa County.

In the foster home of Josh and Lily Spangler there were five other kids, all girls, ranging in age from ten to sixteen. Except for Josie, the oldest, who had been in the Spangler home for six months, all the rest had been placed there within the last three weeks. The reason there had been an influx of girls needing placement was a lack of foster homes available, and the Spanglers preferred girls.

It was summer break, and no one was in school yet, so the girls were kept busy doing housework, gardening, and more housework. No one minded because they all got along, and in a few weeks they would be heading off to school. Zoey had asked to attend church, but the Spanglers refused, calling it "a crutch for weak people."

Chelsey stopped for a moment, took a sip of coffee, and thumbed through her notes.

"Is that the reason she ran away, because she wasn't allowed to go to church? And what's the story about the pregnancy?" I asked.

"No, there's a lot more to this story." She sighed and continued with a narration I would have preferred not to hear.

One night Zoey was awakened by Josie who said she was leaving because she couldn't take it anymore. When questioned, Josie said that what was going on there was wrong and that all the girls needed to be careful. To Zoey this didn't make sense. Why would Josie run away because of the chores?

About a week after Josie left, Susie, the fourteen-year-old, was taken from their room by Mrs. Spangler and wasn't seen again until the next morning. When Zoey came down for breakfast, she found her sitting at the table still in her pajamas. She wouldn't look at anyone or say anything. When Zoey asked her if she was okay, she started to cry, and Mrs. Spangler told her to leave the table, get cleaned up, and get ready to do her chores. After that Susie was often missing from their room at night and rarely spoke to anyone.

When school started, the girls were told that they would not be attending because their parents were not available to sign the admittance papers. They were given some outdated books on history, social studies, and math, but not provided any instruction. Zoey and one other girl were the only ones who could read, so they would read to the others every evening before bed. After some persistent requests, Zoey was given a Bible that she read whenever she could.

One day while pulling weeds in the front yard, Zoey saw Mr. Spangler standing at an upstairs window watching her. A feeling went over her that told her to run. It was the same feeling she had gotten when her father and his friend would watch her play with her friends. She knew she should run but she couldn't leave the others. That night Mrs. Spangler came to her room and told Zoey to come with her. Mr. Spangler wanted to talk to her.

Over the next year both Josh and Lily Spangler molested all the girls, even the youngest. The outings to the mall and the grocery store ended, as well as the chores outside. No one was allowed to leave the house for any reason.

When Zoey became pregnant, Mr. Spangler was happy about the possibility of having a son. This was not the case for his wife. She became jealous about the attention her husband was showing Zoey and would often beat her and lock her in her room.

A week ago, the Spanglers had a big fight and Josh agreed to have the baby aborted. The problem was where they could find a place to have it done. The Supreme Court had ruled in favor of abortion rights, but it was so new there weren't many affordable places available. Lily found an ex-army medic who performed abortions in Vietnam. He operated an illegal clinic in an apartment on the east side of Bellflower Park.

Zoey had been taken there yesterday afternoon, but she refused to get out of the car. Lily drove into an alleyway, pulled her out by her hair, and beat and kicked her. At this point in the account, tears began to run down Chelsey's cheeks.

I reached out and touched her hand, "That's okay. Let's stop for now."

"No." Chelsey wiped her eyes with a napkin. "You need to hear this."

"Okay. Let me get you some water."

Straightening up in her seat, Chelsey took a deep breath and began, "Zoey said she wanted the abortion. She didn't want any part of that man in or near her, but she would sit and rub her tummy and talk to whatever was inside her. Then one night she woke up feeling the baby kicking. Lying there in the dark, she came to realize that there was a tiny human person dancing inside of her, and she owed it a life, one better than the one she had been given.

When Lily Spangler was beating her, she had kicked her several times in the stomach, something Zoey expected. While driving to the clinic, Zoey sat in the backseat of the car and slipped her open Bible up under her dress. When she was on the ground she doubled up and held it against her belly."

"Oh my God. Do you have the address of the Spangler house? Let's go get those girls out of there."

"We know where it is, and Lieutenant Miller is meeting with the DA and Protective Services now. A search warrant is being issued and should be signed later this morning. He knew you would want to be a part, but we need to do this by the numbers. The lieutenant said you can meet him in his office at noon if you want to participate."

"Good. I'll have breakfast with my boys and shoot back here. Thanks again, Chelsey, you have done a fine job."

"I plan on seeing this one all the way through." Chelsey smiled.

"What do you mean?"

"I'm going to ask Angela Doran, from PS, if I could be assigned as her temporary guardian. I have plenty of room and my girls would love her."

"Wow. That's big. I hope it works out. Anything else I can do?"

"No, it's pretty well wrapped up. There is one thing, though, if you get by Bellflower Park, see if you can find Zoey's Bible. She lost it getting away from Spangler."

"Will do."

On the drive home I thought of the decision Zoey had made to have the baby. It would have been more than reasonable to have an abortion considering the circumstances. That fourteen-year-old girl had more courage and compassion in her little finger than I would muster in a lifetime. I wondered how many children would have to make such a dreadful decision because of the actions of depraved and degenerate men? How many tiny unborn people would lose their lives, now that abortion had become a legal alternative to everyone for any reason? Would I even be here to be a small part of Zoey's life if abortion had been legal when I was conceived?

My mother was twenty-seven years old when I was conceived, and my father, fifty. They were married but not to each other. My mother had two children before me, children she abandoned by leaving them with a friend. Her husband was in Europe fighting for the liberation of France during World War II. My father had a daughter who was the same age as my mother, thus there was no love lost there. Two weeks after I was born, I was dropped off with a friend, who babysat me for the first five years of my life. When my father died, my grandfather and grandmother brought me to California where they raised me. As I looked back on those events, and considered the options that were available, it's easy to conclude that only divine intervention was sending me home to my wife and boys.

When I got home, I told Rosie about Zoey and apologized for having to go back to work to assist in serving the warrant on the Spangler house. Her response was a mixture of understanding and anger. She not only felt it was good I go, but also begged to go along with me.

After a breakfast that snapped, crackled, and popped, the boys and I took a morning dip in the Doughboy. Mom said she couldn't join us because she had something important to get done. I knew what it was, and after our swim I wasn't going to get any sleep before going back to work.

In the garage I found Rosie sitting on the floor among a dozen large boxes, each marked with a name and date: Joseph 1970–72, Stefan December 1972–74, and Casey 1974–. Around the boxes were stacks of folded baby clothes and assorted small pants, shirts, coats, and sweaters.

"Bob," she pointed to a stepladder under an opening in the ceiling that led to the attic. "Would you bring down the crib and bassinet. There's also a box of baby blankets and some of the boys' old toys."

"Okay." I knew telling her about Zoey would unleash the empathy monster that lived within her, and I also knew it would give me an excuse to clean out the attic.

By noon the garage floor was covered in baby furniture, clothes, toys, and blankets, and my attic was spotless. Lieutenant Miller called as I kicked back in the old rocker my father-in-law made when Little Joe was born and sipped on a glass of raspberry Kool-Aid.

"Bob, you awake."

"Yes, sir, haven't been to bed yet."

"We're not going to serve the warrants on the Spanglers until tonight. We want to make sure everyone is in the house. I know that you're off tonight, so do you still want to be a part of this?"

"I sure do. I want to get those girls out of there and lock those perverts up. What time are we going to hit the house?"

"Ten. Detective Wilson requested a 'no-knock' night service warrant. The DA said we wouldn't get it because we couldn't justify it. We can't show any risk to the officers or threats of violence to the girls. Wilson went directly to Judge Fairland's chambers during lunch, told him Zoey's story, and Fairland couldn't sign the warrant fast enough. There'll be a briefing at nine, so go get some sleep."

That night in the squad room, Lieutenant Miller went over what had transpired earlier and the importance of going in smooth and quiet. We didn't want to spook the girls. Other than Miller and me, there were two detectives and Officer Defo. We needed a female officer, and Chelsey insisted that it be her.

The Spangler house was fifteen years old, one of two floorplans in a planned community of three hundred cookie-cutter homes. On the screen Lieutenant Miller put the floorplan of a four-bedroom, two-bath, single-story home. The girls would be in the three bedrooms along the right side of the hall, and the suspects in the bedroom at the end of the hall.

"Bob, you started this thing, so you get the front door, and I'll back you up. Wilson, you take the back. Officer Defo, cover the left side rear. There's a sliding glass door off the master bedroom. Because of the girls, we're not going to kick our way in; we're going to knock and let them invite us in."

"Then why the no-knock warrant"? I asked.

"If there is any reason to assume that one of those girls is in trouble, I don't want to be delayed. I want to go in hot and loud."

Shutting off the overhead, the lieutenant looked around the room, "I've made arrangements with Protective Services to be present at the house and when we interview the girls. They are working on finding a home for all of them to expedite their placement and to initially keep them together." A broad grin formed on his face when he looked over at Chelsey, "Zoey has already been placed."

Detective Wilson stood to his feet, "Lieutenant, would you mind if we said a short prayer? Those girls have been traumatized enough. I sure don't want to add to it."

"Sure, by all means."

"Lord, we ask that you protect those girls and guide us in what we must do to bring these sick SOBs to justice. Sorry, Lord, but you know what we need. Amen."

Well, it wasn't very churchy, but it was to the point. I am confident if there is a God, He won't hold it against us.

"Thanks, Wilson, well done," Lieutenant Miller said. "Okay, let's go get those girls."

CHAPTER FIFTEEN

The neighborhood was quiet and the street empty, except for a resident mechanic tinkering on a classic old car a block away. We parked in front of the Spangler house and waited for Chelsey and Wilson to signal us that they were in place. Two clicks on the radio and we were at the front door ringing the bell.

The door opened only as wide as the chain lock would allow. A middle-aged, heavy-set woman in a flowered robe peered out at us. When her eyes looked down at our badges her expression changed from curiosity to panic, "Yes, what do you want?"

"Mrs. Spangler, I am Officer Richards, this is Lieutenant Miller. May we come in? We need to speak with you."

"What about?"

"Mrs. Spangler, we need to talk with you. Please let us in."

"Just a minute." She closed the door. "It's the police," she called out.

A few moments later Chelsey's voice cracked over the radio, "I have a WMA with a child at the slider. Saw me and disappeared back into the room."

"We're going in," Lieutenant Miller said over the radio, as I put my right, size-eleven to the door, causing it to sweep open, breaking the chain lock.

"Police Officer, we're coming in. We have a warrant." I cleared the living room, moving past the kitchen to the hallway. "Step out into the hallway, slowly."

The bedroom doors remained closed, and not a sound could be heard. Mrs. Spangler was also missing.

"Mr. and Mrs. Spangler. This is the Oakland Police Department. We have a warrant to search this house. Step out into the hallway slowly with your hands up." Still dead silence.

Stepping to either side of the first bedroom door, I knocked on and then opened the door. Inside there were two mattresses on the floor, with crumpled-up blankets and tattered pillows. Between the mattresses was a scuffed nightstand with a small lamp and a stack of paperback books. In the corner, next to each bed was a cardboard box with an assortment of clothes and a suitcase, but no girls. Each of the three bedrooms were furnished the same, and in each there were no girls.

We approached the last door at the end of the hall and knocked, then knocked again. Turning the knob, I found the door locked. "Mr. Spangler, please open the door. Mr. Spangler are the girls with you?"

Removing my sidearm, I stepped aside for the lieutenant to force the door open. "We have a warrant, so we're coming in one way or another. Mr. Spangler, we want to make this as easy as possible." Still no response.

With a swift movement, and a solid kick, the lieutenant had the door swinging open. Seated in the center of a king-size bed, with his back against the headboard, was Josh Spangler. On his lap were two small girls, not much older than ten. At his side sat Lily Spangler. Her left hand rested on Josh's leg and her right on a pillow she had on her lap. Over her hand a checkered towel had been tossed loosely, concealing whatever she was holding.

"Mrs. Spangler, please remove your hand from under the towel." I slowly removed my Smith & Wesson .357 from its holster. "Please, Mrs. Spangler, let's not make this situation any worse than it is."

With her left hand she lifted the towel to reveal a black revolver pointed directly at the girls. "I won't make it any worse if you won't."

"Let the girls go and we can talk about this," Lieutenant Miller said.

"No." She let the towel fall back over the revolver. "They're mine, and they're not going anywhere."

Cautiously, Chelsey slid the sliding glass door open, pulled back the curtain and stepped into the room. When Lily looked down and saw Chelsey's gun, her hand tightened its grip on her gun.

"Mrs. Spangler, Lily, I heard what you said. We need to talk about some very serious stuff, and it's not for little ears. Why not let your husband take the girls to their room, then we can talk."

"No. They stay, and we have nothing to talk about. Now, get out, you don't have any right to be here."

Chelsey raised an open left hand, bent slowly, and put her gun on the floor. In a calm, low voice she said, "Lily, we have a warrant to search your house. We aren't going anywhere. I've put my gun down. May I say something to you quietly, just woman to woman? It's not for the little women to hear, or these men. Can I whisper it to you?"

"Is this a trick?" Lily snapped.

"No. There's something really important you need to know. Just between us girls. Okay?"

"Okay, but don't do anything stupid. I mean it."

Chelsey bent down and in muffled tones spoke into Lily's ear. Raising up, Chelsey looked down and said in a tone that bordered on menacing, "Make your decision and make it now."

Lily stared into Chelsey's eyes and saw something that changed her expression from angered confidence to fearful uncertainty. Ever so gradually she removed the towel and lifted her hand away from the gun.

Chelsey picked it up and put it in her pocket. "Josh, it's time for you to take those little girls out of this room."

Josh looked over at his wife, who nodded and turned away from him.

"Officer Richards, would you escort Mr. Spangler and the girls out. I'm going to talk with Lily for a minute."

In the living room Lieutenant Miller took Josh into custody, cuffing his hands in front, and an officer from Child Protective Services was brought in to take charge of the girls. I remained at the bedroom door, in case Chelsey needed assistance, and Lieutenant Miller started a search of the girls' rooms.

Ten minutes later the bedroom door opened and Chelsey, her face pale and her eyes filled with fire, appeared with Lily in handcuffs. Sitting her on the couch next to her husband, Chelsey went into the kitchen and stood over the sink. Her shoulders began to shake as she silently wept.

I waited a few moments and then went in and placed my hand on her shoulder, "You did a great job in there. You defused what could have been a real disaster."

"Thanks," she said, regaining control.

"Mind if I ask you what you said to her?"

In the palm of her hand, she had a tube of lipstick, "I put this up under her chin and told her that at this angle, if she doesn't give up the gun, I was going to blow her brains all over her husband's pajamas."

In the living room Detective Wilson admonished the Spanglers of their rights. "We are going to talk later, but right now I have only one question. Five girls had been placed here. Two have run away, and the two little ones are now in protective custody. Where is the fifth one. Where is Susie, the fourteen-year-old?"

"We don't know. She ran away too." Lily said as Josh began to squirm.

Noting his discomfort, Wilson said, "Officer Defo, would you transport Mrs. Spangler back to the PD. I'll be there shortly. Me and Mr. Spangler need to go over a few things."

Trying to get to her feet, Lily shouted, "No! No! You can't do that! You can't separate us!"

"I'll go with you." Lieutenant Miller took one of Lily's arms and said, "I'll get an evidence team out here too."

At the door she yelled to her husband, "Don't say anything, Josh. You keep your mouth shut. Don't you say a word."

Once quiet was restored, we let Josh sit and silently stew as we talked, just loud enough for him to hear.

"Well, we know he's been molesting the girls, and if we can't find Susie, it isn't a big leap to assume he must have killed her," Wilson said.

"Yep, his poor wife was dragged into all this. I'm sure she will testify against him."

"Have you ever seen an execution? Man, it's ugly. They're using the electric chair again. It's only for special cases like this one. It's a horrible way to go."

"I heard about one guy who . . ." I was cut off by a cry from the living room.

"She's in the shed, out back. Under the floor." Josh began to weep. "Lily did it. She always did it."

I sprinted through the backdoor, across the yard, to a small, windowless shed. Kicking in the door I yelled, "Susie, Susie." Dropping to my knees in the dark, I felt for loose boards and continued to call her name while praying, "Oh God, let me find her." Feeling the raised edge of a board, I wedged my fingers around it and began to pull when the room was filled with light. At the door stood Detective Wilson with Josh.

"You need to move the box, the box." Josh pointed at a rolling toolbox in the corner.

Beneath the toolbox was a hinged panel that opened to a set of steps. "There's a light switch. On the wall, on your right."

I flicked on the light and stepped down into a room with several mattresses. One was rolled up against the wall alongside a jug of water with paper cups, and a bucket for a toilet.

"Susie, are you here? Susie, I'm a police officer. I've come to help you. Don't be afraid. You're okay now."

A slight movement of the rolled-up mattress in the corner caught my attention. "Susie, you can come out now, if you want to." Nothing. "Susie, just peek around and you can see me. I'm not going to hurt you. I've come to get you away from this place."

The mattress began to slowly unfold, and a young, blonde-headed girl appeared. Rubbing her eyes, she examined me thoroughly, focusing on my uniform and badge. Her eyes grew wide as she looked up into my face, then throwing her arms out she ran and jumped into my arms.

We left the scene to the evidence techs and returned to the PD. Susie was passed to the PS officer who had her checked out at the hospital, fed, and placed in a home with the other girls. I had a few hours of reports to do, then I would be heading home for a weekend with my family. Lieutenant Miller had completed his reports and had already checked out. Chelsey booked Lily into County and was hard at work tagging the gun and other evidence and completing her reports. She had just one place she wanted to be, home filling Zoey in about her friends.

Detective Wilson's work had just begun. He would have to write his own report, then gather and coordinate all the others, and itemize and log in all the evidence. After that was done, he had to interview the victims and interrogate the suspects. Overall, it had been a good day.

I didn't get home until noon, and after lunch I took a three-hour nap. I had been up for nearly thirty-six hours and had to get a little rest before we hit the road. This was the first day of a four-day weekend, and I had promised to take the boys to Disneyland. Rosie worked it out to take a few days off, so we had planned on leaving this morning. We would start out late, but we would start out. Mickey, here we come.

Cruising south along a lonely stretch of Highway 5, the boys played in the backseat as Rosie read *Charlie and the Chocolate Factory* to them. The sun began to set, bathing the horizon in shades of orange and gold. It was going to be a beautiful evening, and a good time lay ahead. The miles clicked by and I thought of those girls. That same sun sets for everyone, but not everyone was having a beautiful evening. What lay ahead for some wasn't going to be good.

If there is a God, was He blind to those innocent lives being abused, or did He just not care? I wanted to have the faith I saw in my wife and her father, but when I saw people like the Spanglers, I wondered, what's the point? Why put your life in the hands of a God who ignores the pain or is incapable of doing anything about it?

Then I thought, *Could it have been God's plan all along?* When I was frantically searching for Susie in the dark, groping around in that shed, all I could think to do was to pray. Maybe I did have a measure of faith in me. Then again, maybe it was just something desperate people grab onto in desperate times.

CHAPTER SIXTEEN

When I arrived back at work, I found my report in my locker along with a pair of Mickey Mouse ears and a note.

"Review your report and note areas I believe need further clarification. It needs to be to the DA in the morning. You did a great job. Those little girls are in good hands now. By the way, the Department is issuing new headgear. I've put yours in your locker," signed Lieutenant Miller.

I finished my reports and hit the street. My first stop was Bellflower Park. With flashlight in hand I went on foot, searching the area around the restroom. Heavy foliage had grown around the building and along the paths, with little maintenance. It had been one of the nicer parks in the city until it was taken over by homeless squatters, transients, and druggies. Now even the city maintenance crews wouldn't venture in to clean the place up.

Ten feet off the walking path, tucked between two large shrubs, a beam of light shown through the seams of a green canvas pup tent. It was so secluded it wouldn't have been seen except for the illumination.

I gently shook the tent, "Knock, knock, anyone home." No response. "Hello, I know you're in there. I'm Officer

Richards, I just want to ask you a question. I'm not here to cause you any trouble. I just have one question."

The flap over the entrance moved aside, and a thin, dark-haired woman came out. "What's your question."

"A young girl was assaulted over by the restrooms last week, and . . ."

"I didn't see anything." She turned to reenter her tent.

"We don't need any more witnesses, ma'am. I'm looking for a Bible she dropped around here someplace. You haven't seen it, have you? It means a lot to her."

Ducking into the tent she said, "No I haven't. Now leave me alone."

"Okay. Thank you. I'm leaving my card here. If you come across it, give me a call."

I walked back along the sidewalk looking through the bushes and overgrowth. No Bibles, just discarded bottles, needles, and trash.

"Xray-12, respond to 1475 Carlsbad Drive, a four-fifteen family, possible domestic violence. Xray-5, respond to cover."

"Xray-5 en route."

Sliding in behind the steering wheel, I picked up the mic, confirmed the call, started the car, and began to pull away from the curb when I heard a woman yell, "Hey, Mr. Policeman."

I stopped and rolled down the passenger window as the thin pup-tent dweller leaned in and handed me a tattered old brown Bible. "I didn't steal it, I found it."

"I know. It's all good. There's a little girl who is going to be very happy. Thank you. Can I have your name so I can tell her who found it for her?"

"No." She walked away, stopped, and yelled over her shoulder. "My name is Joyce, and I read the Bible. They won't let me in church, so I read the Bible." Then she disappeared into the park.

I radioed dispatch and asked for Officer Defo to meet me at the Pancake House after I cleared the disturbance call. I hadn't been to 1475 Carlsbad Drive in some time. I thought maybe the Carmichaels had worked things out, and Carl stopped thumping Marylou every Friday night. In front of the house Officer Ralph Carlie's car was parked in the driveway, empty. Inside I could hear Ralph, Carl, and Marylou yelling at the top of their lungs. Opening the door, I stepped in and shouted a little bit louder than everyone else, "Quiet! Shut up or you'll all go to jail."

Silence reigned king for but a moment, then Ralph said angrily, "These two were beating on each other when I got here. I say they both go to jail."

"Okay, let me get up to speed. Officer Carlie, take Mr. Carmichael out on the porch and get his information. I want to talk to Mrs. Carmichael. Then, Carl, I'll come out and get your view on things."

In the kitchen, Marylou sat down at a small dinette table. "I'm done. I want a divorce."

"Has he been hitting on you again?"

"No. He spent six months in jail for it the last time. He learned his lesson."

"How long have you been married?"

"Over a year now."

"A year? I know you two have been together a lot longer than that."

"Oh, we've been together for thirty years, but only married for one. It was so much better before. Things went bad right after we got married."

"He's not hitting you anymore, right?"

"No. Carl has been going to AA ever since he got out of jail. He's really turned his life around. It's that we just don't get along anymore."

"Marylou, sit tight a moment. I'm going to step out a moment and talk with Carl."

On the porch Carl was smoking a cigarette while Ralph stood in the yard.

"Okay, Carl, fill me in. What's going on?"

"Officer Richards, you have been out here a lot, you know what's going on. She's acting up again. I'm sober as a judge, haven't had a drink in over six months. Here look." Reaching into his pocket he removed a bronze coin with the number six embossed in a triangle. "I got this from AA for being on the wagon for six months," he said proudly. "I attend every week and talk to my sponsor almost every day. I'm not going back. I learned my lesson, and you were a part of that. Officer Richards, if you hadn't put me in jail, I don't know where I'd be right now."

Carl stretched out his arms and with a smile started to move toward me for a hug, "That's okay, Carl. I understand, but what's causing the trouble tonight?"

"We just don't get along anymore. I love Marylou, I really do, but I just don't like her."

"She told me that you've been together for thirty years, and things started going south after you got married a year ago. Have you tried counseling?"

"No. She won't go, and I don't think I would either."

"Okay. Well, come on, let's go see Marylou. I know what needs to be done." I opened the door.

In the kitchen I removed my badge and set it on the corner of the table. "I want each of you to stand here at the table." Wearily, Marylou stood.

Refusing to move, Carl said, "What's this about?"

"You'll see. Come over here, Carl. I have the power to resolve the contention between the two of you. Something that should have been done a year ago."

Marylou and Carl stood on each side of the table with my badge between them. "Please place your hands on my badge." They looked at each other, then hesitantly reached out and touched my badge.

"By the authority vested in me by the State of California, and as an enforcer of the law for the City of Oakland, I hear by pronounce you divorced. Your marriage is null and void, effective immediately, until further notice. Any and all property you have accumulated belongs to both of you equally."

Taking two pieces of paper from my notepad, I wrote, "This is to inform the holder that a divorce by proxy has been decreed by the Oakland Police Department." Below I scribbled a name and date and handed each of them a copy. "You now have what you wanted, a divorce."

I pinned my badge back on as they looked at me wide-eyed, "You two are now individual citizens. Any disturbances that take place between you are no longer a family issue. Whatever the problem may be, you will both go to jail. Do you understand?"

Without a word they nodded and looked at each other as Officer Carlie and I walked out the door.

"That's not really legal, is it?" Carlie asked.

I just looked at him for a long moment and marveled at the lack of common sense that seemed to exist in some people. I thought it best for the rookie to figure it out for himself, so I quietly got in my car and left. On the seat next to me was an old well-used Bible that required delivery.

CHAPTER SEVENTEEN

I met with Officer Defo, returned Zoey's Bible to her, and told her about Joyce, the lady in the park. The more we talked, the more apparent was the emotional attachment Chelsey and Zoey had made with each other.

Chelsey was a forty-year-old single mother who at eighteen married her high school sweetheart and gave birth to two lovely little girls. Her husband, a career army officer, was one of the first Americans to be killed in Vietnam. Ironically, it was on the date of their fifth wedding anniversary. She never remarried but had a steady boyfriend for over ten years. Her law enforcement career began as a dispatcher, and when an opening came up for a female officer in the juvenile division, she was a perfect fit.

"I see in Zoey a lot of potential," Chelsey said. "She just needs to be given a chance. I've asked Protective Services to allow her to stay with me until the Spangler trial is resolved. They need to clear it with the DA and the judge that will be assigned the case."

"What do your girls think about having Zoey around?"

"They're delighted. Lindsey will be heading back to school in a few weeks, so her room will be available. Lora will be going to USF in the fall so I'm about to become an empty nester."

With a second cup of coffee in hand, we headed back to the PD, to debrief and go home. It was interesting to see the looks we got from the waitress and some customers when we left the restaurant. Two police officers, heading out the door each with a coffee in one hand, and one with a large well-used Bible in the other. They probably thought we were preparing for a ruckus at a revival meeting.

In the squad room, Sergeant Alan pointed at me. "Gentlemen, if any of you should find yourself in need of a divorce lawyer, first call on Officer Bob Richards. He has a side job that can save you a bunch of money. Isn't that right, Bob."

"Yes, sir." Officer Carlie must have told him about what happened with Carl and Marylou. He was probably checking it out to see if it was legal. Rookies . . .

When I got home, Rosie was at work and the boys were with their grandpa and grandma. It was working out well because I would sleep until four, shower and shave, then pick the boys up. We would get home the same time as mom, have dinner, then spend the evening reading, playing games, or watching a little TV. Lately however, Rosie was getting home later and later. She had been covering for the bookkeeper who recently had twins and was on maternity leave.

Everything went as planned. At dinner I told Rosie about Joyce, the homeless lady who had Zoey's Bible, and asked, "Do you think it would be okay to buy a Bible for her?"

Her response was immediate with a twinge of excitement in her voice, "Sure. That would be a great idea. How about tomorrow?" she said.

"Okay, that's as good a time as any." I had expected more discussion about the idea.

"When you get off in the morning, you could stop by a bookstore and get one. We can bring it to her after I get home, then take the kids for pizza."

"Sounds good." I noted how tired she looked as she leaned back in her chair. "Are you doing okay with all this extra work?"

"Sure, I'm okay. It won't be much longer. Sarah should be back to work in a couple weeks. Then things will get back to normal."

Together we tucked our troops into bed, read them a story, and turned off the lights. Rosie started heading toward the kitchen to wash up the dishes, but I caught her in the hall, "No way, baby. I'll take care of the dishes. You go get ready for bed and I'll come in when I'm done and tuck you in." I could tell she was beat by the lack of resistance I got about the dishes.

With everything washed up and put away, I went into the bedroom to kiss my bride and say good night, but from the door I could see I was too late. Rosie was sound asleep and snoring loud enough to wake the neighbors. Covering her, I kissed her cheek and stood amazed at how fortunate I was.

At the end of my shift, I snatched a couple of donuts and a coffee in a to-go cup from the department's lunchroom and I parked in front of the Lifeway Christian Bookstore. It wouldn't open for another hour, so I settled in for the wait. I probably could have gotten a Bible from any store that sold books, or a used Gideon from one of the rundown motels, but I wanted to get a good one. I've heard that there are a lot of different Bibles, so I thought it best to go to a professional to get a real one.

I had just taken my second sip of coffee when a young man of about twenty walked up and unlocked the door. Turning toward me, he made hand gestures, asking if I was waiting for the store to open. I nodded yes, and he waved me in.

"How can I help you?"

"I need to buy a Bible."

"We have plenty of those. What translation would you like?"

"Translation? A real one, I guess."

"We only sell real ones." He smiled.

It was clear that I didn't have a clue what I was doing, but the young man was gracious and escorted me to a wall filled with Bibles. "There are different versions. Each Bible says the same thing, just in a different way. For an example, the King James Version gives us the Scriptures in the English language of the seventeenth century. The New American Standard gives us the scriptures in modern English. Let me suggest you sort through these." He pointed to two long shelves with Bibles of every size, and with covers of every sort and color. "Take your time. We won't be open for another half hour."

I chose one that had a nice purple cover. I remembered Joyce had a purple scarf on and it looked like there was a purple color in her hair. I thumbed through it and stopped at a random point to see if it was easy to read and made sense. "For God did not send his Son into the world to condemn the world, but to save the world through him." Easy to read, easy to understand, and it's real.

That evening we all piled into the car and drove to Bellflower Park. The sun was starting to set, so I asked them to stay in the car. In the high bushes, just past the restrooms, I found Joyce's green pup tent.

"Joyce, knock, knock, are you home?"

"Who is it?"

"It's Officer Richards, I have something for you."

Cautiously she came out, "You don't look like no cop. Where's your badge?"

"Right here, Joyce." I showed her my ID and badge.

"What do you have for me?" she asked suspiciously.

"Wait right here, I'll get it."

Going to the car I told the boys I wanted them to meet my friend Joyce and to bring the Bible. Little Joe carried the Bible, I carried Sonny, and Rosie carried Critter. As we walked toward her, you could see the apprehension on her face.

"Joyce, this is my family. This is Rosie, my wife, and my sons, Joseph, Stefan, and Casey." Sonny wriggled out of my arms.

Her expression was one of confusion with a twinge of fear. "What do you want?"

Little Joe walked up to her holding out the Bible in both hands. "We don't want nothing, we brought you something."

"What is it?"

"It's a Bible." Sonny stepped up beside his brother. "We wrote in it for you too."

Joyce looked at me, then at Rosie, then back to the boys. Bending down she took the Bible, opened it, and read the only words that could be made out, "Thank you. You are a nice lady." Signed, the Richardses.

"We just wanted to thank you for finding the Bible the little girl had lost. You said you read the Bible, so we wanted to get you a new one."

"Thank you." Her eyes filled with tears.

Slowly she opened her arms, and without any encouragement, both boys stepped into them and gave her a hug. I looked over at Rosie to see her reaction and saw her eyes were beginning to rain too. It was all I could do to maintain a strong male presence. We walked her back to her tent, said our goodbyes, and promised to come again for a visit.

Once in the car the boys were chattering like caged parakeets about their new friend, "She gets to go camping all the time. Can we do that too, Daddy?" Sonny said. "Yeah, we have a tent in the garage," Little Joe chimed in.

"I'll tell you what," I said, "tomorrow I will make you a tent in the living room and you guys can camp out just like Joyce. But now we're going to get pizza." Little did I know that it would take two nights in the Richards Park Living Room Campground, and one night at their grandparents' house before they were ready to go to bed in their own rooms.

Grandpa didn't help detour their desire to be career tent dwellers when he set up a real pup tent in his backyard, with hotdogs and s'mores. It did, however, provide an opportunity for them to sleep overnight, outside in a real tent, and give their mom and dad a night alone.

We were both off the next day, so I went to our favorite Italian restaurant and ordered eggplant parmesan, roasted broccolini, fresh antipasto salad with olive oil dressing. To top it off, I picked up a bottle of Beringer white zinfandel already chilled. At home I put everything on serving trays, placed the parmesan and broccolini in the oven to stay warm, and the salad and wine in the refrigerator. I set the table for two with tablecloth, flowers from the yard, and candles. Then I sat back to watch Kenny (the Snake) Stabler and the Raiders go to town on the Miami Dolphins.

The front door opened at a quarter to nine when Rosie dragged in, put her purse and briefcase on the counter, and saw the dining room table. "Oh baby, that looks wonderful." She hugged my neck. "I'm so sorry for being late."

She had worked all day and I wasn't about to make it worse by grumbling about dinner. "No problem. Are you hungry?"

"I ate a sandwich at work, I'm really not . . ." she hesitated, then with a smile, "It looks wonderful. What's on the menu?"

"Sweetheart, it will all be good tomorrow. You look exhausted, so what do you say you go get ready for bed, I'll put the food in the fridge, and we can have it for dinner tomorrow. Since we can sleep in, I'll pour us a glass of wine and we can curl up on the couch and watch a movie."

"I have to work tomorrow. I'm sorry, but my boss just got some big deal that requires the bookkeeping to be set up for the client's review by next week. Once it's done things will slow down, and when Sarah is back."

Walsh, Harper & Smith, you are starting to interfere with my life. Rosie worked late every day without a break, and the bubbly, happy, and always positive woman I married was starting to change. She would come home, make dinner, then go to bed. There were no more stories about what happened at work. In fact, she avoided talking about her job. Last night, the evidence that there was a problem was clear. She tucked the boys in and went to bed without telling them a story, leaving it to me. That had never happened before.

CHAPTER EIGHTEEN

We decided we would take a short road trip to visit one of Rosie's college roommates in Redding. The boys would spend the weekend with their grandma and grandpa, and tomorrow we would put work behind us for a couple days. Our bags were packed and sitting in the hall near the front door. The boys were in bed and Rosie sat on the sofa watching old reruns. I leaned over and kissed her head.

"You okay?" I asked.

"Yeah, I'm okay." She pulled me down and kissed me. "It's just work. There's a lot on my mind. Go do your job and be safe. Tomorrow when I get home from work, we'll blow this pop stand."

"You got it, sweetheart. Get some sleep." I left and locked the door behind me.

At the end of my shift, I walked into the locker room to find Scott Johnson sitting on the bench, with his head in his hands. I was about to ask if he was okay when I remembered our last conversation. It had ended badly when I told him I didn't want to talk to him again until he broke off his affair with a woman whose husband was in Vietnam. I could only imagine what was on his mind now.

"Bob, can I talk with you?"

I didn't respond.

"Bob, you're the only one who knows what's going on, and I need to talk to someone."

"Have you ended the affair?"

Staring at the floor he shook his head no.

"Then we have nothing to talk about."

"She's pregnant. This time for real, and her husband is coming home." Taking a deep breath, "I told Charlotte. She's leaving me. She's filing for divorce today and asking for custody of the kids. Things have gotten so bad; I don't know what to do."

"You didn't know what to do the last time we talked. You could have brought it to an end then. This time there's nothing for you to do. It's going to get done for you."

Closing my locker, I turned to him and couldn't help but feel some empathy for him. It's easy to get tangled up in the things you want and miss what you already have.

"Rosie is going to a pretty good church, says the pastor does a lot of counseling. I don't know anyone else you might talk to, so I'll get you his number when I get home. He's not the answer you want, but he may be the answer you need. Nothing is going to change that girl from being pregnant or her husband from coming home. Nothing may change Charlotte's mind either, but it may be time for some changes to be made in you."

Walking out the door, I wondered if what I said to Scott didn't also apply to me? I may not be having an affair, but there were some things in my life I had refused to deal with. There were some things I'd buried that still weren't dead.

With that thought in mind my quiet drive home resurrected visions of the past.

It was January 30, 1968. The lunar new year, known as "Tet," was about to be celebrated. Bravo Team, of the 572nd Combat Engineers had spent the last several months cutting a road from Highway 1 to Vung Ro Bay, eighteen miles south of Tuy Hoa, where our home base was located.

It was a clear, crisp morning with the sun rising over the bay. If it weren't for the fact that it was a war zone, you would think you were at an expensive beach resort. It lacked the fancy hotels, expensive shops, and restaurants, but it didn't lack the beauty. The white sand beaches, clear, clean ocean waves, and palm trees provided an oasis in the center of a country torn apart by bullets and bombs.

The sun was cresting the horizon, casting long, slender shadows across the sand. From a distance I saw Kevin "Hillbilly" Stodghill moving my way fast. He had been operating a Caterpillar rigid frame grader on the far side of the beach, leveling an area to be paved with laterite and rock. I was pushing dirt along the road that led out of the bay on a stripped down Caterpillar D7 dozer.

When he was about fifty yards away, I noticed something odd. He looked misshaped and his favorite faded fatigue shirt was darker. When he passed me, I saw that his shirt was covered in blood and his right arm and shoulder were separated just below his neck and hanging loosely at his side. He was as pale as a sheet and stared blankly toward his destination.

I pulled the clutches and dropped the blade, letting the engine die. Raising up from the seat I began to roll backwards over the fuel tank, a practiced method for a quick escape. Halfway through my roll, the world exploded in a brilliant white flash, throwing me backward and away from the dozer. I would learn later that my dozer had been hit by an 90mm HEP round, used to take out tanks.

I landed hard, knocking the wind out of me. Lying there trying to breath, I knew I had to move and quickly. Gasping for air, I crawled into the overgrowth, fell onto my back, and desperately tried to breathe. Slowly air began to fill my lungs, and a pain like sharp needles began to pulse through my right leg. I reached down and felt a tear in my pant leg. Bringing my hand back I saw it was covered in blood.

Behind me I could hear movement, sticks being broken underfoot. Taking the Colt 45 from its holster, I turned over onto my stomach just as a large boot stepped onto my hand, pinning the .45 to the ground.

"Hold up, buddy, I don't want you to shoot me." It was the welcome sound of Specialist 5th Class, John Lucas, a "Screaming Eagle" member of the 101st Airborne, our perimeter security.

Back at camp, our medic, Dr. Alfred Lopez, told me I had a souvenir to take home. There were several small pieces of gearing deeply embedded in my right calf. To remove them would cause more damage to the muscle than just leaving them there and letting them grow over.

"How is Hillbilly doing? He looked bad," I said.

"We dusted him off," Lopez said, "He was hit by a sniper and lost a lot of blood. He may not make it to the field hospital. Truth is, I think he was gone before he even got on the chopper."

I would lose Stodghill and several other friends before I would return home. Eighteen days short of my assigned tour, I got really sick and was put on a medevac flight home. I had dropped a few pounds, from 175 to 128. Between the malaria, blackwater fever, and hepatitis, I was one sick puppy.

I was transferred stateside to Letterman General Hospital at the Presidio in San Francisco. While there, the chaplain would come through on a regular basis. One day I made the mistake of sharing with him the Vung Ro Bay experience. The next day I was wheeled into the psychiatric wing of the hospital and diagnosed with what became known as post-traumatic stress disorder.

I was required to receive weekly clinical counseling for the remainder of my term of active duty and was told to continue biweekly sessions for the next four years of inactive duty. I attended one session, one week after I was discharged, and then I was done.

After Rosie and I were married, she asked me on several occasions to go back to counseling because of the nightmares and anger issues, but I refused. I was firmly convinced that all I needed was to let the past remain in the past.

I was confident that I had handled it well so far, although I must admit there had been times I considered talking to someone. But not today. Today Rosie and I were heading to Redding, to laugh with friends, drink a little wine, eat some good food, and just get away.

At home, I mowed the yard, took a short nap, then picked up the boys. Rosie was late again so I made dinner. She got home at nine, said she had to work late to get everything done so she could have the weekend off. While she tucked in each trooper and read them a story, I cleaned up the dishes and packed the boys' gear for a weekend with their grandpa and grandma.

The next morning, bright and early, we were on the road to Redding. My beautiful bride didn't get enough sleep the night before, so once we were on I-5 she fell sound asleep. Passing the little town of Corning, forty miles south of Redding, Rosie woke up and saw a sign with only one word, *EAT*.

"Eat. Let's stop and eat." She pointed at the sign. "When we get to Mary's it will be after lunch. I can't wait till dinner to eat. Let's stop."

Her wish was my command. She had been so down lately that it was great to see her perking up a bit. We were going to Redding so she could spend some time with an old girlfriend. It would be time that would do her a world of good.

The restaurant under the EAT sign was a small, old-fashioned diner, with booths and a long sit-down counter facing an open serving window into the kitchen. We were seated in a booth and given menus that listed only ten items, four breakfast and six lunch. There wasn't much in variety, but from the number of trucks in the parking lot and the size of the servings I expected to be well fed.

The coffee was rich and strong, the breakfast large and plentiful. Midway through our meal, a tall, blond cowboy in his late twenties came in and took a seat at the counter. He was familiar to me, both in his appearance and in his gait.

"What's the matter?" Rosie asked. "You look like you've seen a ghost."

"I think I have." Pointing to the cowboy, "See that guy in the cowboy hat. He looks exactly like a friend of mine who was killed in Vietnam."

Rosie turned and looked at the cowboy as he turned and looked at us. A broad, toothy grin spread across his face, "Bobby? Bobby Richards, is that you?"

The tall guy spun away from the counter. "It is you." Jumping to his feet, it only took four steps with his lanky legs to get to our table. I was on my feet and wrapped in a bear hug.

"I thought you were dead. They said you died." Turning to Rosie, "Baby this is Kevin Stodghill. We called him Hillbilly. Please sit with us. Please."

We sat, drank coffee, ate, and talked for over two hours. He had been given the nickname Hillbilly because of the stories he would tell us about his home in the hills of Kentucky.

Stodghill's family lived in a settlement called Eagle's Nest located along the Red River Gorge in Eastern Kentucky. He would talk about how as a boy he and his friends would play in the same woods Davy Crockett played in as he grew up.

Kevin and his two brothers, under the supervision of their father, built a beautiful five-bedroom, 3,800-square-foot cabin from timber harvested off their own land. He showed us pictures of his beautiful home and described how his mother had special parking places designated just for her at the furniture, appliance, drapery, tile, and carpet stores. She made the eighty-mile trek to Lexington almost daily and was on a first-name basis with most of the store owners.

When I asked what happened to him "over there," he pulled his shirt off his right shoulder, revealing a mass of scars. After triage and emergency surgery was performed, he was flown to Brooke Army Medical Center, at Fort Sam Houston, Texas. There he had undergone seven surgeries to reconstruct his shoulder and reattach muscles, nerves, and tendons. When he was released from the hospital, he applied and received admission to California State University, Chico. This hick from the hills was about to complete his master's degree in aerospace engineering, then on to a doctorate.

As we walked to our car, we made sure we had each other's address and number, and before parting company we shared a long and emotional group hug.

"Bobby, this wasn't an accident. I have the best doctors in the world, but all they do is put parts together. It's God who gives life to the tissues and brings about healing. There is no way you and I could have planned to run into each other like this. Only someone bigger than us, with a plan in mind, could have orchestrated today's meeting," Hillbilly said.

"It's bizarre, that's for certain." I held the door for Rosie.

"It was good to meet you, Kevin. I hope you come down our way real soon," she said.

"You can count on it, Rosie."

Then catching me at my door, he looked intently into my eyes, "Bobby, this meeting was for you. God wants you to know that He is real and He loves you." After a final hug he walked over to a large, white four-wheel drive truck. Before climbing in he shouted, "I love ya, Bobby Richards, and it's great to see you again. Take care."

CHAPTER NINETEEN

In Redding we were warmly welcomed by Mary and her live-in boyfriend, Eddie. We spent the next couple of hours shooting pool and drinking beer while Rosie and Mary talked about old times. Around five, we got ready for dinner, and by six we were on our way to the Market Street Blade and Barrel, reported to be the best steakhouse in the country. I was looking forward to a good steak, since I ate very little of my breakfast while talking to Hillbilly. Following dinner, we went to a favorite night spot of Mary's and danced ourselves into exhaustion. It felt good to see Rosie so happy. I was getting my girl back.

I woke at nine with the morning, sun filling the room, and reached over to squeeze my bride, but found that I was alone. Rosie had gotten up early and went out to explore the neighborhood. Through our second-story window I could see her across the street from the house, sitting on a bench at the entrance of a community park. I thought of dressing and joining her but reconsidered. She had been getting more and more stressed at work, so she needed a little quiet time to herself.

I laid in bed mulling over what Hillbilly had said about how our meeting was arranged by God. I had to admit, seeing him alive lifted a load off me, but as strange as it was, coincidences do happen. Then I remembered a bumper sticker I once saw: "A Coincidence Is God at Work Incognito."

Eddie had to go to work, and the ladies were going shopping at the local mall, so I had plenty of time to check out Redding. I showered and was getting ready to shave when I heard Mary talking behind me. Standing naked in front of a steamed-up mirror, I spun around to see that the door was tightly closed and there was no one behind me. The sound of Mary's voice was coming from the room below through the heater vents in the floor. The house had been built in 1910, so there was little in the way of insulation, and soundproofing was nonexistent.

Being as quiet as I could, I lathered up and began to shave. Something within me said to make enough noise to alert them that I was right above, listening, but I found this moment of eavesdropping interesting if not intrusive. I was curious about what women talk about when there isn't a man around.

"So, what are you going to do about him?" Mary asked.

"I don't know what I can do." Rosie said.

They were talking about me, and the tone was serious. What did she mean, do something about me? It sounded like I had done something wrong.

"You have to report him. I know you don't want to, but you must. Call the police department, you have friends there. They can tell you what to do. Report him to his boss."

I almost shouted at the vent, "What the hell are you talking about," but held my silence.

Rosie's voice began to crack, "I can't. You don't understand, I just can't. I'll be right back."

I wiped the steam off the mirror and stared at a man covered in shaving cream and guilt. What had I done to cause her such pain? Was it my anger? I sometimes blew up, but I wasn't violent, just loud, and it was short-lived.

I heard the bedroom door open, "Baby, is that you?"

"It's me. I'm just getting my makeup kit. I'll get dressed downstairs. Mary and I are going to the mall. Is that okay with you?"

"Sure." I wanted to ask her what I had done, but that would only tell her I was eavesdropping, one more strike against me.

At the bathroom door she said, "Give me a kiss goodbye."

I threw the door open without thinking and, before she could react, kissed her passionately. Leaning back to look at her I saw that her face was covered in shaving cream. Slowly a smile appeared under where her nose had been.

"Wow. That was fun," she said, "but I'm not going to the mall like this." Without wiping her face, she turned to leave. "I love you, you impetuous beast."

She still loves me, what a relief, but what had I done that she can't come to me about?

"What happened to you?" Mary's voice resonated from the vent.

"I was accosted by a naked, lathered squatter in your attic."

I went back to shaving, trying to ignore the conversation below.

"Rosie, I don't want to keep harping about this, but I'm worried about you. You can't allow him to get away with this. There's probably others he has assaulted."

Wait a minute. She wasn't talking about me.

"I know but he's threatened me. He said he could get me fired, even put in jail."

Curiosity quickly morphed into rage. I wiped off my face and started out the bathroom door when Mary asked about the threats. I stopped and listened carefully.

"Three weeks ago, he came up behind me and whispered in my ear that he wanted me, and he would have me. That's all he did. A week later he walked by me and grabbed my butt. I stopped him and told him that if he ever touched me or talked to me again, I was going to report him. He just laughed."

Now I was on my knees with my ear almost glued to the vent.

"Last Wednesday I was working late, no one else was there, and I didn't hear him come in. He got behind me at the copier and put his hand up my skirt. I pushed him away and he grabbed my breast. I got away from him and picked up the phone to call security. That's when he threatened me."

Rosie's voice quivered. "He said I needed to look at the Stevens account. It was missing over twenty-five thousand dollars, and the only one authorized to move money around in that account was me. He laughed and said if I told anyone, he would see to it that I was arrested."

"Is there money missing?" Mary asked.

"Yes. I checked the account and large amounts of money have been getting syphoned off starting the week I went to work there. I've never had anything to do with that account, but the only ID number allowed to withdraw funds is mine."

I couldn't hold back any longer. I got dressed and went downstairs and waited for Rosie in the living room. When they came out, I asked Mary if she had ever been in the upstairs bathroom when someone was using the one downstairs? She hadn't so I asked her to go up and stand in the bathroom. I stood in the master bedroom and talked to Rosie about the kids. A few minutes later Mary returned with wide eyes.

"You can hear every word as if they were in the same room."

Rosie looked at me and began to cry. I enfolded her in my arms, telling her that it was going to be okay, that we were going to get this thing worked out.

"I'm sorry, Bobby. I should have told you. I just didn't know how."

"Don't worry about it, baby, I'm here now. Who is this lowlife?"

"His name is Chip Nessler, a new hire from Continental Brokerage."

"How does he have access to the accounts?"

"I don't know. I've never heard of a Stevens account until he told me about it."

We spent an hour going over various details, but I saw that my wife needed to get away from all this for now. I sent them off to the mall and sat at the kitchen table going over my notes and making phone calls. My first call was to Continental Brokerage requesting to speak with the head of their HR department. I identified myself and said I was investigating a sexual assault by one of their employees. The phone went quiet for a moment, then Angela Atkins said, "We aren't allowed to divulge names or information about our employees."

"Does that include an ex-employee who may have been given great references just to get rid of him." I sighed. "The next victims may be on you, Miss Atkins."

"If you are referring to Chip Nessler. He was released for cause, and I'm not allowed to go any further than that."

"If I have to get a search warrant and confiscate every record you have for the last twenty years I will. I can assure you I am good at what I do, and I will find every concealed ink spot and blemish. Then I'll file charges against everyone responsible, starting with you, Miss Atkins."

"What is it you want?"

"For starters, Nessler's address, phone number, and date of birth. Then I want you to give my name and phone number to anyone who accused Nessler of assault or harassment. I will leave it up to them to call me if they want to. You do this and I'll leave your name out of it, and you'll never hear from me again."

Atkins agreed to my terms, and with the new information, I called OPD Records for a search of Nessler's past. It turned out he had a history of sexual misconduct. It was petty stuff, but a track record nonetheless. This was followed by a request from DMV for a copy of his driver's license photo, and a list and description of the vehicles he owned. Next I made a call to the Contra Costa, Alameda, and San Francisco county jails for any booking photos.

The creep of the week lived in my district, in beat seven, A. J.'s turf. A quick call to my old buddy and I had photos of his home, his neighborhood, and the length of his grass. To my surprise A. J. also provided me with pictures of his wife and children as he took them out for a day at the beach. What a wonderful family man Nessler was turning out to be.

Our trip home from Mary's was comfortable, taking the coastal route along Highway 1. We stopped often, ate well, and talked a lot. Once home we spent the evening with our boys and got ready to get back to work. Rosie received only one mandate from me: she was to wrap up and come home once everyone else left work, with no more late nights alone.

After I returned to work, Rosie's assault was at the forefront of my mind. At the end of my shift, I went to the investigative division and spoke with Detective Leo Leonard, a specialist in fraud crimes. I told him that I had a friend who was writing a book and wanted to make sure the plot he was developing was credible. I then shared the details of Rosie's dilemma. Leonard said that the account was probably a fake, used only to intimidate potential victims.

I called A. J. and asked if he could hook me up with his son-in-law, a commercial loan broker. Within minutes A. J. called me back and gave me Charles Geter's phone number and said an appointment had been made for me today at two.

Geter's office was in the Global Investment Corporation Building on the tenth floor overlooking Jack London Square. GIC was the largest and most prestigious commercial brokerage firm in Northern California.

When I arrived, an attractive, pleasant receptionist ushered me into a conference room bathed in mahogany and fine art and provided a fresh cup of excellent coffee. The twelve chairs that surrounded the conference table were plusher and more comfortable than my La-Z-Boy. I settled in expecting the customary delay, but to my surprise Geter wasn't late.

"Officer Richards." Geter shook my hand. "I have heard much about you from A. J. He thinks a great deal of you."

"He's a good man."

"Yes, he is. How may I help you, Officer."

"I want to make an appointment with an agent at Walsh, Harper & Smith. I'm looking into a report of threats and harassment, and I need to use your name to open the door."

"I don't quite understand how you would use my name."

"I would like you to call this agent, tell him you have a client that's interested in the Campbell building on Wilshire Avenue that he has listed. Ask if you can refer your client to him. He will agree, so you just give him this name." I passed a note with the name David Lerner. "Tell him that I'll be calling for an appointment."

"That's it? That's all I do?"

"That's it."

I sat across the desk from Geter as he called Chip Nessler and shared the good news of a wealthy client interested in one of his listed properties. Three hours later I called, and an appointment was set for a late lunch meeting the next day at the Velvet Turtle.

I requested a table in the back and was seated in the bar area. It was three in the afternoon, so the room was empty. I sat facing the entrance so I could see Nessler when he came in. At a quarter after three, in walked Mr. Chip Nessler toting a big alligator briefcase and a smile that exposed the whitest teeth I had ever seen.

"Mr. Lerner, I presume." He extended his hand, a hand that had touched my wife.

With the exception of my initial greeting, I didn't say a word for at least ten minutes. Nessler rattled on about the city expansion, low property tax, and the ever-increasing value of commercial real estate. When he finally ran out of steam, I leaned forward and extended my hand.

"I owe you an apology. My name is not Lerner, it's Richards."

"I'm sorry, I thought I was meeting a Mr. David Lerner. I'm a bit confused."

"Well, let me clear it up. My wife works at Walsh, Harper & Smith. You may know her, Rosie Richards."

Nessler stiffened, pushed his chair back, and began to stand.

In a tone that even surprised me I said, "Sit down, Mr. Nessler. We have some business to discuss." Slowly I set my badge on the table.

Looking around, Nessler could see that we were totally alone and slowly sat back down.

"Do you know my wife, Mr. Nessler? Maybe she told you her husband was a police officer, or maybe not."

With a crack in his voice, he said, "No. No, she didn't."

"It has come to my attention that my wife may have been embezzling a significant amount of money, and you may have the evidence to prove it. Is that right, Mr. Nessler?"

He didn't say a word, just stared at me.

"I've had our fraud unit do some checking, and they can't seem to locate any improprieties. Upon further investigation, Walsh, Harper & Smith can't find any either. What do you make of that, Mr. Nessler?"

Again, not a word.

Over his right shoulder I saw A. J. clear the door and saunter up to the bar. Nessler heard the noise and turned to see we were no longer alone. Feeling confident, he began to grin and pushed his chair back.

"There's nothing you can do to me. I may report you for harassment, and there's probably some code against you lying to me." He started to stand.

I removed the 9mm Browning from my shoulder holster and put it on the table, my hand resting on it. "Sit down, Mr. Nessler. Now."

Nessler, wide-eyed, became visibly shaken. A. J. almost fell off the stool. I watched as my friend removed his concealed .38, dropped it to his side, and with a hard look at me, shook his head.

"What are you going to do?" he said softly.

"It's not what *I'm* going to do. It's what *you're* going to do." From my coat pocket I withdrew an envelope. In it was a full confession of the harassment and threats he made to Rosie. It also addressed the manipulation of the firm's computer system as a tool to intimidate his victim. The last paragraph was an open admission of harassing and threatening unnamed persons while employed at Continental Brokerage and during his tenure with Walsh, Harper & Smith.

After reading the document, Nessler pushed back at me, "I'm not signing that."

"That's only the first step. You're a bright guy. I'll bet you can find work just about anywhere. That's good because you and your family are moving. You have sixty days to resign, pack, and get out of California. If you want to stay, then I'm sure your wife and kids will be moving after I put your butt in prison for rape, assault, and threats."

"I didn't rape anyone. My relationship with those women was consensual."

"It's not consensual when there's a threat. It's your call, Mr. Nessler."

Fire lit up his eyes. "I have the power to put your wife in jail." He sneered.

"I have the power to put you in the grave." I slowly lifted the Browning and pointed it at his heart. "You manhandled my wife, give me an excuse, any excuse . . . please."

The breath came out of him as if he had been hit in the gut. Taking a pen out of his pocket he quickly signed it, then looked at me like a deer in the headlights. "Can I go now?"

"Yes," I said, "and this will stay with me for the next sixty days."

Standing quickly, he grabbed his briefcase and headed for the door. Stopping next to A. J. he said, "Did you see that, did you hear it? He threatened me, you're a witness."

A. J. shifted on the barstool, letting his coat open and revealing his badge and gun, "Sorry, sir, I didn't see or hear a thing, except something about you assaulting women and moving out of California."

After Nessler left, A. J. turned to me, "You scared me there, Bobby. I thought you were going to plug him. Worse yet I thought I was going to have to plug you." Slipping off the stool, he left his drink untouched, "The drink is on you, bud. See you in court Monday."

CHAPTER TWENTY

The old clock embedded in the wall above the elevators on the first floor of the county courthouse read ten twenty. I had been sitting on this hard wooden bench outside of Judge Hamond's court for nearly two hours waiting to testify in the Jimmy Hall murder trial. A. J. was called in and released to go home within ten minutes. He said they didn't need him, but he was to be prepared to be called back. Chester Duncan, the crime scene analyst, was called in over an hour ago, and so far, there hadn't been another word.

Sitting across from me was a middle-aged man with a heavy beard, hair in a bun, wearing a plaid brown sports coat, blue bowtie, and gray pants that didn't match. His crumpled shirt looked like he had slept in it, and the overly stuffed, heavily weathered cowhide briefcase was a dead giveaway. He's the shrink for the defense.

"So do you think Jimmy will get a fair shake in there?" I asked him.

He looked at me a long moment, sizing me up, "You the cop that arrested him?"

"Yep."

"He likes you. Said you were a straight shooter, and that you helped him and his mother some time ago. He said you treated him good this time too."

"The kid hasn't gotten any breaks." I sighed. "I don't think this is going to go well for him either."

"His attorney had been talking with the DA, hoping to cut a deal that would put him in Patton State Hospital, in San Bernardino. The big problem was the way he had committed the murder. It showed premeditation and planning. They don't stack well with a self-defense argument or an insanity plea."

"Officer Richards," a bailiff called out from the door.

"That's me." I stood.

"Judge Hamond wants to see you in his chambers."

In the gallery were seven angry-looking family members of the victim and two weary-looking reporters from local newspapers. At the defense table sat Jimmy Hall, in ill-fitting orange coveralls, with *County Jail* printed in bold black letters on the back. His hands and feet were shackled, and he sat hunched over under the watchful gaze of a sheriff's deputy. There was no guessing in this room who was the guilty party.

As the bailiff escorted me past Jimmy, he looked up and smiled, and though his hands were shackled to the table, he was able to give me a wave. "Hi, Officer Richards."

"Hello, Jimmy. You doing okay?" I noted bruising on the right side of his face, and what appeared to be stitches on the left side near his hair line.

"As good as can be expected."

Inside the judge's chambers were Deputy DA Daniel Martinez and Jimmy's lawyer, Jack Cinto. Judge Hamond sat behind a large oak desk covered in papers, photographs, and a dozen bobbleheads of various sports figures. When he put his elbows on the desk, all the heads began to bob, and with them, the intimidation I always felt in his court began to fade away. He really was a human being.

"Officer Richards, I understand you are familiar with the defendant, Mr. James Hall. What can you tell me about him?"

"Well, Your Honor, my first encounter with Jimmy was several years ago when he was just fifteen. He and his mother were living with and being abused by Billy Cook, the victim in this case. His mother had been beaten badly, and the boy had serious facial injuries, a broken arm, and internal bleeding. Cook turned himself in and served six months in County. When he got out, he followed Jimmy and his mother to Reno where he beat them both, killing Jimmy's mother. Reno PD screwed up the case so Cook walked, came back here, and threatened to kill Jimmy."

"Officer Richards, that much I knew. I want to know what you think of the boy himself."

"He's had it rough, but he's a survivor. He's done a bad thing and he knows it, and he's willing to pay the price for it, but he's no killer, not yet."

"Not yet?"

"Look at him. He's just a kid, and not very big. It's obvious that he's been getting kicked around in jail, maybe even sexually assaulted. We leave him in there, or put him in prison somewhere, he'll become the killer he's accused of being."

"Thank you, Officer Richards. I don't believe we will be needing you today but be prepared to be called to testify if we do."

I left the chambers with a better feeling about Jimmy's chances than when I went in. It seemed that everyone in the room had a sincere interest in doing what was best for the boy. Unfortunately, the kid had committed a crime that called for the death penalty. That was going to be hard to work around.

By the time I was excused from Judge Hamond's chambers it was almost noon. I decided to stop by Walsh, Harper & Smith and call Rosie from the receptionist desk and ask her out to lunch. She said she still had a little work to do but would meet me at the Melo Bistro on Grant in thirty minutes. It was at the Melo where we first met. She was with a few friends, one of whom I knew. He was an arson and incendiary specialist with the FBI. I stopped by the table to say hi to my friend and introduced myself to Rosie. Later that day I called him and asked if the beautiful brunette he was having lunch with was married or had a boyfriend. I was informed that he had just met her, and he didn't want any competition. The mistake he made was telling me where she worked and that he had just met her.

That afternoon I made reservations at the Bow and Bell Steak House, where, coincidently, Rosie worked. When I arrived, I tipped the maître d' ten dollars to seat me at a table Rosie would be serving. I scored as much small talk and introductory conversation as I could, then asked her out for dessert. She accepted, and the rest is history. My friend in the FBI, well, we don't talk much anymore.

When I arrived at Melo's I was able to get a table outside under a large umbrella, with a view of the boats in the bay. When Rosie arrived, I noted that the little skip she had in her step was back and her smile went from ear to ear.

"I'm glad you could have lunch with me," I said. "I don't suppose that smile is because of me, is it?"

"Yes, it is." She leaned over and kissed me. "I also have some interesting good news."

"So, what's the good news?"

"The last few days Chip Nessler has been really quiet. He comes in and goes straight into his office without saying a word. All the girls noticed it. He's usually loud and flirtatious, but not lately." She took my hand and looked me in the eye. "Did you have anything to do with that?"

"What would I have to do with that? Maybe he's not feeling well."

Without taking her eyes off me she said, "He didn't come in today, and the blinds in his office are closed. The rumor is he resigned and that he received a job offer somewhere in Nevada." Those beautiful blue-green eyes had a question lurking behind them. "Does that make sense to you?"

"Sure. He probably got a better job. I don't see a problem here. Why are you concerned about that dirtbag? I thought you wanted him gone."

"I do. I just don't want you to do something rash."

Sitting back in my chair, I took a pose, "Do I look like I'm breaking out in a rash?"

"No." She tilted her head slightly. "Thank you, Bobby. Thank you for protecting me."

After lunch I walked Rosie back to her office and then went to the PD to pick up my service revolver. It was time for my quarterly qualification, so the next stop would be the range. On my locker was a note from Deputy DA Martinez asking me to come by his office as soon as possible, regarding the Jimmy Hall case. Since I would be passing his office on the way to the range, I made that my first stop.

The district attorney had branch offices located in several places within the county, but the main office was on the fourth floor of the county courthouse. Martinez's office wasn't much bigger than one of the secretarial cubicles that were just outside his door. He sat behind a small desk surrounded by filing cabinets, stacks of folders, and framed law degrees on the wall. If the paperwork continued to pile up, there was a good chance Martinez would completely vanish, never to be seen again.

"Have a seat, Bob." Martinez pointed to a wicker chair in the corner with a stack of folders on it. "Just set the files on the floor there."

"Are these all cases you're working?"

"No, not all, but most. Some just need closure, with a statement of resolution or plea agreement. Most will be negotiated out, but a few," he pointed to a stack of folders stuffed with papers on his desktop, "like these, will go to trial."

"Wow, you guys need more help."

"No, we just need less crime. Officer Richards, I asked you to stop by because I want to get your feel on something. I also wanted to talk to you about it face-to-face. Too often we make decisions on cases that pass our desk and never talk to the officers involved. You guys saw the victims, and you have a perspective we often miss, and even more often ignore."

I was starting to like this guy. "I assume it's about Jimmy Hall?"

"Yes, Judge Hamond heard what you said, and it moved him. He's seen a lot of throwaway kids come through his court, and all the system can do is send them to an institution of higher learning to become real bad guys."

"So, what do you and His Honor have in mind?"

"Why did you book Jimmy Hall into County Jail?"

"What do you mean why? Because he killed Billy Cook." I stared at Martinez dumbfounded. "He took Billy to Reinhardt Redwood Regional Park, tied him to a chair, and blew his brains out. Then he called us, admitted to the killing, and told us where we could find the body. I think we had plenty of probable cause to arrest Jimmy and book him in County."

"I agree. I'm not questioning the justification you had for the arrest, but what would you have done if I were to tell you he was a juvenile?"

"Juvenile? He's eighteen."

"Yes, now. According to the coroner's estimated time of death, he would have been seventeen when he killed Cook. Due to the circumstances surrounding this case—the beatings, threats, and killing of his mother—we are looking at treating him as a juvenile. We may be able to get the case sent to Juvenile Court with a self-defense plea. If he behaves himself, he will serve three years until he's twenty-one at California Youth Authority. The family of Cook aren't going to be happy, so Judge Hamond wants to know how you and Officer Jackson feel about that?"

"I think that's fair. The kid needs a break if he's ever going to get his life in order."

"Good to hear you say that. I spoke to Officer Jackson earlier and he's in agreement too. I'll speak to Hamond, and Jimmy's attorney, and have the case sent to Juvenile Court. We should have this wrapped up by the end of the week."

"Is there any chance I could talk with Jimmy?"

"I'll see what I can do. It will be up to his attorney, but probably not until the case is settled."

I left the DA's office with a renewed confidence in the system, until I got out of the elevator on the ground floor. As the doors opened, there stood Curtis Mitcham, dressed in cargo pants, slip-on shoes, a Hawaiian shirt, and a pair of Aviator sunglasses. He looked like a tourist that had just walked off Venice Beach. Next to him stood two black-suited FBI agents.

I stepped out, and he smiled at me. "Hello there, Officer Richards. What have you been up to?"

I watched as he entered the elevator with his two companions. Looking back at me, he removed his glasses. "I'm going up to make a deal." Then with a broad grin, "How is your lovely wife and those boys of yours doing?"

"You son of a . . ." One of the agents stepped between me and Mitcham as the doors closed.

I stood, fists clenched, and shook in anger. When I realized that I was blocking the elevator door, I walked over to a bench, sat down, closed my eyes, and focused on breathing. What kind of deal could possibly be made?

Martinez was the DA assigned to the case and he didn't say a word about any deal while I was up there. A raging debate was taking place in my head. Do I stay and wait for Mitcham to come back down, or do I go to the range and take out my anger on a defenseless silhouette? Do I go back up to Martinez's tiny office and demand to know what's going on, or leave it to him to contact me?

I could hear Rosie's voice echoing in my mind, "I just don't want you to do something rash."

A hand rested gently on my shoulder, "Are you okay, son?"

I looked up and saw a man in his fifties sitting next to me. His disheveled graying hair, heavy rimmed glasses, and tweed coat gave him a warm, friendly appearance.

"I'm fine, thanks."

He handed me a business card. "I'm sitting right over there if you want to talk. You can also call me any time you want to. Bless you, son, and thank you for all you do. I know it's hard to be a police officer in times like these, but I suppose that is true about any time."

He walked back to the bench along the window, and I read his card, "Howard Hays, Senior Chaplain, California Penal System."

I decided to go to the range and spend the afternoon annihilating paper bad guys with hundreds of rounds of ammunition. When I was through, I went home to a world absent of guns, chaos, and crime, but full of little boys' laughter and love.

Joe, my father-in-law, once read to me a Bible verse when I was angry and depressed about what I had seen on the streets: "Whatever is true, whatever is noble, whatever is right, whatever is pure, whatever is lovely, whatever is admirable—if anything is excellent or praiseworthy, think about such things." Good advice.

CHAPTER TWENTY-ONE

I opened one eye just enough to see the clock on the night-stand. It was four-thirty in the afternoon, and I had slept a good portion of the day away. I knew it was time to get up, but I had found that rare place where the bed, the sheets, and my pillow were harmonizing in a symphony of exquisite comfort. I could not bear to leave them.

A scream came from just outside in the hall, shattering the tranquility of the morning. The door flew open, and all the Richards Warriors stormed through, leaping and climbing onto my restful refuge, attacking its powerless occupant.

"Wake up, Daddy, wake up." Critter stood at the side of the bed with his face an inch away from mine. I forced open one eyelid and looked into a pair of bright green eyes, just above a button nose, and couldn't help myself. I grabbed him up, rolled over, and covered us both in blankets. "Gotcha."

The squeals and giggles began to flow as the other two joined the battle. After several minutes of hand-to-hand pillow combat, the commander in chief came in and ordered a truce. It was Good Friday, and because we were not going to be available on Easter, we were having dinner at the in-laws before I headed off to work.

The meal was wonderful as expected, but Alberta was not happy with me for arranging to have the family away on Easter. We planned to come by in the morning so the boys could do their customary egg hunt in the backyard, but that wasn't good enough. Easter, according to Alberta, is a family holiday like Christmas and Thanksgiving. I believe if she had her way, every day would be a family holiday.

A. J. and Betty had invited us to dinner every year since I joined the department, but we always turned them down. Not this year. I figured A. J. was about to pull the plug and retire at the end of the year. He had been making comments about wanting to travel and fish more and see more of the children and grandchildren. Betty recently had a bout with breast cancer, and that seemed to change A. J.'s heart for the job. He had made his bones and deserved to spend the next twenty years exploring the country with his bride.

After dinner, I dropped Rosie and the boys off at the house, tucked everyone in, and headed for work. It was one of those clear, beautiful, star-filled nights, so before the streets were filled with over-indulged inebriants, I took a cruise into Oakland Hills. Finding a spot where the horizon lights didn't defuse the night sky, I got out, leaned against the car, and marveled at the wonder of heaven.

I had never really put much thought into where the world and everything around it came from. I kind of figured the "big bang" was as good an answer as any. However, standing here looking at the celestial landscape before me, it was becoming harder to imagine it was all an accident. To my right, spread across the valley, was the city of Oakland with its nearly four hundred thousand residences.

It was lit up like a Disneyland parade, with rivers of streaming lights interwoven along its streets and highways. If I was told all that shined and sparkled in the valley below was an accident, I wouldn't believe it. Someone had to have planned it out. Why was it so hard for me to believe that it might also be true about me and that I'm not the result of some celestial accident?

The night went smoothly with the usual drunk drivers, corner brawls, and family hate fests. The only excitement was in Berkeley at what had become known as "People's Park." Several OPD officers were dispatched to back up BPD in quelling another in a long line of "peaceful protests" that never stayed peaceful.

At the end of my shift, I pulled into the Corp yard to refuel and parked at the gas pump, across from A. J., who was grumbling to himself about the newly installed streetlight over our heads.

"Is there anything I need to bring tomorrow, food, dessert, beer?" I asked.

"Nope, just those three little terrors of yours. Make sure they have their suits. I'll have the pool warmed up. Bring yours, too, if you want to go for a swim."

"No, I've eaten your barbecue and Betty's cooking. When I'm done gorging myself at your table, I'll sink like a rock."

"Xray-12, respond to a motorist assist on State Route 13, just south of the entrance to Joaquin Miller Park."

"Dispatch, that's outside of the city. Can CHP or Alameda SO handle it?" I radioed back.

"Negative, CHP has a major accident on I-80, and SO is at People's Park assisting BPD. The report is that the motorist is lying on the ground. He may be injured."

"Ten-four, en route."

"Bob, I'll take the call. You live a lot further than I do. Go on in and check out. I'll cover it."

"Are you sure?"

"Yep. Betty is out with some of her friends so I'm home alone anyway. Go on."

"Okay, thanks."

A. J. took his mic. "Dispatch, this is Xray-7, I'll handle the motorist assist. En route from the Corp yard."

"Ten-four, Xray-7."

A. J. left, and I finished filling and cleaning up my unit for the next shift. While leaving the Corp yard, I heard A. J. report in that he had arrived, but the transmission was garbled and difficult to understand. What caught my attention was one word—Mitcham—but the transmission was broken up so badly it could have just been my imagination.

There's a three-mile stretch along State Route 13 where the hills and power lines interfere with police communication. Berkeley PD has requested a radio bouncer installed in the area, but it has been denied by the city council.

"Xray-7, please repeat. Xray-7, come in. Xray-7."

"Dispatch, this is Xray-12, I'm en route to his location."

"King-3 is en route. I'm close," Gary Alison said.

"Ten-four, King-3. Xray-12, you can stand down."

I didn't respond because something in me said this is all wrong. I turned on the lights, floored it, and my Plymouth Gran Fury took off like a rocket.

I was within two miles when I heard Gary yell into his microphone, "Officer down, officer down, get an ambulance out here now! Officer down!"

Within moments I rolled up to a scene I will never forget. Gary's K9 unit was parked at an angle behind A. J.'s, along with several cars stopped in the middle of the road and along the shoulder. Gary was bent over A. J., who was on his back, legs stretched out and arms lying loosely at his side. Turk was going rabid in the back of the K9 wagon, barking at those gutsy enough to get close. I jumped from the car and ran to A. J., dropped to my knees, and assisted Gary, who had begun CPR. In the background I could hear sirens coming from every direction.

There was a dark stain on his chest, so I ripped open his shirt and discovered a large wound just below his ribcage. I tore off my shirt and held it tightly against his chest.

I leaned over him and whispered in his left ear, "Come on, buddy, stay with me. A. J., you're going to be fine. You're cooking tomorrow, remember? We're bringing the boys. Come on, man."

I heard what sounded like a sigh, the kind he was known to make to emphasize his frustration. I leaned back with a smile to look him in the face, but his eyes were wide and blank, as though he were looking at something in the distance. Blood had pooled around the right side of his head, and on his forehead above his right eye, was a hole the size of a dime. There was no doubt in my mind, I had seen this empty blank stare countless times before. A. J., my mentor and friend, was gone.

On my knees at his side, I held my shirt to his chest and did everything I could to control myself. Tears began to flow, and I cried so hard I couldn't breathe. Police and emergency vehicles were screeching to a stop all around us, as ambulance personnel took over for Gary, rendering aid that was no longer necessary. One of the ambulance crew told me to back away, but I wasn't able to let go yet, not yet.

Hearing a loud and demanding voice at my side, I was about to take out my rage on a defenseless man who was only trying to help, when Lieutenant Miller said, "Bob, come on, Bob, let these guys do their job." He gently put a hand on my shoulder and said, "Come on, I got ya."

Lieutenant Miller walked me back to his car, sat me down in the passenger seat, and squatted like a father to a child with a bruised knee. "Bob, I understand, but we have a lot of work to do here right now. I need you clearheaded, so stay put awhile. We're going to be out here all night. I've called dayshift in early, and the SO will assist. When you're ready, come and see me and I'll give you an assignment."

"Sure, LT, sure."

He reached into the backseat and removed a small black case, unzipped it, and took out a new Bell autophone. From the glove compartment he retrieved a long cable that he attached to the phone case. Handing me the handset, he said, "We just got these. They'll be in all the command vehicles soon. I want you to call your wife and talk to her. Tell her what has happened and that you're okay. This is going to hit the radio and TV news within minutes, and she needs to hear that you're okay. She needs to hear what happened from you. Talk with her awhile and defuse, then come and get me."

"Yes, sir." I felt like I'd wake up from this because it was all just a bad dream. A. J. couldn't be dead, because I had just talked to him. Besides, he was A. J.

Rosie took the news hard. We talked and cried and talked some more. Before I hung up, Rosie asked if she could pray with me, and at first, I was reluctant and saw no need to call upon someone who either didn't exist or didn't care. A. J. was a churchgoer, and his belief in God hadn't done him much good. Then she said that we needed to hold Betty up in our prayers for her well-being. Somehow that made sense, because what else could we do for her?

I knew Rosie would call Betty when we got off the phone, but I counseled her to hold off awhile. The chaplain would be going over to break the news and needed to spend some time with her.

I hung up and sat watching the crime scene techs and detectives mill around, setting out evidence markers, taking photos, and getting statements from witnesses. Off in one corner a group of brass, including the chief, had gathered to discuss how to feed this to the media. Bright yellow tape had been stretched around the entire area and several officers were posted to keep the crime scene buffs, the curious, and the morbid away. Reporters and cameramen were everywhere, and several helicopters hovered overhead. The California Highway Patrol called in extra help to fight a losing battle getting the morning commuter traffic flowing again.

The county coroner arrived and released A. J.'s body to be taken to the morgue, where he would be dissected like a lab rat. He was placed under a white sheet and put into the ambulance for transportation, which was usually against policy. The coroner had a large black, windowless van with the words *Alameda County Coroner* in bold white letters on the side. The chief ordered the ambulance to be used to cut the media's dramatic edge a bit.

I had talked and watched more than I needed to, and it was now time to get back to work. I approached Lieutenant Miller, thanked him, and said I was ready.

"Bob, I want you to go back to the PD and hook up with Detective Wilson. We have a number of people who witnessed this thing go down, and we're getting dozens of calls. He's doing the interviewing and getting statements, but he needs help."

CHP cleared a lane for me to get by, and while maneuvering through the congested traffic it occurred to me that I hadn't thought once about who killed A. J. It was like combat in Vietnam. Your focus is on your injured comrades and avoiding being shot. You don't know who's shooting at you and you don't care. You just want to survive and keep your buddy alive.

In Interview Room A, I met with Clark and Hattie Howard. They were on the east bound side of the freeway going to the airport. They saw a man lying on the ground and a policeman standing over him. Clark pulled to the side of the road and, being a retired emergency room medic, thought he could help. He got out of the car and waited for traffic to clear so he could cross over the highway. He saw the officer walk to his car, get something, and walk back.

Hattie began to cry, "That's when he shot him."

"Shot who?" I asked.

"The police officer," she screamed, "the man shot the police officer."

"Yes, the man shot the officer in the leg. He fell and started to reach for his gun when the man shot him again." Clark dropped his head, "The officer didn't move."

"But it didn't stop there. Those other men came . . ." Hattie cried.

"Other men, what other men?"

Clark put his arm around his wife to console her. "Three motorcyclists came up and stopped, but they didn't get off their bikes. I thought they were going to help the officer, but instead, they watched as the man took the officer's gun, rolled him over on his back, and shot him again."

"They laughed." His voice broke. "I have seen some of the most horrible things while working the ER, but I've never seen anything like that. They laughed, they all laughed."

Dropping his head, he began to cry along with his wife. "The man who shot the officer got on the back of one of the motorcycles and they left." His voice began to trail off, "They just left the police officer to die alongside the road."

Speechless, we sat for several minutes in silence. My mind began to race with images of my friend being slaughtered on a beautiful sunny morning along a lonely stretch of road, simply for trying to help. Then a word exploded in my brain, "Mitcham." A. J. had said Mitcham on the radio when he arrived at the scene.

"Did you see what the men were wearing?" I asked, "Was there anything distinctive about their clothes?"

"Well, they were wearing the usual motorcycle stuff. Helmets, jeans, boots, and vests, the usual stuff," Clark said.

"How about the vests. Was there anything distinctive about them?"

Hattie nodded. "They all had the same design on their vests."

I excused myself and ran to the locker room. In my locker was the envelope of photos I used when Little Joe identified Rosko Tanner and Curtis Mitcham as the men who gave him a bullet to intimidate me. My next stop was Records where I got a picture of the Savages motorcycle club patch.

Back in Interview Room A, I set the picture of the patch in front of the Howards but said nothing.

"That's it. That's the patch they had on their backs. That's it," Clark said excitedly.

"I'll be right back." I slipped out the door and walked to Interview Room C. Picking up the red wall phone by the door, I called Detective Wilson and asked him to step out for a moment.

Outside he asked, "What's up, Bob?"

"Come with me."

"I'm in the middle of an interview. Can't it wait?"

"No. Come with me."

I introduced Detective Wilson and asked the Howards, "Have I shown you any pictures other than the one of the patch you have in front of you now?"

"No," they both said.

"Good, now I'm going to ask Clark if you would mind stepping out for a moment. I'll have an officer show you where you can grab a cup of coffee. I want you both to look at some pictures, but you must do it independently."

Clark began to protest leaving his wife alone, "Why? What's the point of that?"

"If by chance you see a photo of anyone involved in the killing of Officer Jackson and you are not together, the detective and I can validate your individual observations. Together it would be construed that one of you influenced the other."

When Clark left the room, I spread out the nearly fifty pictures of members of the Savages motorcycle club, "Mrs. Howard, please look over these and tell me if any of them are the men you saw this morning when the officer was killed. Take your time, there's no rush."

She slowly sorted through them, taking a couple of pictures out and putting them on the side. Then she stopped, and the blood drained from her face. "That's him. That's the man who shot the police officer."

Staring at the picture as if it were alive, she lifted it and turned it over for us to see, "This is the man who killed the officer."

It was a booking photo of Curtis Mitcham.

"Thank you, Mrs. Howard," Wilson said. "Please continue to look through the pictures for the three bikers. If you would excuse us a moment, I need to speak to Officer Richards. Can I get you anything, coffee, tea?"

"No, thank you." Hattie sorted through the photos, inspecting each one thoroughly like a grandmother scrapbooking her grandchildren.

Once in the hall, Wilson said he would get another detective to finish up the witness interviews and then put out the word to be on the lookout for Mitcham and his friends. He'd call the DA's office for an arrest warrant for Mitcham and a search warrant of his home, car, and the Savages' clubhouse. I was to get IDs of the three bikers and complete the interview of the Howards. My taped narrative and the Howards' recorded interview would be fast-tracked through for transcription. It was needed in order for a judge to sign the warrants.

Hattie picked out four pictures. One was of Mitcham and the other three were who she thought were the three bikers. Two of the pictures were of a couple of scruffy dudes with long curly hair and dark beards that covered eighty percent of their faces. One of them was Rosko Tanner.

When Clark returned, he spread all the pictures out on the table and stood looking down on them. Within five minutes he had pulled out four mugshots, the same ones Hattie had picked out. Holding Mitcham's photo in his hand he began to shake, "This is the animal that murdered one of our heroes."

CHAPTER TWENTY-TWO

Although I didn't always agree with them, I honored and appreciated the work our lieutenants and sergeants do. Today was a prime example why. All the shift sergeants and the district commanders put on their work uniforms and hit the street, allowing those officers who worked closely with A. J. to have the night off. It was good for Gary and me not to be on the street tonight. We hadn't gotten any sleep and our attitudes weren't up to par.

When I got home, I wanted to crash but was too wound up to sleep. The television was on but the sound had been muted. The boys were at their grandpa's, and the only noise in the house was the icemaker dumping cubes into the tray and filling back up.

Rosie told me that she had cried all day at work and didn't know if she had any tears left. Fortunately, her job puts her in a room where she is usually alone, but she went to her supervisor anyway, apologized for her emotions, and explained what had happened.

Just before Rosie was about to leave for the day, Mr. Walsh and Mr. Smith of Walsh, Harper & Smith, Inc., came into her office. Everyone, including her supervisor, the receptionists, and the secretarial pool were stunned because the big brass had never been seen venturing beyond the executive offices on the top floor.

Both men came to express their heartfelt sympathies for the loss of her friend and their appreciation for her husband's service in protecting their community. They told her to take the rest of the week off, and if she needed more time, they would accommodate her. This of course brought Rosie to tears again, and to her surprise, both men began to tear up as well.

It was a clear spring evening, so we sat out on the back deck and watched falling stars streak across the sky. I reverted to my childhood a little and hung a wish on each one that went by. I looked over at Rosie and caught her lips moving as she pinned a wish on a few as well. We both knew our wishes would go unfulfilled.

Gazing upward, it seemed as if the night sky was darker than usual, and the stars a bit brighter. I wondered if A. J. was somewhere out there looking back at me, asking as he had once before, if I believed in God. Some days I'm sure there is a God because everything is going so well, then other days I question if there could possibly be a God. Because a good God would have intervened.

We went to bed around ten, and although I was beat, I just lay there staring at the ceiling fan. In the dark Rosie scooted over next to me and put her head on my chest. I could feel her tears running down my side as she silently wept.

"Don't die on me Bobby, please."

I stroked her hair and kissed the top of her head, "No, baby, I won't. I promise."

In the morning, Rosie made me breakfast and went to work in the kitchen putting together a food basket we would take over to Betty. We were both concerned that she would be alone, so after checking on the boys, our next destination was Betty's.

We rounded the corner and found there wasn't a single parking spot near A. J. and Betty's house for two blocks. The driveway and street on both sides were jammed with black and white police cars, unmarked police cars, private vehicles, and news vans. In the front yard, news reporters talked with folks from the neighborhood about what great neighbors A. J. and Betty were, and how comforting it was to have him next door.

In the house, it was standing room only, as family gathered in small groups and children ran through the crowd like squirrels through a forest. The back patio and yard looked like a police convention. I couldn't help but wonder who was protecting the city. Maybe crime took a day off in honor of our fallen comrade. It was clear that the entire city of Oakland was concerned that Betty might be alone.

Rosie stood at the front door with her basket trying to determine the best route to take to get to the kitchen. Tables covered with finger food, cakes, pies, and fruit were in every room. Betty was moving from one person to the next greeting them, hugging them, and consoling them. Looking up she saw Rosie, and with the speed and dexterity of a ferret she weaved her way through the crowd. When she reached us, she looked intently into Rosie's eyes, then wrapped her arms tightly around her, silently enveloping her in an almost cocoon-like embrace. After a long hug Betty took Rosie's basket and handed it to a teenage girl to be put on a table.

Taking Rosie by the arm, Betty guided her up a flight of stairs, to a room at the top, where they disappeared for the next twenty minutes.

On the patio, Lieutenant Miller and Sergeants Helmer and Alan called me over.

"How are you doing, Bob?" Lieutenant Miller asked.

"Better today, thanks."

"Great job in identifying Mitcham and his crew. That's good investigative work," Sergeant Helmer said.

"You are one of A. J.'s projects, aren't you?" Sergeant Alan asked.

"Projects?"

"Yeah, wasn't A. J. your TO? The two of you worked together on a number of cases, and knowing A. J., you would have learned a lot."

"Yep, I'm definitely one of A. J.'s projects." I smiled.

"I hate to do this to you, Bob, but I need you to come in a few hours early tonight and read over the initial report and all the witness statements. I want to make sure everything is in line. I don't want Mitcham slipping out of our hands again," Lieutenant Miller said.

"What about the Feds? Every time we pop him, he's back out on the street before the ink is dry on the arrest report."

"Not this time. The chief has made some calls, and whatever Mitcham was feeding the Feds for a get-out-of-jail-free card is done. There's no negotiating when you kill a cop."

On the way home Rosie and I talked about how good it was to see the overwhelming response and support Betty was receiving. She told Rosie that she knew that it would fade and eventually she would be alone. She had seen it played out for other police widows in the past. We made a pact that when that time comes, we would make a point to be there for her.

After dropping Rosie off and getting some desperately needed hugs and kisses from my troop, I left early for work. Sitting alone in Interview Room B, I spread out the six eyewitness statements on the table and began by reading Lieutenant Miller's and Detective Wilson's reports. Then, to better understand what the witnesses may have seen, I read over the coroner's initial narrative.

Next, I took each witness statement and first read the interviewing officer's cover sheet that gave a brief description of the witness, and where they were located as they watched what took place. Closing my eyes, I envisioned the scene along State Route 13 and imagined that I was standing where they stood, then I began to read.

They all began describing how A. J. was talking to Mitcham, who was lying on his back on the hillside by the rear of his disabled car. They stated that A. J. had gone back to his car to use his police radio, then casually returned to Mitcham's location.

They detailed how Mitcham had surprised A. J. by pulling a gun from behind his back, and how A. J. had fallen when the first bullet entered his left kneecap. While on the ground, A. J. struggled to lift up and reach for his gun, when he was shot a second time. This bullet entered his chest.

They described how Mitcham stood over A. J., taunting him and calling him names. According to several of the statements, Mitcham looked at the witnesses who were crouched behind their cars and yelled that he was going to kill himself a cop.

They said that the three motorcyclists, all identified as members of the Savages biker gang by the patches they wore, showed up almost on cue. When they arrived, they pulled in front of the police car, a few feet from the officer's body, and turned off their engines. They never got off their bikes, just watched as Mitcham took the officer's gun and rolled him over onto his back.

A. J. was not dead or unconscious. He slowly lifted himself onto his elbows as Mitcham stood over him pointing his service revolver at his head.

Each account of the events was more graphic than the last. The horror of those last moments of A. J.'s life was depicted in minute detail from every possible angle. I was experiencing every emotion at once, from rage to heartbreak. My stomach was starting to turn, and I was about to get sick.

Looking at his terrified audience peeking over hoods and from car windows, Mitcham had laughed and shouted, "Ever see how you make bacon? You first kill the pig." Turning to the three bikers, "Right boys?" They all roared their approval.

A. J. looked up at Mitcham and began to plead with him, "No, no, please don't do this. Please."

"Please?" Mitcham laughed and pulled the trigger. The sound of the Smith & Wesson .357 echoed through the valley, along with the laughter and cheers from the leather-clad animals who watched.

My stomach rebelled and I ran from the room, reaching the bathroom just in time. Bending over the toilet I vomited so hard I expected to see my guts in the bowl. Falling against the wall in the stall, I let the tears flow. My friend, my mentor, was gone.

I didn't hear Lieutenant Miller come in, but above my own sobs I heard the water running in a sink. Trying to regain some measure of composure, the restroom door opened, and two officers came in talking about their cars.

"Gentlemen, I'm sorry this restroom is out of order. Please use the one in the locker room," Lieutenant Miller said.

"Sure LT," they said and left.

I heard footsteps walking toward the door and then Lieutenant Miller's voice.

"Bob, take your time. When you're ready, bring the reports and statements to my office." The door opened, "And bring the 'Out of Order' sign too."

I sat on the floor for about a half hour reflecting on the different situations A. J. had walked me through. I don't know why he took a liking to me, but I am truly thankful he did. He deposited what we call "street smarts" into me that most police officers take years to glean. He once told me I should never be afraid of being afraid. That fear properly handled is a warning sign to the mind like pain is to the body. It must exist, but not be shown.

Gathering up the paperwork, and reassembling it in the proper order, I went to the district commander's office. Putting the small mountain of papers on Lieutenant Miller's desk, I handed him the "Out of Order" sign.

"Thank you, sir." I lowered my head. "I'm sorry for my reaction."

"You have nothing to be sorry about, Richards. I sat in the stall next to yours when James Asher was killed in a hit and run on I-80 ten years ago. We weren't the only ones to use those stalls, and we won't be the last."

"Losing A. J. is hard, but reading the whole account of how it all went down is like a kick in the gut."

"I know, but you needed to hear it all. You need to know the truth, all of it. I'm sorry it's so painful, Bob, but if you don't know the truth, you'll get bits and pieces, and a hell of a lot of rumor and false crap for months. Over time that can dismantle you."

"You're right. I sure don't need to hear what happened on the 'installment plan.'"

"Think of the good times. Remember the positive. Go and be safe out there, Officer Richards."

The squad room was unusually quiet. Both swing and grave shifts had taken their respective places without the usual conversation and banter. I walked in and sat down at my usual spot next to A. J.'s chair. It had a black ribbon draped over it. Sergeant Helmer came in and, instead of taking his place behind the podium, stepped to one side while Chaplain Michael Blackhall stepped up.

"Gentlemen, yesterday we lost one of our own, a man deeply respected and loved. There are no words I can say to relieve you of this loss. I truly wish there were."

The chaplain dropped his head. "Please allow me to pray for A. J.'s family and for you." Every head bowed. "Lord, we come before you with humble and broken hearts. We ask that your gentle presence fill A. J.'s home and rest upon Betty and each member of their family. I ask that the peace you promised that would rise up in times of adversity would rest upon the hearts of each of the peacekeepers who sit before me. I ask this, Lord, in your name, amen."

Sergeant Helmer returned to the podium and said, "Listen up, arrest warrants have been issued for Curtis Mitcham, Rosko Tanner, Harry Heckle, and Louis Hanson for the murder of Officer Alford Jackson. Anyone wearing Savages' colors is to be arrested and booked for aiding and abetting, and as an accessory to the murder, pursuant to Penal Code Section 31. If you make an arrest, expedite your arrest reports and get them to the detective division, ASAP." A loud cheer filled the room.

"Okay, settle down. We have added two extra floaters for the next three days. Any traffic stops are to have two back-ups covering them. Do you understand? These are some bad boys, and there may be some wannabees out there looking to make a name for themselves."

Sergeant Helmer then moved aside as Lieutenant Miller walked into the room and took the podium.

"Good evening, gentlemen. 'No Knock' search warrants have been issued for the homes and vehicles of Mitcham, Tanner, Heckle, and Hanson. In the morning, at 3:10 a.m., Oakland and Alameda SWAT teams, along with assistance from the CHP tactical team, FBI, and ATF, will be hitting their homes, as well as the Savages' clubhouse. Anyone and everyone who breathes, including their dogs, will be arrested. Depending on the number of arrests, they will be brought to Alameda, Contra Costa, and San Francisco county jails to be segregated and housed. We don't want them to be talking until we can interrogate them individually."

"Can we attend the party, LT?" came a voice from the back.

"Unfortunately, no. The first question that came up during the planning of this was your involvement. The loss and manner of A. J.'s death could—and most likely will—stir emotions that might jeopardize the case. We want these guys on death row. You will have your shot at them in court."

A collective groan waved across the room. "I'm sorry. I wanted to be there too."

"When will there be a service for A. J.?" asked another voice.

"That is being planned with Mrs. Jackson. You will all be given plenty of notice. Polish your brass, and make sure your dress uniform is cleaned and still fits. We owe A. J. the best so be sharp. Let's go to work. Be safe."

CHAPTER TWENTY-THREE

On the way home I swung by Dee's Country Store to get some of her sweet rolls and to let them know that although Mitcham was out, and on the run, he would soon be in custody. I didn't think they would ever see him again, but it didn't hurt to bring them up to speed just in case. They had been hearing the news about A. J. and were probably in need of a little reassurance. John was working in the garage and told me that Dee was home preparing for a brief stay in the hospital. She had been diagnosed with lung cancer that she attributed to thirty years of smoking. Her chemo treatments were starting tomorrow.

John handed me a slip of paper with a phone number on it. "I know you have a lot on your plate, but do you think you could call her sometime? She thinks highly of you. Says you're a churchgoer so you know how to pray. It would mean a lot to her."

Where did she ever get the idea that I was a churchgoer or that she wanted me to pray? She'd be better off coming to me for the chemo. "Can I use your phone? I need to call my wife."

In the office, in the back of the store, I sat behind a large antique wooden dining table Dee used as a desk. I called Joe and said I would be late picking up the boys. Then I called Rosie and arranged to meet her in her office and together we would call Dee. It would be best for the prayer to come from a woman, I reasoned. Besides, I'm not a member of the "party line" to heaven. The Big Guy, Jesus, would never answer my call.

In a small conference room, I dialed Dee's number. After a brief conversation I introduced her to Rosie, who got on the other line. From that point on I was just a spectator. The tears that flowed were contagious. Dee's concern wasn't for her illness, but for her family. After thirty minutes my bride began to pray, while I searched the office for tissues. Bringing Rosie into the equation was the wisest move I could have made. I was a lucky man. No, it wasn't luck. I was a blessed man.

That evening after dinner, while the troop watched the *Mickey Mouse Club*, I called in to find out what the raids had accomplished. Curtis Mitcham, Rosko Tanner, Harry Heckle, and Louis Hanson—the four involved in A. J.'s death—were all in custody, along with sixteen others.

Drugs, weapons, stolen property, and a huge amount of cash were seized. Mitcham was asleep when his house was hit by SWAT. He scrambled out of bed and reached for his pants that hung on a hook on the wall. In the pocket was a .380-caliber automatic, believed to be the one he shot A. J. with. In a dresser drawer was A. J.'s .357 Smith & Wesson.

The district attorney's office was filing every charge they could justify on all of them, including first-degree murder, or the aiding and abetting of the murder of a police officer. They would be held for seventy-two hours and arraigned Thursday morning in Judge Fairland's court. The judge specifically requested that the arraignments be assigned to his court.

On Thursday morning, I showed up at Judge Fairland's court to find the benches in the gallery filled with uniforms. There wasn't a seat left, and little standing room along the walls. Two attorneys sat at the defense and prosecution tables going through papers and writing notes. The stereographer and court clerk were getting ready at their desk, and the bailiff stood like a bar room bouncer at the door leading into the judge's chambers. Both the jury box and the judge's bench were empty.

"Bob, Bob, over here," came a voice from the sea of blue uniforms. "We have a seat for you," Gary Alison said.

Sliding past a couple officers on the front row, "Thanks Gary, where's Turk. I would think he'd want to be here."

"He is here. He's out front growling and barking at anyone on a motorcycle, or in leathers, that shows up."

"He's a good dog, and a good cop."

I looked around, nodded, and acknowledged all the different uniforms that were there. Multiple city and county law enforcement officers had come to show their support.

"Doesn't look like they would get in if they did show up."

"That's what we had in mind."

The door to the chambers opened and the bailiff said, "All rise," as Judge Fairland took a seat behind his large mahogany bench.

Looking around the room, Fairland surveyed the audience and smiled. "Good morning, ladies and gentlemen. This morning we will be arraigning those men charged with the murder of one of your own. I understand your pain and anger, but in this room, it will not be expressed. There will be no outbursts or loud comments or conversation. We are going to get our business done and get these men back to their cells. Do you understand?"

I stood, "Yes, Your Honor, we understand."

"Bailiff, bring in the first defendant on the docket."

A door on the left side of the courtroom opened and Louis Hanson and Harry Heckle shuffled in, dressed in orange coveralls and shackled in chains. Each had an armed deputy at his side and behind them walked a well-dressed attorney.

The three stood facing the judge. "I assume, Mr. DeSantis, you are representing both Mr. Hanson and Mr. Heckle?" the judge said.

"Yes, Your Honor," the lawyer said. "The firm of DeSantis, Whitehouse, and Davis will be representing all the defendants in this action, Your Honor."

Lifting a stack of manila file folders, Judge Fairland asked the court clerk. "Mary, are these all the files on this matter?"

"Yes, sir," she said.

After thumbing through the files, Fairland looked up and said, "Mr. DeSantis, there are a total of twenty defendants, each one with various charges. Are you and your firm going to be the attorney of record for them all?"

"Yes, Your Honor. We have twenty-five attorneys associated with our firm and twenty paralegals and staff."

"Okay, Mr. DeSantis, you are now Attorney of Record. Mr. Hanson and Mr. Heckle, you are both charged with 187, 37, and 141 of the California Penal Code, First Degree Murder, Aiding and Abetting a Murder, and Evidence Tampering. The murder charge includes special circumstances in the killing of a police officer. If you are convicted, you can be sentenced to life in prison without the possibility of parole or the death penalty. Do you understand?"

"No." Hanson pulled away from the deputy and moved toward the judge until both deputies grabbed him. "I didn't kill anybody. What are you trying to do, frame me?"

"Mr. DeSantis, get control of your client. Mr. Hanson, keep your comments between you and your attorney. How do you plead, guilty or not guilty?"

"Not guilty!" Hanson shouted.

"Mr. Heckle, how do you plead?"

"Not guilty," Heckle said.

"Your Honor, my clients have families and are respected in . . ." DeSantis began to say.

"Save your breath, Mr. DeSantis. There is no chance I'm going to set bail on charges like these. That will also hold true for the rest of your clients involved in the killing of Officer Jackson."

Hanson and Heckle were returned to their cells as Curtis Mitcham and Rosko Tanner took their turn before Judge Fairland. Like the previous two, the charges were read along with the potential penalties. Both said they were not guilty. When they were being led away, Mitcham turned to his audience in blue and stopped. He scanned the room until he saw me. Not taking his eyes off me, he raised his hands as high as the shackles would allow and pointed two fingers, mimicking a gun, and pretended to shoot. The deputies responded by jerking the shackles hard enough to cause Mitcham to stumble backwards, landing on his butt. Then they grabbed his collar and dragged him back through the door. Laughter and applause erupted but was quickly quelled by the sound of Judge Fairland's gavel and the stern look on his face.

In a firm tone, Judge Fairland said, "That will be enough." He looked down with a slight grin on his face.

For most of the morning we sat and watched as twenty scruffy-looking Savages in orange were brought before the judge's bench, pled their innocence, then returned to their new home. On the way out I shook hands with every officer and deputy in attendance and thanked them for their support.

I stood at the top of the marble steps that led out of the courthouse and down to the street, watching a sea of blue, brown, and green uniforms descend into the parking lot below. Thinking of those early days of training with A. J., I remembered him telling me not to expect police work to be just a job. It was much more than that. It was a way of life. Those who wore a badge, whether I knew them or not, were more than fellow employees. They were family. Today we shared the same heartache, not because we were all close to A. J., or even knew him, but because he was a member of our family, and he was taken from us.

The courthouse was built on a hill rising above the financial district, and the bodies scurrying around were fulfilling their daily routine. For them it was just another day. No one stopped to give even a moment of silence for a warrior lost.

"You gave your life for them, my friend. I hope they are all worth it," I said to the wind.

CHAPTER TWENTY-FOUR

I got home in time for a late lunch, but the house was empty. On the refrigerator door was a large note that said Rosie and the boys had gone to visit Dee at the hospital, then they were going to run by Betty's to check on her. It was signed in various motifs, in three colors of crayon by each of my troop, and one in ink by the commander in chief. That's my girl, always checking on someone in need, and my gang always at her side.

It had been two weeks since A. J. was killed, and tomorrow would be his funeral service at Sacred Heart Catholic Church. Officers from the San Francisco and Berkeley police departments along with deputies from the Alameda County Sheriff's Department would be covering the city while every OPD officer would attend the service.

Bedtime would be early tonight because Rosie and I would be going to A. J.'s home early in the morning to pick up Betty for the service. The boys began to put up a fuss until they were told that Grandpa and Grandma were taking them to Fleishhacker Zoo in San Francisco in the morning. You would have thought it was Christmas Eve and they had to be in bed before Santa showed up.

I awoke to the aroma of Rosie's perfume, a soft kiss, and a whisper in my ear, "Wake up, Bobby, we need to get ready. I put your coffee on the counter in the bathroom."

She knew if she put it on the nightstand I would stay in bed and drink it there. The kiss and the coffee were just lures to get me moving. Smart girl, that Rosie.

Putting on my dress uniform, I could hear Joe's and Alberta's voices in the kitchen and the boys all talking about their favorite animal. Critter was taking his favorite animal with him, a faded tan teddy bear named Bert, with one ear stitched on and his right eye missing. That little bear had made the rounds. It started with Little Joe, then went to Sonny, and even though we bought Critter a new one, he only wanted Bert.

When we arrived at Betty's, we again found the street lined with parked cars. Inside I met a couple dozen ladies and a few men, half from the neighborhood, and the other half spouses of Oakland police officers. They were all busy preparing for the gathering that would follow the service.

One of the neighbors noticed my surprised look and came over to me, "We will have this all set up with food, drink, and seating by the time you get back. We have a crew all set to clean everything up when we're done too," he said.

"Wow, that's great," I said. "Thank you so much."

"That's what neighbors do. Jesus told us to love our neighbors, and this is how it's done."

"It might be a big crowd. I don't know where they're going to park."

"You shouldn't have a problem finding a parking space. Every homeowner on the block, and a full block on either side, are either putting their cars in the garage or parking them at Smith & Son's truck lot a couple miles up the road. Mr. Smith lives four doors down. We have a crew that will direct the parking, both on the street and in the driveways."

"I'm sure Betty is truly thankful for you folks."

"A. J. was more than just a neighbor. He was our friend." A tear ran down his cheek.

I dropped off Rosie and Betty in front of the police department, where they were escorted into the building, and pulled away expecting to park several blocks down the street. To my surprise I was directed to a spot on the side of the building by several California Highway Patrol officers. They had a plan all laid out, and the manpower to make it come to pass.

"Thank you, gentlemen," I said. "Will you be escorting us to the church?"

"Yes, sir, and to the gravesite as well."

"Thank you again." The thought of being a part of a family in blue gave me a tangible sense of peace and security.

A cadet stationed at the door checked a clipboard and told me to report to the squad room for instructions. Inside, there were thirty officers, most from the early morning shift who worked with A. J., and a group who had been trained by him.

"Attention," commanded Sergeant Helmer as Deputy Chief Woodard entered the room. Everyone snapped to attention.

"At ease. Please be seated," the DC said. "In forty-five minutes, we will be departing for Saint Mary's church. You will all be in the lead cars. Bob Richards and Chelsey Defo, you will ride in the limo with A. J.'s family. This was his wife's request. CHP will be directing traffic and clearing the path. According to CHP Logistics and Assessment Division they're expecting two hundred marked police vehicles, fifty motor officers, seventy unmarked and transport vehicles. Only God knows how many personal vehicles. Lights on but no sirens, as this is not a parade."

Taking a sip of coffee, he looked around the room, his expression hardening. "What I'm about to say stays within this room. Do I make myself clear?"

"Yes, sir," the room echoed collectively.

"The department has received a number of threats and warnings of possible disruptions during today's services. This is not uncommon. However, two alerts came to us via FBI intelligence, from sources they have within out-of-state branches of the Savages motorcycle club. The Feds are tracking the movements of SMC members around the country, and several groups have entered California in the last week. It is believed they're here to show support for the members of the Oakland club that we have locked up. Remember, this is not to get out. We don't want to frighten Mrs. Jackson or her family. Threats like these are usually all bluster, but keep your eyes open nonetheless."

In front of Sacred Heart Catholic Church, the thirty officers who had been briefed by Deputy Chief Woodard lined up along the walkway that led to two large open wooden doors entering the sanctuary. There were fifteen on each side facing one another. The rest of the OPD officers in attendance formed eight rows of forty-five on the opposite side of the street facing the church. Several more rows of officers in full dress uniform flanked each side of the church. Behind them stood officers and deputies from agencies all over Northern California, and some from Southern Cal, Nevada, and Oregon. It was an awe-inspiring sight of unity.

At precisely 10:00 a.m., two motorcycle officers with lights flashing passed along the street in front of the church, followed by a long black limo that stopped at the church's walkway. Lieutenant Miller opened the doors, while I took a position opposite him. Police Chief Robert L. Boon exited and extended his hand to Patricia, A. J.'s daughter, followed by Betty.

The moment A. J.'s widow stepped from the car, a voice rose up in the silence, "Attention," and a single muted sound of movement could be heard, as hundreds of men and woman snapped to attention. As she began her trek toward the church doors, the voice was heard again, "Present Arms," and all raised their hands to salute her. The limo slowly pulled away, followed by several large black sedans dropping off various members of the family.

The church inside was much larger than I had expected. I counted twenty-five rows, each with four long wooden pews, that could easily seat twelve. Betty and her family were ushered to the front row, center right with Rosie behind her. On the front row, center left sat OPD Chief Boon, along with the chiefs from San Francisco, Berkeley, and Richmond. Beside them were the sheriffs of Alameda, San Francisco, Contra Costa, Marin, and San Mateo counties. Seated behind them and on the outside pews sat a variety of high-ranking stars and bars. OPD officers entered in military fashion and stood along the side wall under tall semicircular arched stained-glass windows.

Each of the windows across from me depicted the trial, beating, and crucifixion of Jesus, in brilliant color. *Aren't churches supposed to be places where hope was dispensed?* I thought. This place seemed to focus more on pain and death.

"Attention," came the order, and everyone, except the family, stood as the casket, draped in an American flag, moved slowly down the center aisle. On either side were the pallbearers, family members, and a few lifelong friends.

Once they were seated, a heavyset, mature woman stood and began to sing "Amazing Grace." I had heard that song so many times, I could sing it myself, but the way she sang it made me feel like I was hearing it for the first time. Following the song, a priest in a long light blue robe and green vestments stepped to the podium.

"We have come to celebrate and reflect upon the life of Alford Fergus Jackson. We all have come to know him simply as A. J."

Fergus? I never knew what A. J.'s middle name was and was glad I didn't ask. I probably wouldn't have gotten an answer.

"A. J. rarely attended Mass because of his work schedule, but every week for over eleven years, he would come to the presbytery with two cups of coffee, and we would spend a little time together. He once shared that he had put to memory a verse from the Bible and that it gave him peace when dealing with difficult situations on his job. It was from the book of John, the third chapter, verses sixteen and seventeen. 'For God so loved the world that He gave His only begotten Son, that whoever believes in Him should not perish but have everlasting life. For God did not send His Son into the world to condemn the world, but that the world through Him might be saved.'"

There was much more read from the Bible, and the sermon was interesting, but those verses that A. J. had memorized kept ringing in my ears. He was a good cop, a real cop, gentle when needed and tough when it was called for. I knew he and Betty would go to church on Easter and Christmas, but I never saw the religious side of him. Now thinking back on it, I guess it was always there.

After the sermon, Chief Boon, Lieutenant Miller, and a host of friends and family took the podium and shared some laughter and some tears. The most moving moment came when A. J.'s ten-year-old granddaughter, Allison, stepped up onto a stool and read a letter to her grandpa. There wasn't a dry eye in the room.

When the priest gave the final prayer and blessing, the casket was moved back down the aisle, followed by Betty and the family. Lieutenant Miller signaled me to break from the rank and accompany Rosie and the family.

In the limo I took a seat facing the back window, next to Chief Boon and Officer Chelsey Defo. Across from us sat Rosie, Betty, and Patricia, with Allison on her lap. During the entire procession, the chief made small talk while I stared out the window at crowds of people who lined the streets. Large signs held by children and adults proclaimed appreciation for Officer Jackson's service, and sorrow for the loss of his life. Little old ladies were praying and making the sign of the cross as the hearse passed by.

The trip to St. Mary's Catholic Cemetery would have covered the mile and a half in less than five minutes, but this was a journey that required a much longer route. Heading north, rather than east, the procession slowly snaked its way through North Oakland, Emeryville, Clawson, West

Oakland, North Gate, Lakeshore, and Piedmont. Within forty-five minutes we passed through all of OPD's twelve districts.

At each intersection, CHP stopped traffic, allowing the procession to pass uninterrupted, causing a serious back up of traffic. At the intersection of Hollis and 40th, motorcycles were parked along both sides of the street for a block and a half. On the sidewalks bikers gathered, clad in leather and sporting the Savages' colors. Beside our car two San Francisco motor officers rolled up on either side. Looking over my shoulder I could see a line of police motorcycles taking positions on either side of the cars that transported the family.

Betty looked at me and smiled. "Impressive, isn't it? A. J. always felt that he was part of something much bigger than himself."

"Yes, it is. I'm just sorry the officers had to be here for protection."

"Those gang members being here simply demonstrates the power you have over them. You frighten them," Betty said.

"I never thought about it that way."

"Officer Defo, thank you for accepting my invitation to ride with me today. A. J. thought a great deal of you. He said that he saw you as the cutting edge to bring more women into law enforcement. He would often tell stories about cases you two would work together, and how confident he was when you backed him up."

"Thank you, ma'am, it is a true honor to be here with you." Chelsey's voice quivered. "I will truly miss him."

When we arrived at the cemetery, the family was escorted to a series of chairs on either side of the gravesite where the casket had been placed. It took another fifteen minutes for the rest of the procession to arrive. Some fifty yards away I saw two familiar faces standing between two deputies from the county jail. The smaller, thin man in a black suit, two sizes too big for him, was Jimmy Hall, and the well-dressed man was Jack Cinto, his attorney. Judge Hamond had granted permission for Jimmy to attend the graveside service.

After a brief homily and the reading of the Twenty-Third Psalm, seven riflemen fired three volleys into the air. A seven-man honor guard removed the flag from the casket and began the thirteen folds of the triangle. Upon completion it was handed to Chief Boon, who presented it to Betty. Stepping back, he saluted, and the honor guard marched away to the sound of "Amazing Grace" being played on bagpipes in the distance.

It was a fitting ceremony for a man who had touched so many lives. The ride back to the PD was quiet because all that could be said had been said. Rosie and I took Betty, Patricia, and Allison home to a gathering large enough to spill over into all the neighboring yards. There was enough food to feed the entire city of Oakland.

I found a space halfway up the stairwell and settled in to consume a large plate of finger food. From here the front door, entry, and living room were in view. From my lofty perch I could watch people, both uniformed and civilian, flow in and out like the tides on the bay. Off to my right a big guy was cutting a wake through the congestion toward me. It was Scott Johnson with his wife, Charlotte, close behind.

"Bob, Bob." He waved his hand and excused himself to the people he weaved around.

Standing on the floor below me looking up through the rails, he put a big meaty arm around his wife and pulled her close. "Bob, I want to thank you, but first I need to apologize to you. I know I was wrong, real wrong, and I offended you big time. I'm sorry, Bob, I truly am. I hope you can find your way clear to forgive me some day."

Considering where we were, and why we were here, it seemed foolish to hold a grudge against someone who was out there fighting the battle with you. His relationship with a woman whose husband was away in Vietnam angered me, but it was time to move on. Our battle was here and it was not with each other.

"This is Charlotte, my wife."

"Yes, we've met. Good to see you again, Charlotte."

"Bob, the advice you gave me was right on. It didn't make sense at the time, but now I can see it was the only way to make things right."

"Advice?" I asked.

"You asked me if I attended a church and suggested I get counseling from a pastor. Well, I went and met with my mother's pastor, Lester Pearly at Trinity Assembly of God. He told me if I was serious about straightening my life out, I needed to confess my sins and ask forgiveness from two people. First, God, and second, Charlotte. That was a big order, but it had to be done. God forgave me, but with Charlotte, it took a while, so I moved out and stayed with a friend.

"I told Vicky Harper that I was prepared to support her and the baby, but I couldn't marry her. It turned out that she wasn't pregnant. She said that to just keep the relationship going."

Scott looked down at Charlotte, pulling her tighter to his side, "She forgave me, and we're continuing the counseling together. The church has become our second family."

"That's good to hear. You two look great together."

"Thanks again, Bob, for being willing to stand for what's right. I'm sorry for what I've done and for the loss of A. J. I know you two were close. Well, we have to get home. Maybe we can get together some time for dinner."

"That sounds good." I spied Rosie across the room greeting and serving everyone within her reach.

Gradually she worked her way through the crowd to the foot of the steps. Slowly she ascended and stopped in front of me.

"You want anything else, sweetheart?" she asked.

"No, thank you. Everything looked so good I took more than I should have. This has been some kind of day, hasn't it? It's really great that there were so many here for Betty."

Rosie looked at me, and a sadness washed over her face, "Bobby, you promised me, remember? What we are doing for Betty is good, but the price is too high. I don't want anyone to do this for me. I don't want there to ever be a reason. You promised."

"I promised." I put my plate down and wrapped my arms around her.

CHAPTER TWENTY-FIVE

It had been nearly a year since A. J.'s service, and the reality of him not being there to back me up just hadn't fully set in yet. I expected to see him wander in five minutes before briefing and flop down in his customary seat, but he never did. It wasn't ever going to be the same.

Mitcham and Tanner hadn't gone to trial yet. It had been nothing but legal haggling and delays. Most of his crew had their day in court or pled guilty and were serving out their sentences. I was told by the DA that because it was a capital murder case, with the death penalty in the balance, they needed to dot every *i* and cross every *t*.

At least they were in jail, and not on the street, but the word I had gotten from a few deputies who worked in the jail, was that Mitcham and Tanner had become big deals behind bars. Being members of a biker gang who killed a cop had given them street creds and made them real popular.

After another year had gone by, Sergeant Helmer began the briefing by introducing a new member to the graveyard shift.

"Gentlemen, we have two new additions to our early morning romp, a lateral transfer from LAPD, Officer Abel Glasser." On the far side of the room, a large guy with a military-style haircut waved his hand as if swatting away flies.

"You all know our next addition. She has been with OPD for six years and has requested the opportunity to work patrol, Officer Chelsey Defo." Chelsey stood and gave a gentle wave to all in the room.

"Abe, why don't you tell us a little about yourself? What brought you up North?" Sergeant Helmer asked.

"Well, to begin with, Sergeant, my name is Abel, not Abe, and able is what I am. I've worked the streets of LA for ten years and wanted to go someplace a little quieter for the next ten."

"Well, welcome to the quiet streets of Oakland. Try to stay awake out there. Things can get pretty boring, especially for an experienced LA cop, like yourself," Helmer said sarcastically. Turning his attention to Chelsey, "Officer Defo, tell us a little about yourself."

She stood and was about to speak when Abel said, "That's something you won't see in LA, women cops on patrol."

"Officer Glasser, you had your two minutes of fame. Now we want to hear from someone else. Since you are unaware of the protocol, let me bring you up to speed. When I talk, you don't. Do I make myself clear, Officer Glasser?"

"Yeah, loud and clear, Sergeant," Glasser snickered.

Chelsey smiled. Her feathers weren't ruffled a bit. "My great-grandfather worked the streets of Oakland, and my grandfather was killed investigating a homicide in the Produce Exchange, what we now call Jack London Square. My father, James Defo, retired as a patrol watch commander of the Second District five years ago. He hoped for a boy but fathered three little girls. It is my intent to fulfill my father's legacy as an OPD patrol officer."

"Welcome aboard, Chelsey," one officer shouted from the back. "Good to have you with us," said another, and others clapped.

The uproar quieted when Lieutenant Miller walked into the room and approached the podium. "Good evening. I have some important business to conduct. Officer Bob Richards, would you step up here for a moment please?"

A bit bewildered, I walked up to the front, as my supporters called out to me, "What did ya do now, Richards?" and, "It was nice knowing ya, buddy," and "We'll miss ya around here, Bobby."

"Officer Richards, it is my privilege to announce that effective the first day of June, you will be promoted and assume the roll of Patrol Sergeant. Congratulations, Bob." He handed me three gold chevrons that would soon be on my sleeve. A number of officers applauded, others called out their approval, and from the back of the room Sergeant Helmer shouted, "Aw crap, they didn't fire him."

After a few minutes of well-meaning harassment, Sergeant Helmer brought the briefing back to order. "Officer Glasser, you will be assuming Beat 7. You will be riding with Officer Prager who can show you the beat and introduce you to some of the folks in the area. He has been working the beat for a year now. He's moving back to swing shift. It's been good serving with you, Prager."

Glasser rolled his eyes and sighed.

"Officer Defo, your TO is Senior Officer Richards. You will be working Beat 12. Anything you wish to add, LT?"

"Nope. Just be safe out there," Lieutenant Miller said.

Defo and I spent our first few hours getting reacquainted and cruising the darkened Oakland streets waiting for a call for service and looking for trouble. I had known her since I was hired but realized I knew very little about her. She was born and raised in Oakland, like her father and his father before him. She had a police science degree from Mt. Diablo Junior College, a bachelor's degree in criminal justice from Cal State, Sacramento, and was presently working on a law degree at the University of San Francisco. She wasn't sure if OPD was her life's career, or if it was working as a deputy DA once she passed the bar exam.

Her greatest achievement and primary focus were her boyfriend and her daughters. In her personal life she was known as Chelsey Defo Ballesteros. She kept her maiden name while working with OPD in honor of her heritage. At the end of our first shift together it was clear that this young lady was a cop to her core.

As became our custom over the next year, I asked Chelsey to clean up and refuel the car, as well as submit the shift's incident reports while I hit the locker room to change clothes. This day was a big day, and I got home just in time to get Little Joe to school. He sat next to me, wide-eyed, and with a grin from ear to ear. The backpack on his lap had all he needed to breeze through the next four years successfully. Today is his first day at Valley View High School. Every night for the past month, the topic at the dinner table was what high school was like. The kid was so excited about school starting, he all but missed three months of summer vacation.

"Dad, would you mind dropping me off here?" Little Joe said, three blocks from the school.

"I don't mind taking you all the way up, son, and if you want, I don't mind walking you in," I said as seriously as I could.

"No. No. That's okay, Dad. I just need to walk a bit, you know, stretch my legs. I'll be sitting all day."

"Oh, yeah. You're right. You don't want to get all cramped up on your first day." I tried not to smile.

I pulled to the curb. "Okay, buddy, here you go."

"Thanks, Dad." He opened the door and jumped out.

"Hey, bud, I love you. Have a good day."

Looking around to see who was close by, he bent down and in a low voice, "I love you too, Dad. Thanks."

I sat there watching him walk away behind a procession of other kids and remembered the day I dropped him off for his first day in kindergarten. Time had gone just too fast.

Rosie had taken Sonny and Critter to school for their first day and was going to meet me at our favorite spot for a little "we time" over breakfast. I sipped my coffee and waited, as I looked around the room remembering Dee's Country Store, those sumptuous sweet rolls, and that sweet lady.

Gone were the small wooden tables, hard-backed chairs, long counter with its stools, and the cash register. In their place were cushioned booths along both walls and individual tables with comfortable wicker chairs in the center. The tinted pane window and the old wooden front door had been replaced by a set of large decorative French doors that led out to a patio, with outdoor furniture surrounding several fire pits. Inside, the earth tone walls had been painted over with beautiful frescoes of the Oakland hills as they looked before asphalt and concrete took over.

Dee's grandchildren had given the place a new facelift for the new decade we had entered. Dee would be proud of what they had done. The Flying A station and tow service had moved two miles down the road and was now Steller's Shell and Tow Service. Dee lost her battle with cancer a few years ago, and shortly after, her son, John Steller, had a stroke that confined him to a wheelchair. It was not the same place anymore, but the smell of Dee's sweet rolls still lingered in the air.

Through the French doors I could see the most beautiful woman on the planet walking my way across the patio, and I was compelled to thank God for the gifts He had given me. I have heard what He had done in the lives of others and have seen His hand at work in mine, but I still had a lot of questions. There must be someone looking out for me, because if it were left to me, I would have screwed it up a long time ago. I once thought of becoming an atheist but gave up the idea. They don't have any good holidays.

"They're baking up another batch of sweet rolls. We'll get a couple right out of the oven."

She took a seat across from me.

"You going to be working late today?"

"No. The IT department is shutting the system down to do work on our mainframe, so I have my team doing some sorely needed housekeeping. Hopefully tomorrow I'll walk into a bay of clean desks."

Rosie worked as a temp for a large real estate firm for six months when their bookkeeper took time off for maternity leave. They liked her work so much they asked her to come back. Once all the boys were back in school, and Critter was in sixth grade, she went back part-time. That lasted a year. Shortly after going full-time, she was promoted and moved up the ranks. Today, my brilliant little colleague in life is the Senior Corporate Accountant for Walsh, Harper & Smith, Inc.

"Guess who's back, but only for a broker's conference?"

"Your old admirer, Chip Nessler?"

"Yep, but I won't see him. The conference is being held at the Sheraton on the other side of town, and I'm not going to be attending."

"How did you hear he was going to be there?"

"He sent a note to a couple of the girls in the office, inviting them to dinner. What a worm."

I really didn't want to dwell on a character like the Chipster during the few precious hours I had alone with Rosie. So following breakfast, I took her to an early movie. It had to be something light, not too serious, and not a love story or a cop flick. She said it was my turn to pick, so we were off to meet E. T., the Extra-Terrestrial. I would soon learn that all I needed was a finger that would glow to bring civility back to those I dealt with on the street.

We picked up the boys from school and spent the afternoon barbecuing in the backyard and listening to what the new school year had to offer. Little Joe, who now wants to be known only as Joe, showed us the list of his classes, and Sonny gave us a permission slip to sign for a field trip to the California Art Museum. Critter had already forgotten about school and only wanted to know if we were going to make s'mores after we ate.

By six o'clock I was getting ready for work. It was only three years ago that I was promoted to sergeant and assumed the role of Felony Shift Watch Commander, from

8:00 p.m. to 4:00 a.m. It was the shift that saw most of the action and looked good on a resume when it came time for advancement.

The eight to four shift wasn't responsible for a particular beat area, nor was it restricted to a specific district. This team of twenty officers was assigned to areas that experience higher than normal crime stats. If shootings, robberies, drugs, assaults, and the like were on the rise in a particular neighborhood, then it would get a higher level of police presence. The goal was deterrent over detention. Stop the problem before it started. Unfortunately, what it really meant was when we showed up, the trouble was just going to move to another neighborhood.

Before I would brief my team, I would meet with Lieutenant Miller, who would soon be pinning on captains bars, and Sergeant Kip Boxer, the swing shift watch commander. Together we determined where we needed to place our suppression team within the city.

We had just begun our meeting when the door opened and the evening desk officer poked his head in, "Sergeant Richards, I'm sorry to bother you. There's a lady in the foyer that has been waiting to see you. She's been waiting for over an hour. Says she's an old friend."

Our meeting was quickly wrapped up, and I went out to the foyer and met an attractive woman in her early fifties, simply dressed but with a flair of elegance. She looked familiar, but I couldn't place where I had seen her before.

"Officer Richards?"

"Yes, ma'am, it's Sergeant Richards. I'm sorry you had to wait so long. What is it that I can do for you?"

"You don't remember me, do you?"

"I'm sorry, ma'am, I know we've met before, but I just can't place it."

"Maybe this can help." She removed a dog-eared, purple-covered Bible from a large sling bag on the seat next to her. "You gave this to me five years ago. It changed my life."

"Joyce?" I opened the cover and saw three little scrawled signatures of my boys. "Joyce, you look wonderful. Please come into my office. I have a briefing to do, but if you don't mind waiting a bit longer, I'll get you a cup of coffee and be right back."

"Take your time, Officer, or I mean, Sergeant Richards. I have some good reading material." She lifted her Bible.

I spent an hour hearing how Joyce had been given an opportunity by the Salvation Army to move out of her tent into a shelter, and how she received job training and rehabilitation. The foundation that her new life was built upon was a deeper understanding of God's Word and His desire and plan for her life. Joyce served four years as a Salvation Army soldier and was recently promoted full time to the rank of Lieutenant. It was wonderful to see and hear the positive changes that had been made in her life. However, that wasn't the reason she came to see me.

"Sergeant Richards, there is a man who has come to the mission that I'm concerned about. He was recently paroled from prison, but he has no family and isn't doing well."

"Has he threatened you or harmed anyone?"

"No, but I'm afraid he could hurt someone, or be hurt. I just don't understand why they would let him out like that."

"What do you mean?"

"He fought in the Battle of Normandy and was wounded at Omaha Beach. He was hospitalized in France until the war was over. He was sent home to find his wife with another man." She shook her head. "He killed them both. He was sentenced to life in prison and served nearly forty years. He's now seventy years old and in bad health. He has no one, no place to go, and no future."

"Honestly you and your organization can do far more for him than we can, but I'll keep an eye out for him. What's his name, and where does he live?"

"It's Harold Dowling. He goes by Hoot. I believe his parole officer put him up in the Blue Gulf Motel, with another parolee."

I took Joyce's information and gave her our home phone number, asking her to call Rosie in a few days and share with her the story of her new life. I knew my bride would enjoy it far more hearing it from her.

Once I hit the street, I drove into the parking lot of the Blue Gulf Motel and watched as small groups of gang bangers scattered like roaches when the lights came on. It was your standard two-story fleabag, with the doors to each room facing out toward the street. Lights were on in most of the rooms, and half of the florescent bulbs on the motel's sign were out. I parked for a few minutes and watched as the ladies of the night strolled past me on the sidewalk, smiling, waving, and making catcalls.

Across the parking lot an old man with scraggly gray hair and beard shuffled out of a room on the ground floor. His clothes were two sizes too big, and he kept pulling up his pants as he walked. Stopping in front of my car, he just stood and stared at me, raised his hand, gave me a single finger salute, turned slowly, and walked away.

I think I just had an introduction to Mr. Harold Dowling, better known as Hoot.

It was a quiet night with little to do but back up patrol in a few domestic disturbance calls and a couple of drunk driving arrests. There was a chill in the air that lent heavily to getting people off the streets.

I was home by a quarter to six and crept in without waking the boys. I woke Rosie up with a kiss, a fresh cup of coffee, and one of Dee's sweet rolls. I told her a little about Joyce and that she would have to get the whole story directly from the source when she called.

"Looks like I'll be going to the broker's conference after all."

"Really? What changed?"

"The attorney that was going to speak on the responsibilities of CFOs, Controllers, CIOs, and Accounts Managers has come down sick, so I have been asked to step in. I think it's good because at every conference they tell them what they shouldn't do. I want to tell them what they should do."

"Attagirl." I smiled. "So, when is the unveiling of my beautiful virtuoso going to take place?"

"Tonight. There's a dinner at five, and I speak at seven. I would love to avoid the dinner, but I can't. I didn't think you could get off with such short notice, so I've asked Dad to go with me. You okay with that?"

"Sure. I'm glad he'll be there, especially with your office Casanova hanging around. Do me a favor. You'll finish dinner before I go to work, so give me a call, if you can, and tell me how you're doing."

"You got it." She kissed me. "Daddy is going to be bored to tears."

That evening the phone rang just as I cleared the shower door. Dripping wet, with nothing but a towel, I streaked across the bedroom, slipped on the throw rug (what an appropriate name), and slid up to the nightstand. "Hello?"

"Are you okay?"

"Yeah, baby, I'm fine. How was dinner?"

"The food's pretty good. Daddy was introduced to a couple of gentlemen who were in the army serving in Europe the same time he was, so he's having a great time telling war stories."

"Have you run into Chip?"

"We sure did. He asked me who my old boyfriend was. Said if I wanted someone younger, he was still around. I thought Dad was going to punch him." She giggled. "Daddy told him to move on or he'd see just how old he was."

"He's not bothering you, is he?"

"No. He's off talking it up and drinking as much of the free booze as he can hold."

"Okay, be safe and call me at work if you need me."

"Will do. I love you."

"Love you too."

I went to work early and retrieved my gear from my locker, then stopped by the watch commander's office to talk to Sergeant Kip Boxer.

"Sergeant, how are we doing this evening?"

"Good. It's been an uneventful evening. What are you doing here so early?"

"Kip, I have to make a quick run across town. Would you mind holding down the fort if I'm running late? I don't think I will be, but it's possible."

"Yeah, no problem. Is everything okay?"

"Sure, everything's fine. I just need to talk to a fella about some personal stuff."

My first stop was the front desk of the Sheraton Hotel.

"Good evening, Officer. How can I help you," the desk clerk said.

"Do you have a gentleman by the name of Chip Nessler registered here?"

"Just one moment." The clerk scanned the register. "Yes, room 312. Is there something wrong?"

"No. No. You wouldn't happen to have a conference of some type going on here, would you?"

"Yes, we do. It's the Northern California Broker's Conference."

"Well, it looks like he's up to his old tricks again. He hasn't charged anything to his room, has he? You know, like meals, drinks, tickets, stuff like that?"

Thumbing through a stack of papers, his face flushed, "Yes, he has, several meals and a bar tab. He also got two tickets to a musical at ATC in San Francisco for tomorrow night, and he rented a car through our concierge service. What's going on; what do we need to know?"

"Oh, nothing, sir. I'm sorry. I didn't mean to alarm you. To my knowledge he has been doing well since his parole. I have no evidence that he's done anything wrong. Not yet, anyway." I turned and looked at the two large doors to the conference room. "I'm just going to take a quick look. You folks have a good evening."

"Good evening," I said to a young lady seated at a small table just inside the entrance. "Northern California Broker's Conference?"

"Yes, sir."

"Mind if I take a quick look around?"

"No, sir. Is everything okay?"

"Yep, it's just a courtesy visit we give to our hotels and their guests."

From the back of the room, I could see my beautiful wife's head, and the shiny bald spot on her father's next to her. He tried covering his glossy dome once with some stuff in a spray can he bought off a TV ad. He looked like an Elvis Presley wannabe.

To my left, midway to the stage sat Chip, just three tables away from Rosie. He was yucking it up at a table of like-minded drunks, guzzling as much of the free booze as they could. Out of the forty tables in the room, theirs was the loudest, and the brashest voice belonged to Chip. I felt a bit sorry for the speaker as he tried to ignore the heckles and laughter.

I walked to the greeter table. "Miss, are you familiar with Mr. Chip Nessler?"

She sneered. "Yes, I am."

"Would you please step over to his table and tell him that an old friend of his is here."

She looked at me as if to ask, you're his friend? "Yes, sir."

I returned to the back of the room as she worked her way around the tables, leaned over Chip's shoulder, then pointed at me.

When he turned and looked at me, I smiled, nodded, pointed two fingers at him with my thumb up, mimicking a gun, and made a gesture. He went pale and turned back to the table quickly, knocking over several glasses. The commotion caught everybody's attention, including Rosie's. She looked to see what had happened and saw me in the back of the room, waved, and threw me a kiss. I waved back, pointed at my watch, and left the room. I had to get to work.

CHAPTER TWENTY-SIX

As I slid behind the wheel and was about to radio in that I was on duty, dispatch put out a call of an older man threatening customers with a knife at Mickie's Diner, not far from my location.

"Dispatch, this is Alfa-3, I'm a few blocks away, I'll cover," I radioed.

"Ten-four," came the response. "The Reporting Party requested to know if you were on duty. Said she knew you. She will be out front, please meet her there."

"Ten-four, en route," I radioed back.

I arrived at the same time as Officer Charles Williams and was met by Joyce, the Bible-reading pup-tent dweller from the park who was now a skid-row missionary. Mickie's Diner was an old-fashioned box diner once seen along the interstate highways. Through the front windows I could see six frightened patrons seated around two small tables. At the end of the counter stood the short, disheveled old man I saw in the parking lot of the Blue Gulf Motel. Over his head he swung a large meat cleaver as he yelled obscenities at the cook.

"Sergeant Richards," Joyce called out. "Thank you for coming. The man I told you about, Harold Dowling, came to the Mission for our Saturday evening service, and afterward we invited him to join us for coffee. He was doing fine until they brought him his bill. Then he just went crazy. Please, Sergeant, don't hurt him. He is just lost out here and has no one."

"I promise we'll do everything we can," I sighed. "Williams, stand by the door. Come in only if you have to. I don't want to corner him or put too much pressure on him. I want to get those people out first."

"You got it, Sergeant." He glanced around. "Ma'am, would you please go and stand behind my police car. Thank you."

"Hoot." I eased in through the front door. "What's going on, man?"

He spun around and froze, "You know me? How do you know me?"

"You're Harold Dowling, right?" I smiled. "I've been told you're a pretty good guy. So, what's going on?"

"That so-called cook back there wanted three bucks for a cup of joe and a sandwich. I made better joe than that when I was inside. I was a cook's assistant and knew how to brew real coffee, not this mud he gave me."

"Okay, but is that any reason to scare your friends? Let's get these folks out of here so you and I can talk. They brought you here because they're your friends. They shouldn't be treated like this. It's not their fault they don't know what a good cup of joe is."

"What about him?" Hoot pointed at the cook.

"Well, if we get him out of here, maybe we can go back there, and you can make us a real cup of coffee."

He stood silently looking at the six people sitting around the tables, "I'm sorry. You all have been nice to me. I'm sorry."

"That's good, Hoot." I moved between him and the six. "Ladies and gentlemen, the restaurant is now closed. Please exit and see the officer out front."

Without a word, all six stood and moved behind me to the door. The cook slid cautiously from the kitchen, around the counter, and hurried out.

"Hoot, you need to put the meat cleaver down and step away, okay?"

"I don't think so." He sat on one of the stools. "I think I'd just as soon have you shoot me."

"Hoot, you don't want me to shoot you. I'm such a bad shot, I couldn't hit the water if I fell out of the boat. All I'd do is wound ya, and you'd be in pain for months, maybe even lose a limb. I will make you a deal though."

"What kind of deal?"

"Where were you the cook's assistant?"

"Folsom State Prison. I'd been there for twenty-two years. I was the chaplain's helper too. I did all his errands, delivered the Bibles and letters, and set up the chapel for Sunday services."

I keyed my portable radio, "Williams, do not move in no matter what you see. It's all under control. Please confirm."

"Okay, Sergeant," he responded with a question in his tone.

"Hoot, here's what we're going to do. When I tell you to, you are going to stand up, take one step toward me, and swing that meat cleaver at me, but by God, you better miss. Do you understand me?"

"You want me to try and chop you up?"

"No, I don't want you to try to chop me up. All I want you to do is swing it at me so everyone outside can see it. Then I'm going to arrest you for attempted murder of a police officer, assault with a deadly weapon, violation of your parole, kidnapping, and petty theft."

He had the look of an old lost puppy, wide-eyed, as his head tilted to one side.

"Kidnapping and petty theft?"

"Yes. You held those people here against their will by force and fear, that's kidnapping. You didn't pay for the coffee and sandwich, that's petty theft. I'll be talking with your parole officer and the DA. If I get my way, you'll be serving some hard time, most likely at Folsom. With the attempted murder of a police officer in your jacket, you'll probably become a pretty popular fella in there."

He sat there, both hands wrapped tightly around the handle of the meat cleaver, staring down at the floor. Slowly a smile formed across his face as he raised his head, "How close should I get?"

"If I can feel the breeze of that blade go by me, the deal's off and I'm going to shoot ya."

"Okay, tell me when."

"Now."

Hoot jumped from the stool, took not one, but two steps toward me and swung the meat cleaver. It may have been my imagination, but I'm sure I heard a gasp from the people outside as a button on my shirt was severed off. The weight of the cleaver caused Hoot to spin, and I thought he was going to screw himself into the floor. I caught him when his back was to me and brought him to the ground.

Handcuffing him, I said, "Hoot, you're under arrest. You have the right to remain silent, what you . . ."

"Yeah, yeah, I know," twisting his head around to look up at me. "Thank you."

"You came a little too close."

"Yeah, I'm sorry, I got excited."

I walked him outside as a small crowd gathered and began to applaud. Hoot thought they were clapping for him, and maybe they were, so he straightened up, put on a big toothy grin, and winked at all the ladies as he went by.

"Williams, this is your collar. I'll write up my end of the narrative, and you make up the arrest report. I'll get the witness statements, and you admonish and interview Hoot. We'll get together and lay it out when we get back to the PD. Any questions?"

"Nope. I was told about Hoot by the folks out here. He's been having a pretty rough time of it. I know what you did, Sergeant. It was a good call."

Placed in the backseat of Williams's patrol car, Hoot turned to look out and gave a last wink and smile to his fan club as it pulled away.

I asked for Joyce and the six who had been around the table to meet me back inside the diner. The cook locked the door, put the closed sign out, and went back into the kitchen, brewing each of us a little of his mud.

"Ladies and gentlemen, I'm afraid Hoot will no longer be attending services at the mission. I need you to write down what you know about Hoot, how you have seen him act, and what you witnessed here tonight. Joyce, would you assist if anyone needs help?"

"Will we have to go to court? I don't think any of us want to cause him more trouble."

"He is in a lot of trouble, but it's good trouble. He was tossed out of his home into a world he knew nothing about. He's been institutionalized. Inside those prison walls he had food, shelter, and purpose. Out here he has nothing and no one. Tonight, he bought his ticket home."

I dropped off the witness statements with Officer Williams and returned to the darkened streets of Oakland. After several passes through some of our more volatile areas, I parked in my favorite spot at the end of the driveway at Grace Lutheran Church. It was one of the highest points in the city, and I loved the spectacular view of the lights below. Pouring a fresh cup from my thermos, I began to record my account of Hoot's arrest.

I went through the narrative of the evening's events, excluding my direction of Hoot's assault, and began to reflect on Pastor Conor's sermon last Sunday. We had been attending New Hope Christian Fellowship for the last year or so and had made a number of friends. Rosie had wanted us to attend as a family for some time, and the boys loved it. As for me, I liked the way Pastor Conor put things. He read a lot from the Bible, but then he explained things in a way that made sense. Last Sunday he talked about law and grace. The law was needed to set boundaries, to point out wrongs, and to assure peace. Grace was how we were to apply the law, with wisdom and understanding. A. J. would be proud. I believe I fulfilled them both this evening with Hoot.

In the cityscape that spread out before me, there was happiness and heartache, compassion and conflict, and my job was to mediate between them. When those who lived within the glow of those lights had no place else to turn, they turned to me. A feeling of inadequacy washed over me like a tidal wave. Who was I to take on the world's troubles?

CHAPTER TWENTY-SEVEN

Sitting in the bleachers overlooking the football field of Valley View High School, I tried to make out which of the mortarboard-covered heads was mine.

"There he is, Dad." Critter pointed to the left side of a sea of maroon-draped graduates of the class of 1988. Two in, on the fourth row, sat my boy. He was easy to spot once I knew where to look because on the top of his square hat were the letters *UCLA* in silver glitter.

Where had the time gone? In a month, we would be flying to the army's Fort Leonard Wood, in Missouri, to attend Little Joe's graduation from military police school. Today it was Sonny's turn, and next year we'd be sitting here again for Critter's graduation. Our lives had passed us by just too fast.

"You must be proud, son. You raised three fine men," Joe said.

"They couldn't have had a better grandpa, Joe. You loved them and showed them what a real man was. I can never thank you enough for always being there when I couldn't."

"Are you still planning to attend the Full Gospel Businessmen's Dinner with me tomorrow night?"

"Sure."

The next evening at precisely 4:45 p.m., Joe was at the door to pick me up. He was always fifteen minutes early. He once told me if you're on time, you're late. He saw anything other than an early arrival as disrespect.

On the ride over to the dinner, we drove quietly for nearly twenty minutes. I had always enjoyed that about him, that he wasn't afraid of the silence. When he spoke, he had something to say. He was never good at small talk.

"Bob, have you ever thought about what you will do when you retire?"

"Rosie and I have talked about it. The department is planning on offering early retirement packages to some of the upper-level administrative staff."

"Have you ever considered the ministry?"

"Joe, I'm not a minister."

"Yes, you are. I've watched you with your friends, the men at the church, and with the other officers. You have a gift, son. You're a born leader, and you have a heart for others."

"That's nice for you to say, but it's not for me."

The conference room at the Holiday Inn was full of local businessmen, and quite a few had brought their wives. The food was good, but the speaker was dry, and after fifteen minutes I began to nod. Fortunately, I had brought with me a pocket of chocolate mints for just such a time as this.

The next speaker was a man I had met early in my career, Chaplain Howard Hays. His presence and presentation were interesting and stimulating. He addressed the concerns of overcrowding, gang wars, racial unrest, and the desperate need for Christ in the hearts of both the prisoners and the guards alike. In his conclusion, he spoke of how short-handed the chaplaincy was and that he was looking for those who might have an interest in working to bring the gospel into the California prisons. A young man in a business suit handed out interest cards to everyone. I placed mine under my plate.

"What do you think?" Joe asked me.

"Are you kidding? I put them in there, I'm not about to join them." I said, surprised that he would even ask.

The ride home was quiet, and when he dropped me off, I stood on my lawn and watched his taillights disappear around the corner. I wanted to tell him that Deputy Chief Allan Hart blew into my office like a winter storm to congratulate me on my future promotion to Lieutenant. I didn't tell him because the news was to be kept quiet until a public announcement was made.

In the family room, on the sofa in front of the TV, bundled up in a multi colored Oakland Raiders blanket, lay the love of my life. I didn't have the heart to wake her, so I sat across from her and watched her breathe.

When I was a small boy, my grandmother would tuck me in, kiss my forehead, and as she turned off the light, tell me to count my blessings. Every night, I would go through a list of my toys, my friends, and my puppies. It wasn't a long list, but long enough to put me to sleep. Now the night doesn't provide enough time to even scratch the surface of the abundance of my life.

"Are you okay, baby? What's wrong?" came Rosie's soft, gentle voice.

"Nothing is wrong. I'm just counting my blessings."

She pulled the blanket back and smiled as I stretched out beside her and kissed her. "What do you say we trade in that old wagon of yours and get you that new Chrysler LeBaron convertible you fell in love with?"

"Bobby, that's out of the question. We can't afford that."

"Little Joe is out of the house and will probably be stationed somewhere along the east coast. Sonny is heading down south to school, and Critter will be wrapping up his senior year soon and he'll be gone too. Just think of the money we're going to save not having to feed those gluttons. Just what we're going to save in milk could buy the car."

"Let's wait and see. Remember, Little Joe is the only one paying his own way."

"Okay, but I have just one request."

"What's that?"

"Start referring to me as Lieutenant Richards."

Her eyes widened as she leaned back and looked at me. "Lieutenant Richards?"

"Yep."

Putting her head on my shoulder, she tilted her head, kissed my neck, and whispered softly in my ear, "Jenkins Chrysler is open at nine. My car's on the showroom floor."

Rosie and I were able to coordinate vacations, so for the next two weeks we explored the California coastline, from Eureka to San Diego, in our—I mean, her—new baby blue convertible. Sonny was flying to UCLA for orientation and to check out the available housing, and Critter was traveling north with his grandpa for a couple weeks of fishing on majestic Nehalem Bay. We would then all board a plane to Missouri to cheer on our soldier at Fort Leonard Wood.

Following three great weeks of exploring, resting, and fishing, it was time to get back to work. Parking a half block from the department, I approached the stairs leading up to the backdoor and noticed an empty parking spot just to the left of the steps. The sign on the wall above it read, "Lieutenant Parking Only," and a warm feeling radiated through my immense ego.

In my mail slot were a dozen phone messages requesting ride-alongs, extra patrols, and interviews for student papers. There were the usual complaints, from the usual complainants, and two messages from the office of Chaplain Howard Hays.

"Chaplain Hays's office. This is Clerk Pasquil. How may I help you?" the young man said.

"My name is Bob Richards. I am returning Chaplain Hays's call."

"Yes, Sergeant Richards, we are in need of some additional information in order to complete your background check. If you will hold for just a moment, I'll pull up your file."

"Back it up, what background check? What are you talking about?"

"We're following up on your interest in working with Chaplain Hays and the California Prison Chaplain's Association. A complete background is necessary, I'm sure you must understand, Sergeant Richards."

"Yeah, yeah, I understand the need for a thorough background, what I don't understand is why you're calling me?"

"Well, as I said, we're just responding to the interest card you submitted to Chaplain Hays at the Full Gospel Businessmen's Dinner last month."

I knew where that card had come from and who filled it out. It was my sneaky father-in-law, Joe. If he wasn't such a great guy, this would tick me off. It looked like I was just going to have to bless him with four or five vacuum cleaner salesmen appointments and a couple dozen free magazine subscriptions.

"I'm sorry, but that was a mistake. I'm not interested in the slightest in working within the prison system in any fashion. Please remove my name and pass on my apologies to Chaplain Hays for the confusion."

"Okay, sir. I'm sorry to have bothered you. Have a good day, sir."

Leaving my office, I walked through the communication center and dropped off some audiotapes for transcription. Cindy McDaniel, Dispatch Supervisor, waved me over.

"Sergeant Richards, we received a call from a Mrs. Sharon Pace who said that her fifteen-year-old son got angry, struck her, and hid somewhere in the house. The beat officer and his backup are making a DUI arrest, so I sent Reserve Officer Reeves on the call. He radioed in that he was there, but I haven't been able to raise him for a safety check. Would you mind running by there? It's only two blocks away."

"Sure, his portable may not be working."

The reserve officer's car was parked in the driveway, the lights were on inside the house, and the front door stood open. Broken glass from a vase was strewn about throughout the entry, and a coffee table and pole lamp were overturned in the living room.

"Oakland Police." I shouted as I walked through the house. At the end of a long hall the door leading into the garage was partially open. "OPD, Police. Is there anyone here?"

The door opened slightly, and a frail woman in an old house dress, sporting a swollen black eye, slipped into the hall, shutting the door behind her.

Turning the bruised eye away from me, she nervously said, "Hello, Officer. I'm sorry we bothered you. Everything is okay now. We don't need to take up any more of your time."

"Where is the officer, and where is your son?"

"Oh, he left. My son is in bed. He wasn't feeling well. He's had a cold."

"The officer left already, and your boy is in bed?"

"Yes. That's right."

"Who is in the garage?" I stepped toward the door.

"No one," she almost shrieked, jumping between me and the door.

"Get out of the way now," I growled through my teeth and clenched jaw. Gently but firmly, I moved her aside.

On the garage floor under an open hatch that led to the attic was Reserve Officer Reeves lying at the foot of a ladder. Blood had pooled around his head.

"Dispatch, I have an officer down. Roll an ambulance to my location. It appears to be a head injury."

Kneeling at Reeves's side I could see a deep laceration on his forehead but found no other injuries. His breathing was steady and pulse appeared strong. On a makeshift clothesline strung from the side of the door to the corner wall, hung five tan housedresses like the one Mrs. Pace was wearing. I grabbed two of them and gently placed them on his wound, applying only enough pressure to stop the bleeding.

"Mrs. Pace, is there anyone else in the house? Where is your husband?"

"He is at work. No, there is no one else here."

"What about your son?"

A thump, then movement could be heard above us. "He's gone too." She looked up at the ceiling.

Just then, the EMTs arrived and took over. They bandaged Reeves's head and placed him on a gurney.

"Mrs. Pace, get your husband on the phone. I want to talk to him."

"Oh, I can't do that. He's never to be disturbed when he's at work."

"Mrs. Pace, I'm not asking you. I'm telling you, get him on the phone, now."

Her hand shaking, she dialed then handed me the phone, "Mr. Pace, this is Sergeant Richards of the Oakland Police Department. Your son assaulted your wife, and it appears he also assaulted one of our officers. He has hidden himself in the attic above the garage. I need you to come home and get him down."

"I can't come home now. I have appointments with some important people this morning. Can't you handle it? I'm willing to pay you whatever it costs. Do your job, so I can do mine, now put my wife back on the phone."

Taking control of my emotions, I took a deep breath. "Thank you for your cooperation, Mr. Pace. I will do my job."

I handed the phone to a crying Mrs. Pace. "Charles, I'm sorry for bothering you at work. The policeman made me call you. I'm so sorry. He also used two of my dresses on the officer's wound, but I think I can get the blood out. It won't cost anything, I promise. Please don't be mad."

"Mrs. Pace, what is your son's name."

"Sammy," she wept, holding the phone near her ear. I could hear the dial tone. He had already hung up on her.

In the garage I yelled toward the ceiling, "Sammy, this is the police. Come on down, son. We need to talk. Sammy, did you hear me?"

"Yeah, I heard you, pig. Come on up here and I'll bash your head in too."

I'm a patient man, always wanting to go the extra mile, and couldn't help but see the similarities between father and son. Looking at the blood on the floor and then at his mother's black eye, I figured we pretty much had covered a mile and a half already. Going back in I told the lady of the house to make herself comfortable on the sofa and not to move. I would be back with her son shortly.

In the bedroom, I threw off the bed covers and pulled the mattress out into the garage. Taking the rake I tapped the drywall on the ceiling, noting where the beams were located.

"What are you doing down there, pig? You might as well stop knocking. I'm not letting you in."

"I'm sorry, Sammy, I can't hear you very well. Move back a bit so I can make a hole we can talk through." I could hear him shuffle back, so I drove the end of the rake handle through the drywall several times, leaving a hole about six inches in diameter.

"Talk to me now, Sammy."

"I don't want to talk to you, pig."

"I'm sorry, I didn't get that. Move back again." I poked a few more times through the sheetrock. Now the hole was a little more than a foot wide. "How's that?"

Sammy, the attic rat, started spewing obscenities, using some words I had never heard before. While he demonstrated his seemingly inexhaustible litany of profane expressions, I moved the ladder to the other side of the mattress, out of sight from Sammy's angle of view.

"You seem to have a lot to say, but I still can't hear you very well. It must be all the insulation up there."

I climbed up four steps as Sammy leaned down close to the hole, spit, and tossed a few more choice descriptions of his views of law enforcement.

Quickly I grabbed the collar of his shirt, weaved my fingers tightly into the material and jumped off the ladder. My weight brought little Sammy crashing through the drywall, landing hard on the mattress. A bedrail followed close behind, bouncing off his shins. The tears began to flow. I rolled him onto his stomach, handcuffed him, jerked him to his feet, and all but dribbled him out to my car.

I left him in the backseat to cry while I instructed another officer to take pictures and collect the bedrail as evidence. I gave Mrs. Pace my card and told her to give it to her husband. She looked at the large hole in the ceiling. "Charles is going to be so mad."

When Charles showed up at the PD, his first words were, "I'm going to sue you and the city of Oakland for the destruction you caused to my home."

He had even more to say about lawsuits when I handcuffed him and walked him down to the county jail and booked him for neglect and abuse. It might not fly, but it was Friday evening, on a holiday weekend, so he wouldn't be getting out until late Tuesday.

Sammy was spending some time with other boys like himself, in the county's juvenile detention, perfecting his language skills.

Reserve Officer Reeves regained consciousness shortly after arriving in the emergency room. The prognosis was good, and he was expected to be back on duty within a few weeks.

Dispatch Supervisor Cindy McDaniel came to my office and said she had talked with Mrs. Pace, and it looked like there was going to be a restraining order against Charles Pace while she filed for a divorce.

It looked like it was going to turn out to be a pretty good day. Thank you, Lord.

CHAPTER TWENTY-EIGHT

The ceremony promoting two of my team to Sergeant, and myself to Lieutenant, was wonderful. Little Joe was home on leave, Sonny drove up from LA, and Critter bailed out of a football game, where he was needed, to attend. Our table included Rosie and me, the boys, their grandparents, and Deputy Chief Allan Hart and his wife, Maybell.

At first when the Harts sat down, I thought, *oh boy, this isn't going to be fun*, but to my surprise, the Harts were great conversationalists, funny, warm, and personable. Grandpa Joe and Deputy Chief Allan hit it off right away. They were both avid fishermen and started telling some whopper fishing adventures. Not really sure how much truth was shared but they enjoyed themselves.

Rosie, Alberta, and Maybell joined a small group of ladies at another table, where they talked about their children and their husbands. The boys weren't bored either. There were quite a few good-looking young ladies in attendance.

Watching the boys brought back a lot of memories of days past when I would try to get the attention of some attractive young lady walking down the halls of our local high school. Now the only young lady's eye I wanted to catch would soon be sitting right next to me with her hand in mine.

"By the way, Bob, have you noticed the increase in vacuum cleaner salesmen showing at your door with bogus invites?" Joe sneered.

"No, Joe, I haven't." I smiled.

"How about the number of magazines chocking up your mailbox?"

"Nope, haven't noticed that either."

It had taken me a couple of weeks to acclimate myself to the new job and get a routine down that assured I got everything done. On my first day I walked into a paper mountain of reports, interviews, articles of interest, and communiques. I had thought of running it all through the shredder, but once I got into it, I found a lot of valuable and important paperwork that had not been properly routed.

This morning the answering machine on my desk had two messages from Chaplain Hays, with little information other than asking me to return his call. I put it at the bottom of my to-do list because he was probably calling to apologize for the call I had gotten from his office a couple of months back. I felt it was unnecessary to put him through the "I'm sorry" gauntlet for a practical joke my father-in-law pulled.

It was five o'clock when I was finally able to see my office door from my chair through the sea of paperwork. It had been a long day, and assuming there wouldn't be a major fire in this wing of the PD, I should have the rest of the paper mill bound, filed, or shredded by noon tomorrow.

"Lieutenant Richards, are you still in your office?" the intercom asked.

"Yes. Deanna, what's up."

"I have a Chaplain Hays on the phone for you."

You had to hand it to him, he sure was persistent. Might as well let him get his apologies over with. "Okay, I'll take it."

With a sigh, I pushed the button on the speaker phone, "Hello, Chaplain Hays, good to hear from you."

"Hello, Lieutenant Richards. Congratulations on your promotion."

"Thank you, sir. What can I do for you?"

"Well, for starters, are you available next Saturday?"

"Yes, I believe so." I almost bit my tongue. Why did I say that? I just responded without thinking. I should have said I needed to check my schedule. Then I could have made something up.

"Great, I would like you to attend an orientation that includes a basic training session here at the prison next Saturday starting at 10:00 a.m. It will only take a few hours."

"What kind of training session? Is this something I need to clear with Command here at the department?"

"Everything has already been approved. I have spoken with Deputy Chief Hart, and he was very pleased to hear of your interest in the chaplaincy program."

"What program?"

"Working in the prison as a chaplain."

"Oh no, I'm not interested in any part of that."

"Well, you put in an interest card and then provided your personal information for the background. I'm sorry, Lieutenant, you have given us every indication that you wish to be considered for a position on our staff."

"Chaplain, I received a call from a man in your office and I asked him to remove my name. I'm sorry, but I am not interested."

"Hold on a minute." He put the phone down.

I could hear file drawers opening and closing, and the sound of papers being shuffled.

"Here it is. The man you spoke with was one of our trustees. He didn't note anything on your card about not wishing to follow through with your initial interest. Some six weeks later my clerk called a woman who identified herself as your wife, and she provided the information we needed."

"That would have been my overly helpful wife, Rosie."

"We have spent a great deal of time and money on clearing you up to this point, and I understand your reluctance to get involved. However, I would greatly appreciate it if you would attend the orientation. I believe you will find it of interest, and it may give you some insight to another facet of our legal system."

Oh, I really didn't want to do this. I wanted to be polite but wasn't about to go into a prison. "I really don't think . . ."

"Bob, we have gone through a great deal of trouble because we were led to believe you were interested in being a part of our team. As a police officer, your background required a significant amount of follow-up, and several contacts with the administration of Oakland PD. As I said, all the way up to the deputy chief. Now if you're not interested, you're not interested, but I'm asking you to just give me a few hours this Saturday. I know you will find the information valuable and the time a good investment for your law enforcement career."

I rubbed my hand through my hair as a splinter of guilt passed between my ears, "Okay, Chaplain, where am I to go for this orientation?"

Once directions were given, I knew I had to reaffirm my disinterest in becoming a chaplain. Why would I want to go inside a prison, let alone help those I have spent most of my life putting in there?

"Sir, I mean no disrespect to you or your ministry. It's just that I would not be comfortable locked up in there. I'll attend your orientation, but that's it."

"Good. I'll see you Saturday at ten."

Although I would only be going into one of the training centers, I struggled with the idea of going into San Quentin. I couldn't shake the trepidation I felt, and for two nights after I accepted the chaplain's invitation, I had a hard time sleeping. It wasn't fear that kept me awake, but something I just couldn't put my finger on.

That reservation rose in my heart as I crossed over the Richmond-San Rafael Bridge and took the first exit off Interstate 580. I kept telling myself that in four hours I would be home tinkering in the garage on my '51 Ford Six Series Club Coupe, and San Quentin would just be a memory.

At the prison I felt my heart pound as I approached the end of the road. I didn't like the idea of being locked up with the bad guys. I guess I had worked the streets too long. At the end of the road stood three uniformed guards in front of a wrought-iron gate. A sign that directed me to the visitor's parking lot rested against a building that hadn't been refurbished or painted since the Great Depression. A large sign on the left of the gate gave the name of the warden, and an admonishment to keep personal information private. Names, addresses, license numbers, or any other personal data was not to be divulged to anyone. The sign went on to list items considered to be contraband, as well as the crime and punishment if any were found being smuggled into the prison.

I identified myself and told the guard that I was there to attend a chaplain's training session. His demeanor changed. He shook his head, rolled his eyes, and then directed me to a two-story, newly painted building just inside the gate. Too bad he wasn't under my command at OPD. He'd have been spending the next two weeks sitting with the second graders at Miss Penelope's School of Etiquette.

At the door I was met by a young man in an orange jumpsuit with CDCR printed on the back. He was a member of the club known as the California Department of Correction and Rehabilitation.

"Mr. Richards, Chaplain Hays and the others are in the training room. Please follow me."

Inside, the walls were covered with old photos depicting the history of the prison, and some of the events that had taken place there. Glass display cases dotted the room containing memorabilia, writings, photos, and artwork. The largest number of displays contained makeshift weapons. There was everything from knives made of melted down Styrofoam cups to elaborate zip guns and smuggled bullets. Yup, I really didn't belong there.

In the training room I was greeted by Chaplain Hays and introduced to five others who came for the orientation. Following a lengthy presentation by Hays describing the duties and responsibilities of the chaplaincy, we were introduced to Warden Earl Kilpatrick. Initially he said that he would only take a few minutes of our time, and for the next forty-five he touted the merits of the chaplain's program. This was followed by fifteen more minutes describing his commitment and involvement to his local church. For some reason everyone seemed to feel it was necessary to point out their spiritual side to anyone who might represent the clergy.

While on a break, Chaplain Hays showed and described for us some of the various types of weapons, drugs, and illicit contraband that had been discovered within the prison. I must admit, I was surprised to see that the variety and quantity nearly matched what was available outside on the streets.

In the main lobby, a full corner was dedicated to the San Quentin Six. On August 21, 1971, six inmates attempted an escape that led to one of the biggest, if not the biggest, riots in the prison's history. When the violence was finally quelled, it was found that six people had lost their lives, three guards and three prisoners. The trial of the six was one of the longest in California's history and cost over two million dollars. Only one of the six was actually convicted of murder.

Back in the training room we watched a film about the different ways chaplains could be manipulated and the dangers that existed within the prison walls. A booklet was handed out to each of us that described, in detail, events where guards were won over by inmates and found themselves in prison or unemployed. Contraband is not always drugs or weapons. It may just be restricted magazines or notes from a prisoner's family. The entire session gave me some insight into prison life and reassured me that it was not my cup of tea.

I found the three hours interesting and thought that it might make some good training for the officer on the street as well. It never hurt to know more about the life and experiences of those they would be dealing with when they were released.

I spent the next half hour looking over the pictures, articles, and criminal keepsakes with the others, learning of their various professions and interests. All were quick to express their enthusiasm about being a part of the chaplain's program. I smiled, acknowledged their passion, but remained neutral in my response.

Returning to the training room I thanked Chaplain Hays for his time and inquired about the possibility of sending some of my officers to the training. I was provided an itinerary of upcoming classes and a stack of pamphlets, booklets, and flyers.

Hays asked that we not leave until he could have a moment of prayer with us. I stood around, getting anxious to be homeward bound, planning my next stop. It was going to be Jake's Smoke House, the finest meat market on the planet. His seasoned steaks were to die for, and on my patio was a new Weber grill, a gift from Rosie for my promotion. But for some reason, I just couldn't shake the premonition that my time at Casa San Quentin wasn't over.

CHAPTER TWENTY-NINE

We closed with prayer, handshakes, and well wishes, gathered up the reading material we were given, and headed for the door.

"Mr. Richards, hold up a moment," Hays said. "Let me grab my bag. I wish to speak with you."

In a few minutes he was back with an old rawhide bag slung over his shoulder. With his hand on my shoulder, he walked me out onto the porch, "Lieutenant, I would like you to accompany me on my rounds this afternoon. I'm sure you will find it of interest."

"No, sir, thank you, but I'm really not interested in going inside. Maybe one of the other guys? I'm sure they would love to go in there."

"They're gone. Bob, I hope you understand this, but I believe you are to be with me today. For the last week God has been putting you on my heart and I don't know why. Please, come with me. It won't be long. I just have a few men to see and then we'll be done."

"Chaplain Hays, I have come this far, way beyond anything I wanted to do. I have no desire of any kind, physically or spiritually, to improve the lives of those incarcerated in this prison. I have dealt with their victims and seen the wake of pain and destruction they have left behind. I have committed my life to catching them and putting them in here. So as far as I am concerned, they bought the ticket, and I don't intend on riding with them."

Hays dropped his hand from my shoulder as I turned toward the Bay and watched a small group of visitors move slowly toward the massive walls of the prison. From their expressions, and the way they shuffled along, I expected to hear the melodious sounds of a funeral dirge.

I looked back to see Hays bow his head and his lips move. He was praying. I wasn't sure what to say or do, so I just stood there. Then he looked up at me and smiled. "Let's go, Bob."

I honestly don't know what happened, but there I was, marching briskly along behind him. "This isn't going to take long, right?" I asked as our pace picked up.

Within moments we stood in front of what looked like a medieval fortress with two towering stone turrets on either side of a large archway that was once used to bring in supplies by horse-drawn cart. It had since been filled in, leaving just a single iron door. To the right of the door was a small shack, just large enough to protect the guard stationed there from the elements.

"Hello, Steve. How is the family and that new baby boy?" Hays said to the guard.

"Fine, sir, just fine. He's sure keeping us up at night."

"That's a rehearsal, Steve. He's just getting ready to join the church choir. This is Bob Richards. He's going to accompany me on my rounds this afternoon."

The guard stepped up next to me, "Sir, please raise your hands above your head and stand still. I am going to search you."

He patted me down and, with some effort, opened the door. Clearing the threshold, I found myself in a concrete tunnel with three sets of iron bars and another steel door on the other side.

Chaplain Hays stepped back outside. "Bob, I'll meet you on the other side. Just wait for me there. I have to go through the administrative entrance to pick up a few things."

With just a hint of panic in my voice, I said, "Wait a minute, you're not going in with me?"

"Yes, I'll be there," he said when the guard closed the door, "I'll meet you on the other side."

Under the strain of the door's weight, the hinges creaked with a high-pitched groan. It was relieved only when it slammed shut with a resounding clang that echoed through the tunnel then fell deathly still. I was sealed in a cement tomb, eight feet wide and twenty feet long. It was divided by three sets of iron-barred gates every five feet. I stood in a space a half a foot larger than the cells that the residents of this place called home.

I never thought that I was claustrophobic, but the irrational fear of becoming trapped in the walls of San Quentin had become a reality. Something I had seen earlier hanging on the wall of the training room flashed across my mind. It was a newspaper article from the early 1900s entitled "Modernizing San Quentin." It described several construction projects including the filling in of the archway. A photo accompanied the article, which had been taken outside looking through the newly installed door and the gates inside.

The caption underneath read, "The prisoners referred to this area as 'the Three Gates to Hell.'"

The silence was unnerving; not a sound of any kind could be heard. Fortunately it was well lit. Two lightbulbs, inset behind Plexiglas in the ceiling, cast a harsh bright light. A concrete bench ran along the wall on the right side, and everything was painted a washed-out gray. It gave the space a macabre aura that reminded me of the old black-and-white horror films from the 1930s.

After several minutes I was about to bang on the door and demand they let me out when a crackly voice from a poorly connected microphone sputtered, "Mr. Richards, can you hear me?"

In the corner above the other door was a small wooden box speaker, which was painted to blend in with the walls.

With what I am sure thinly veiled my irritation and twinge of apprehension, I responded, "Yes, I can hear you."

"Okay, when you hear the buzzer, open the gate. Once inside, shut the gate securely and move through the next gate when its buzzer sounds. Do you have that, sir?"

"Yeah, I got it." The buzzer sounded, and the barred gate was unlocked with a clank. I stepped in, closed the gate behind me, and heard the lock slide into place. Another buzzer sounded and the next gate opened. Two down, one to go.

After a couple of minutes, I began to wonder if they had forgotten me.

"Hello, I'm still in here." The irritation in my voice, no longer veiled, was now abundantly apparent.

After a few more minutes, "Hey, is there anyone out there? Can you hear me? Hello!"

Ten minutes passed and no one was responding. I was not in panic mode yet, but my frustration level had begun to peak. "Hello out there! Can anyone hear me!"

To my relief I heard the speaker begin to crack and hiss, "Mr. Richards, I apologize. There has been an incident in the yard, and we are in lockdown. I will not be able to clear you until the lockdown order is lifted. Please make yourself as comfortable as possible."

"Wait, how about buzzing me back out the way I came?"

"I'm sorry, sir, that is not allowed. It shouldn't be long."

"Wait a minute." The hissing sound in the speaker faded into oblivion. "You still there? Hey! Hello!" The deafening silence had returned.

I began to pace and every few minutes searched my watch face for any sign of its hands' forward movement. I was certain time had slowed down, if not stopped altogether. What seemed like an hour had only been fifteen minutes. This was one of those times I needed to put my watch in my pocket and leave it there.

The only place to sit was the concrete bench, and the only thing to look at was the wall. I stood, paced, sat, laid down as best I could, measured, and remeasured my cell, counted the bars, the cracks on the walls, and the stains on the floor. After wasting some of the quietest time I had ever experienced, I began to do what I should have been doing all along, reciting my memory verse and praying.

In church the previous Sunday, the pastor told us to put to memory James, chapter 1, verses 2 and 3. I usually listened to the messages, but rarely did the memory stuff, until this last Sunday. Closing my eyes, I could see the words in front of me, "Consider it pure joy, my brothers and sisters, whenever you face trials of many kinds, because you know that the testing of your faith produces perseverance."

Could any words be more appropriate to my current situation than these? Pastor said the Greek word for *perseverance* was the same word used for *patience*. I guess I was still in the classroom.

Taking a deep breath, I leaned against the wall and began to pray out loud, "Lord, thank you for this opportunity. There are no interruptions, no phone calls, no business to conduct, no emergencies to rush to. It's just you and me, Lord."

I sensed a need to change my posture. It was as if true humility required a humbler position. I stood, bent down on my knees, placed my elbows on the bench, put my face in my hands, and began to pray. In the stillness something began to happen—I started to weep. Overwhelmed with gratitude for all that God has given me, and in contrast the knowledge of how I had failed Him, my heart broke. When I asked God to forgive me, it was done in part to satisfy my wife. I brought Jesus home to my family when I should have brought my family to Jesus. I sang God's praises, but only for a few minutes in church. There should be praise on my lips every moment of the day, and not just for what He has done, but for who He is.

Tomorrow is Easter Sunday, a perfect example of how my life could so easily become distracted from God's true purpose. Tomorrow would be a day when we would celebrate the single greatest event in human history, but we would be distracted by imaginary bunnies, candy, and multicolored eggs. Tomorrow, I was to play the part of a centurion replete with helmet, sword, and all, crucifying Jesus, but it wasn't an armed soldier who crucified God's son; it was my sin that had nailed Jesus to the cross. For the first time the reality of this truth pierced me to the core of my being.

Words flowed from my mouth as my heart felt like it was being ripped from my chest, "I'm sorry, Lord. Please help me not to wander down my own path, but to walk rightly before you."

The tears ran down my cheeks, as my lips and my mind became as silent as my lodging. I knew it was time to listen, yet for some reason I pulled my watch from my pocket. It was ten minutes after three.

A memory long since buried rose up, bringing with it pain, heartache, and anger. On a lonely stretch of freeway in the Oakland hills, one of the finest men I had ever known was surrounded by a gang of bikers. After being shot twice, once in the leg and once in the chest, he was then beaten. His own service revolver was used to shoot him in the arm and in the stomach. All this was accompanied by the cheers and laughter of those who watched this slaughter take place. The final shot had been to his head.

On Saturday, the day before Easter, at ten minutes after three, Curtis James Mitcham brutally murdered my friend and mentor, Officer Alford Fergus Jackson. Mitcham was now housed just yards away on San Quentin's death row.

Rage coursed through me like lava through a forest, burning away everything I had thought, prayed, and uttered in the last hour. I was on my feet pacing back and forth, kicking the air, and swinging my fists in every direction. I was fighting against the ghosts of the past, shadows with no true substance. Yet in this moment, they were as real and solid to me as the concrete walls that had entombed me.

Turning around and around in my cage, I grabbed the bars and leaned my head between them, exhausted. Then I heard a voice in my head, low but clear. It was mine, "You are here for such a time as this."

"No!" I yelled at the top of my lungs, "No! Where is the justice?"

Dropping back down on the bench, I lifted my fist high over my head, "A. J. believed in you. He trusted you. Where were you?" I shouted, throwing my fists into the air. "You could have stopped that, but you didn't. Why? What divine purpose could A. J.'s death possibly have accomplished?"

I curled up on the bench, placed my head on the cool concrete, and pulled my legs in tightly. "Where were you then?"

A still small familiar voice that could not be heard, weaved its way through the darkness of my thoughts, "Where was I? The same place I was when they crucified my son. And I didn't stop that because I love you, and you are mine."

I all but whimpered, "I don't belong here. What am I supposed to do?"

"Love one another, as I have loved you," echoed through my soul.

A light crackling and a hiss could be heard from the speaker on the wall, "Mr. Richards, you doing okay in there?"

I raised myself up onto my elbow, "Yeah, fine. Doing fine."

"Good. The lockdown is being lifted. We'll have you out of there in just a minute."

The sweet melody of the buzzer resonated throughout the tunnel like a choir of angels playing a kazoo. I was being paroled. As the gate opened, I looked at my watch. I had been held captive for two hours and twelve minutes.

The steel door opened with a creak, and there stood Chaplain Hays.

Through gritted teeth, I said, "I really don't want to go in there."

He saw the look on my face. "Let's sit over here for a moment."

We took a seat on benches that were around a fire pit in front of a freshly painted building with the word *Chapel* over the door. Spread out before us was a well-manicured lawn with flower beds and several small trees. It was a tranquil scene not unlike what you might see illustrating a book of poetry. That was until I looked around us. We were surrounded by fourteen-foot-high concrete walls topped with razor wire. On each corner was a taller tower with two armed men in uniform. Any sense of peace and tranquility was quickly shattered.

We sat quietly for a few minutes before Hays spoke. "Bob, I have one stop to make, and after that I'll get you out of here."

Clasping his hands together he bowed his head and began to pray, "Lord, you have ordained this moment in time, and you have appointed the events that have and will take place. You, Lord God, have called us both to such a time as this. Walk with us, guide our steps, and give the peace that only you can give to my brother's heart."

CHAPTER THIRTY

A sudden slip along the San Andreas Fault caused a sharp jolt, bringing me out of my yesterdays, and back onto the bench in front of the chapel. It was from this bench that my life took a dramatic turn.

"Chaplain Richards, sir, are you okay?" came the familiar voice of Cadet James Kilpatrick.

"Yes, I'm fine." I realized the San Andreas hadn't moved California any closer to Hawaii. It was Cadet Kilpatrick's not-so-gentle nudge that rescued me from my near coma-tose reflection of years past.

"We have been calling around everywhere for you, sir. Chaplain Hays had to leave due to a personal emergency. He asked us to find you and see if you could cover his shift this evening."

"Yes, certainly."

"He said he had a couple of things to get done—paper-work stuff. The details are in a folder on his desk."

"Okay, thanks. I'll be heading over there momentarily," with that, Cadet Kilpatrick did his customary about-face and marched smartly off into the evening.

Looking out over the walls into the darkened sky, I remembered the day that brought me to this place in my life. Nearly five years ago I sat on this very same bench with Senior Chaplain Howard Hays and reluctantly agreed to accompany him while he made his rounds. On that fateful night I met Matthew Fielding, a twenty-five-year-old, who was about to be paroled after serving five years of a ten-year stretch for armed robbery.

While standing some thirty feet away, to provide some semblance of privacy, I waited for Chaplain Hays to finish a meeting with an inmate on the third tier of North Block. Sixty-six barred cells lined one side of the tier, and a three-foot-high railing lined the other. The catwalk that ran between the cells and the railing provided barely enough room for two moderately sized people to comfortably pass each other. The third tier rose nearly thirty feet above the floor, giving me a queasy feeling in my gut. It wouldn't take much to hurl my five-foot, ten-inch frame over that rail.

A cell block is just that, a block. Except for a series of small slits in the wall allowing slivers of natural light, it's comparable to walking into a large hollowed-out brick. Crammed into San Quentin's four cell blocks are 5,247 inmates at any given time. The tightly packed mass of humanity deposited in each block creates an unremitting thunderous rumble that bounces off the solid interior walls. Any chance of clear understandable communication was out of the realm of possibility.

"Are you a chaplain?" came a shout behind me.

Turning, I gazed into the face of a boy with the uncanny resemblance of my youngest son. He could easily have been mistaken for Casey with his shaggy blond hair and his mother's blue-green eyes. Although he was the same height and build, that was where the similarities ended. His neck from ear to ear was a series of black inked tattoos that disappeared below the collar of his blue prison-issued shirt. On his face, under his left eye, were two inked teardrops, and a small cross was etched on his right cheek. From his cuffs to his fingertips the ink flowed. It was apparent that the rest of his body, although covered by prison garb, had become a canvas for someone's handiwork. I would learn later that such markings were intended to act as camouflage, concealing a young man's attractive appearance.

With a touch of disdain in my voice, I said, "No, I'm not a chaplain."

"Can you get one for me, man?"

"The chaplain's up there." I pointed toward the end of the tier. "He's busy today, and he'll be leaving as soon as he's done."

I didn't want to get into any conversation with this kid, and I didn't want Hays to get hung up on him or anything else. All I wanted was to get out of there now.

"If you're with the chaplain, then you must know about God and stuff. Would you pray for me, man?"

"What? No, I'm not a chaplain, man." Inside I began to feel a little regret for my harsh retort.

"Come on, man. I get paroled in two weeks, and I need some prayer."

"If you're getting out, what do you need prayer for?" I said, wanting to add, *it's the people you're going to hurt out there who need the prayer,* but I held my tongue.

"Look, my old lady is going to show up with a hot car, a gun, and a needle, and I'll be back here in a month serving out my stint with a bunch more added."

He leaned against the bars of a cell, turned his face away from me, and began to cry, "I need help, man, big help."

I couldn't get over how much he looked like Casey. Only by the grace of God have my boys sidestepped the enticements and circumstances that brought this young man here. Would I want someone to pray for my son if he were in a hellish pit like this? Of course, it would be the prayer of any father, so slowly and somewhat reluctantly I turned and stepped toward the boy.

"What's your name?" I asked.

"Matt, Matt Fielding."

I put my hand on his shoulder. "Okay, Matt, I'll pray for you. I'm not a chaplain, but I know the One you're really searching for, and I'm pretty sure He's been looking for you too."

As I prayed, his grip tightened, and his head remained pressed against the iron shafts. His body began to convulse as he wept like a baby. His emotions were contagious. The chatter between cell mates and the competitive volume of televisions and radios went oddly silent in several of the cells that were on either side of us.

Taking a deep breath, and wiping away the rainstorm from my eyes, I tried to remember the prayer my pastor always said at the end of his sermons. I didn't know if they were the right words, but as closely as I could, I led Matt in a prayer, asking Jesus to forgive him and to come into his life and give him new direction and purpose.

I knew I had to do more for Matt, so to avoid his girl-friend and any number of other hurtles he had to overcome, I met him at the gate when he was released. Our first stop was to his parole officer, then to our church to attend the men's gathering scheduled that night. I introduced him around and was surprised how open and receptive the guys were toward him. You could see in his face that he was taken aback, too, but in a good way. One of the men—a contractor by trade—offered him a job doing cleanup work on his con-struction sites, and the church's benevolence fund provided a month's rent on a small studio apartment. That had been five years ago. I had been a chaplain's assistant ever since.

Matt and I kept in touch, and a year after his release, he left a message on my answering machine saying he had to talk to me right away. It was important and he needed my help. He sounded excited, and the number he left wasn't the number I had for him. I could only imagine the trouble he had gotten into.

I called the police department and asked the watch com-mander to check the booking sheets for the last forty-eight hours for a Matthew Fielding. When the answer came up negative, I called the Alameda and Contra Costa county jails, and they didn't have anything either. Whatever he did, it hadn't been done locally.

That night when I got home, I told Rosie about the call. We sat on the bed and prayed for Matt. We asked for his safety and wisdom for me in how to deal with him and his situation. With the grace of an angel, Rosie handed me the phone and gently closed the bedroom door behind her. It was a call I didn't want to make.

"Hello, Matt? This is Bob Richards. Are you okay?"

"Yeah, I'm fine. How are you? You don't sound so good."

"What's up, Matt? What's going on? You said you needed my help." I lay back on the bed with the phone at my ear. I closed my eyes, anticipating a dissertation of the trouble he had gotten himself into.

"Yes, sir, I sure do. I'm going to the courthouse next month . . ."

The word *courthouse* echoed in my ear, and I cut him off, "Courthouse? Why?" I heard my voice rising to an angry crescendo.

What had he done? Did he have a lawyer? He must have bailed out, but where did he get the money? My mind reeled with the possibilities. I had been so confident that Matt was going to make it. He seemed so committed to God and to turning his life around. A. J. used to always say, "Once a con, always a con." He could be intolerant sometimes, but I knew that wasn't how he really felt. I had seen him go out of his way on numerous occasions to help parolees.

With my voice lowered and controlled, I said, "Matt, just lay it out. What's going on?"

He could tell I was getting wired up, "Lighten up, Bob. I have a handle on this. I'm expecting to get a life sentence, but that's good with me."

"Life sentence," now my voice was really exposing my emotions. "For what?"

"Being in love, Bob. Just for being in love."

"You don't get a life sentence for being in love, and you don't get out of jail that easy either. What in heaven's name did you do?"

"It's not what I did, it's what I'm going to do, and I don't want to get out."

Confusion was now added to the emotional goulash bouncing around inside my skull. "What are you talking about?"

"Love, Bob. I'm getting married, and I want you to be my best man."

Bolting upright, "Married? What?" I was torn between chewing him out for hanging me out to dry or breaking out in tears. "Wait a minute. So, you're not in any trouble?"

"Nope, at least not yet. My future bride is a beautiful girl who keeps me walking the straight and narrow. So how about it, Bob, are you going to stand with me?"

"Your best man? Matt, I would be honored to be your best man. What day next month is the wedding?"

"It's not next month. It's in May."

"You said you were going to the courthouse?"

"Yeah, to get the license. I was wondering if afterward you and Rosie would let us take you to lunch. I want you to meet Laurie."

"You got it. Just let us know when and where."

After getting filled in on how his job was going and an assortment of other guy things, I hung up and walked into the living room, dropping my head sorrowfully. With a deep sigh, I flopped down on the sofa and covered my head with a throw pillow.

"What is it, Bob? Is it bad? Is there anything we can do?" Rosie pleaded.

I lay there under the pillow and groaned. "He said he expects to get a life sentence. From what he told me, I'm pretty sure he will." I shared a little of what Matt put me through.

The pillow slowly slipped down to my chin, and I looked into Rosie's blue-green eyes, which were filled with compassion and tears. I had definitely played this out too far, and I knew I was in trouble.

"Baby, it's okay, really. He's getting married, and he wants me to be his best man."

"Married? Are you telling me the truth?" she sniffled.

"Yes, he's doing great. I'm sorry, baby. We're going to have lunch with him and the soon-to-be Mrs. Fielding next month. It's all good."

I put my arms around her and pulled her close to me, to comfort her and to keep her fists from being free. Her punch is like getting hit with a sharp stick. It hurts.

The wedding was small and personal with just a few family members and close friends. Laurie was beautiful and Matt looked better than I had remembered. There was certainly something different about him.

Leaning over, I whispered into Rosie's ear, "Do you notice something different about Matt?"

"Yes, don't you, Mr. Policeman? Aren't you supposed to be the observant one in our house?"

I examined Matt, his polished shoes, navy blue suit, white shirt, striped tie, and . . . Wow, the tattoos below his eye and on his cheek were missing.

"Is that makeup?" I asked Rosie.

"A little, but he's been getting laser surgery to remove them. Said he doesn't what his children to see them on their dad. Isn't that wonderful?"

It sure was, and it only got better from there. Every Christmas and birthday we would get cards from him and

Laurie and a letter every few months. Matt was now a journeymen carpenter, and in training to be a site supervisor. According to his last letter, Laurie had given birth to an eight-pound, four-ounce baby boy. It was their second son. At the bottom of the letter Matt had written, "We are going to name him Bobby."

The sound of men returning to their cells after dinner drew me back to my park bench and the envelope in my hand. I looked toward heaven. "Lord, thank you for the memories. I have much to be thankful for. I needed to revisit my blessings so my heart would be in accord with yours."

I stood, took a deep breath, and headed toward the general administrative offices to get instructions from Chaplain Hays, along with a security vest and safety glasses. I also needed to deposit my watch and wedding ring for safe keeping. Then it was on to the Adjustment Center where San Quentin's notorious death row was located. I was to meet a man who was about to die. Inmate number P-68473, Mitcham, C., condemned to death for the murder of an Oakland police officer.

Mitcham earned his membership into the AC Country Club, where the most dangerous and violent felons in the state of California were housed. He had assaulted his cell mate in East Block. What had been the motive? The man snored too loudly. Mitcham now had a room of his own.

Although it was the most secure building in the state, its residents were creative and had plenty of time to devise and implement ways of causing harm. Several guards had been medically retired after being attacked with weapons made from everything from toothbrushes to Bible covers in the Adjustment Center.

The security vest was to protect me from being stabbed in the upper torso. Unfortunately, there were other vital organs that would be deprived of the benefit of a stab-proof vest. The safety glasses were to protect my eyes if I was "gassed," which is what inmates call throwing human waste into the faces of the guards. "Wow, what a great place to call home," I thought as I walked across the yard.

I had been confident that my meeting would hold no physical threat to me, but facing Mitcham again did have me emotionally on edge. I hadn't laid eyes on him since that morning in Judge Hamond's court nearly ten years ago, when he had been sentenced to death. My pace slowed as I remembered that day and the look he had on his face. He turned and glared at me, then a sardonic grin gradually formed on his face. I truly believe if I were to describe what pure evil looked like, it would be that smile on his face.

There was only one way in and one way out of the Adjustment Center. Through what is known as a "sally port." It was a chamber similar to the entry tunnel known as the "the Three Gates to Hell." There was a series of gates, with the entrance operated by a guard who I showed my ID to, along with the note I had received from the assistant warden. Just inside, a guard at a desk rechecked my ID and note, then called the warden's office to get confirmation. While this was taking place, another guard searched me thoroughly. Once I was cleared to go in, my right hand was stamped with a mark that could only be seen under a black light. It was a way of identifying those leaving the Adjustment Center as the good guys. It was referred to as my "get out of jail free card."

Once I exited the sally port, I was standing in a court-yard looking at a long, off-white, three-story building with barred windows. An overwhelming feeling of urgency rushed though me, and all I wanted to do was run. What was I doing there? I was a volunteer. This visit was requested by a murderer who had just hours to live. This was nuts!

"Are you okay, sir," asked the guard at the exit gate.

Sarcastically, I said, "Yeah, I'm fine, thanks. Just taking it all in."

I felt like my legs were encased in concrete. What was going on? Why was I so hesitant? I wasn't fearful of going into the Adjustment Center, and I was certainly not fearful of Mitcham, although it would be nice to have had a roll of quarters in my pocket.

The chaplain's words rang once again in my ears, "Bob, you may be here for just a time as this."

CHAPTER THIRTY-ONE

Crossing a short walkway from the sally port exit to the Adjustment Center's entrance, I pressed a button on the right of a large, green steel door. A voice from a small speaker above the door asked me to identify myself.

"I'm Assistant Chaplain Bob Richards. I'm here to see Curtis Mitcham."

"Stand by."

After a couple of minutes, the door swung open and a tall muscular guard with biceps about to rip his shirt sleeves extended a hand. "Good evening, Chaplain Richards. I'm Sergeant Roman. We've been expecting you. If you don't mind, would you please raise your hands high for me, sir," and once again I was given a thorough search.

Inside there were no tiers or armed catwalks like those in the other cell blocks. The Adjustment Center was made up of three individual floors with access to each via an enclosed stairwell, just wide enough to accommodate a single individual. To the right of the stairwell was Sergeant Roman's office. It was large enough to accommodate a small desk, two chairs, and a filing cabinet. On the wall behind the desk hung the headshots of a hundred inmates in the order of the cells they were housed in. I spotted Mitcham's photo immediately. He had aged some, but still had that arrogant sneer on his face.

"Mitcham has only hours left, hasn't requested any family, and from what I know of his friends, I doubt any of them would be allowed in," Sergeant Roman said. "You, sir, are the only one he said he wanted to see."

"Did he give any indication of why he wanted to see me?" I asked.

"No, sir. From what I've read, you are a lieutenant with Oakland PD, is that correct?"

"Yes."

"And you dealt with him on the street?"

"Yes."

"According to protocol, just before his execution, a condemned man has the right to have a private meeting with the spiritual counsel of his choice. If you don't mind me saying so, sir, I think it would be unwise for you to be that spiritual counsel."

"Thank you for your concern, Sergeant, but as much as I would like to, I can't pick and choose who I pray with, particularly in their last hours." I heard the words that fell from my mouth and how noble they sounded. Clearly my hypocrisy had risen to new heights and began to shine through. Curtis Mitcham was the last person I wanted to provide any comfort to. I could have rejected this meeting, and no one would have thought any less of me for it. So why was I here? Curiosity, I guess, or maybe I just wanted to stand before him and flaunt my victory as he awaited his execution.

"So where do we meet?" I asked.

"There is a holding cell converted into an interview room on this tier at the far end of the block. It has a table and two chairs. They are bolted to the floor. You will be seated in the chair closest to the entrance."

"Okay, can I bring in a Bible, that is, if you have one?"

"We normally don't have one here, but the inmate can bring one in if he wishes." Rotating in his chair, he opened the bottom drawer of the filing cabinet and withdrew a well-worn brown leather Bible. Removing a sticky note, he read it and tossed it into the trash. "Looks like Mitcham had one. I'll make sure it's in the room for your meeting."

I went to reach for it when Roman put his left hand on top of it, "Sorry, sir, I have to bring it in for you. Our protocol requires it."

"Certainly." I appreciated the high level of security.

As he picked up the Bible, the cuff of Roman's shirt lifted slightly, revealing what appeared to be a series of dark jagged tattoos, possibly lightning bolts. On the flat surface between his knuckle and the first joint of each finger was a small letter tattooed in old style script: *MISÓ*. I found that unusual because very few of the employees were adorned with tattoos because of departmental policy. I was about to comment on it when he turned to the photos on the wall.

His expression went cold, and the pleasant welcoming tone in his voice was gone, "Chaplain Richards, you are dealing with a 'B' class inmate. He is violent and unpredictable. He is in the Adjustment Center because he attacked his cell mate and put two of our guards in the hospital. I am required to let you meet him privately, which I strongly feel is unwise. The inmate has requested that a guard not be in there with you, but that's not his call. It's yours." Sitting back in his chair, shaking his head, "I wish to encourage you to rethink this, and if you intend to continue, at least allow a guard to be present with you."

"Believe me, Sergeant, I have thought long and hard about this. I'll meet him alone," I said and mumbled, "Just make sure he doesn't have a roll of quarters in his pocket."

"Quarters, sir?"

"Sorry, Sergeant, it's just a personal joke."

"Okay then, Mitcham is on third tier. We'll bring him down, but it will be a few minutes. Make yourself comfortable." Picking up the Bible and tucking it under his arm, he turned to leave. "I'll come and get you when we're ready."

Sitting alone I could hear the usual garbled sound of voices and music resonating from the cells. Closing my eyes, I took a deep breath and asked God to guide me, to speak through me, and to protect me.

Although I had some sense of peace, I still had this lingering awareness that I was about to walk into the lion's den. I had always had a premonition when things weren't going to go well. My grandmother used to say I had a third eye. Of course, everyone thought Grandma was a little wacky.

The last time I had experienced that same feeling so strongly, I was being dropped into the jungle somewhere near Tan Phu along the Mekong Delta. It was a two-week campout in the thickest, bug-infested foliage I'd ever been in. On day five I was told to participate in ambush and reconnaissance maneuvers. With my gear and rifle in hand, I joined the team just as my gut began to churn and that feeling of dread washed over me.

We began to load onto a truck when the CO, Captain Craig Rodgers, came out of his tent, saw me, and ordered me to remain behind because I was the only one who knew how to operate a bulldozer. Relieved, I went to the sergeant in charge of the team with my hunches and was, as expected, brushed off as some kind of nut case.

Three hours after they left camp, rifle fire could be heard in the distance. The CO sent out a squad of men to see what was going on and to assist in the firefight. The team that had gone out for training had set up an ambush along a trail commonly used by the Viet Cong. They were told not to fire, but to remain concealed. When a group passed by, one of the soldiers thought he would make a name for himself and took a shot.

It turned out not to be VC or enemy soldiers, but a troop of baboons. A troop is normally fifty baboons but can number as many as five hundred. They're extremely protective and fierce fighters, who work in unison to defend themselves. They attacked the soldiers with their dog-like muzzles, heavy powerful jaws, sharp canine teeth, and razor claws. They killed two of our men and seriously wounded six others.

Once again God's protective hand had overshadowed me. Maybe it had been for such a time as this. I'm no longer in the center of a bug-infested jungle, but that same unease pounded heavily in my chest. Today my jungle was not trees and bamboo, but concrete and iron bars. There were no fanged baboons, but the men who had been caged like animals for decades, many without hope.

The sound of a metal latch echoed along the corridor as a steel door leading to a stairwell at the end of the block opened. I leaned back to see Sergeant Roman stepping out, and behind him two large guards. Between them was Curtis Mitcham. He was shackled in handcuffs that were linked to leg irons. He was bent over slightly, and his movements were staggered by the restrictions. However, the way he carried himself and the attitude on his face showed the same arrogant defiance of the animal that had murdered my dear friend and colleague.

Turning back to the desk, I put my face in my hands and tried to swallow my anger. "Lord, you have to do this, I can't. I just can't."

My mind began to flush with the memory of Mitcham's threats, the bombs in my home, and the taking of my family as hostages. Once again, I was holding A. J. in a pool of blood, looking into his eyes as he took his last breath.

My emotions were conflicted. On the one hand, I wanted nothing to do with him. All I wanted to do was leave and never look back or give Mitcham another thought. On the other hand, I wanted to meet him and rub in, with as much malice as I could muster, the fact that he was about to die. It wouldn't bring A. J. back, but in some small way, it might balance the scales just a little.

I leaned back again and watched as Sergeant Roman unlocked and swung open a green door located at the end and on the opposite side of the corridor from the cells. Mitcham and the two guards disappeared inside as Roman remained at the door observing what was taking place, assuring that everything was secure.

After several minutes the guards came out, spoke to Roman quietly, then left the way they had entered, through the door leading to the stairwell.

Roman looked back down the hall at me, smiled, held up the Bible, and said in a loud voice, "Chaplain Richards, we'll be ready in just a minute." Then he went back into the room.

"Yeah, give me just a minute," I muttered. I could use more than a minute, maybe a week. Then it would be too late. Mitcham would be dead.

Closing my eyes, another voice spoke to me. It wasn't audible, but I heard it all the same. "I want to talk with him." I knew exactly whose voice that was, and exactly what was meant.

The interview room door closed with a clang and my eyes shot open as the footsteps of Sergeant Roman echoed off the cell block walls.

"Okay, we're all set. Let's go," Roman said.

Pushing my chair back, I noted that the usual chatter had ceased. The corridor had become deathly silent. I rose and followed him past a long line of what appeared to be empty cells. They were not barred like the cells in the other blocks but had large steel doors with a small slit of a window and a hatch where food trays could be passed through.

My peripheral vision caught movement in one of the windows. Slowing my pace, I looked to see if I was just imagining things, fearing I could be losing my mind. To my surprise I saw partial faces staring out at me from every cell. The thick glass slit in the door only allowed the occupant one eye with which to see out, and everyone was watching.

"Why did it get so quiet?" I asked.

"They're all condemned to die soon, and they know the next one to go is on their tier meeting the chaplain."

At the end of the corridor, I stood with my stab-proof vest and safety glasses in front of a solid steel door with an even smaller glass window above the latch. With the use of a large flat key, Roman opened the door and there sat Curtis Mitcham, in a windowless, stark white room. He was seated behind a small metal table with his hands under the table. They were cuffed and chained to the shackles on his legs.

I took a seat opposite him as the door closed with an ear-popping clunk. The air in the room was stale and tense as we sat in silence, staring at each other. A decade back I would have paid for this opportunity. To be locked in a concrete block alone with this scumbag was once my greatest wish. Now I was close enough to see that his years in prison had not been kind to him. He had aged poorly. The picture in Roman's office must have been taken years before. His hair and beard were gray, uncut, and unkempt. Several facial tattoos had been added, and his eyes expressed a ghostly absence. I felt as though I was staring into a dark and bottomless abyss.

"Okay, Mitcham, you called this meeting. What do you want?" I asked, not really caring what his answer would be.

"Aren't you going to pray for me?" he smirked. "Isn't that what you God-pushers do? Get me to confess all my sins and turn from my wicked ways?"

I said nothing and just sat there as he glared at me. This man clearly hated me as much as I hated him. I wasn't about to give any response that would show him that he was hitting a nerve. I wasn't going to allow Mitcham to get any satisfaction from this meeting, no more than he had gotten from our first encounter.

"I have a question for you." I glared. "Why me? According to your record you've met a lot of cops, and you've been busted on bigger beefs than a five-and-dime grocery store burglary."

Mitcham's nostrils flared like a bull seeing red, "You dissed me bad."

Suddenly the lines had been drawn. I had pushed the right button, and now I was in control. "You mean the wetting-your-pants thing?"

His eyes widened, as he began to shake. His neck flushed red as he was filled with irrepressible rage. I honestly had expected him to explode.

"You could have left it alone, but instead you ground it in. You wouldn't let it go, not even in front of my own, not once but over and over again." He leaned forward, getting as close to my face as he could, then he screamed, "I'm going to kill you, Richards, and everyone and everything you love!"

"That's it. I'm out of here. You want a chaplain, then call one who cares." I stood and turned to the door.

Just as I was about to bang on the door, that voice I had heard in my head earlier spoke again. "I want to talk with him."

Looking down at Mitcham as he continued to rant, I suddenly felt pity for him. I felt sorry for the life he had lived, and the life he was about to lose. I actually had compassion for this man who just moments ago I had reviled. A peace washed over me that was greater than the conflict of the moment. It captivated me and soothed my mind. I had never felt this way before.

Everything that Mitcham had done to me, to my family, even to A. J., wasn't as important as the life of this man who sat before me. Standing there as he beat on the top of the table with his fists, and cursed at me, I just felt empathy, even pity for him. How was that even possible?

I opened my mouth and with a calm, controlled voice said, "Curtis, I'm sorry that I offended you. It was wrong.

The humiliation and disrespect I showed you was not in line with the love I am to have for you."

What did I just say? I stood there dumbfounded by my own words. I said it, I heard it, and I knew it was me because it was my voice. What was even stranger was I felt and believed what I had said.

Mitcham looked at me like I had morphed into a tulip, lifted his head, and once again began to shout obscenities. It was clear that our conversation was over and that I had said what I had to say. Turning my back to him, I pounded on the door, alerting the guards that I was ready to leave. Peering through the small glass slit, I couldn't see anyone in the corridor. I banged a little louder, with no response.

Behind me I heard Mitcham shriek insanely and turned just in time to see him leap from the tabletop with his hands reaching out for me. Wrapping both arms around me, he drove my head into the concrete wall, and everything went black.

CHAPTER THIRTY-TWO

Someone was talking to me, but they sounded as though they were far away. I heard my name but couldn't make out what else they were saying.

I sat on the floor, but why? Where was I? My eyes were closed, and my nose was running. I wanted to wipe my nose, but I couldn't move my arms. They were pinned behind me, and no matter how hard I tried, I couldn't move them. A dull throbbing began in my head that slowly became a skull-splitting headache.

Shouting. Getting closer, but the pulsations in my head had drawn all my attention. I was about to throw up, but I couldn't move. The yelling continued, so I yelled back, "Shut up!" With that exclamation, an excruciating flare of pain shot through my temples like an ice pick. Oh, dear God, how that hurt.

I groaned and opened my eyes to brilliant and painful flashes of light. Squinting and blinking, I slowly took in the room around me. Coughing and spitting vomit all over myself, I struggled to draw deep breaths into my lungs.

"Oh, that's disgusting, Bobby," came a voice next to my side. "Looks like that nose of yours will never be the same again."

Tilting my head back, I looked up into the face of Curtis Mitcham who sat on a chair backward. I tried to move, but my hands were cuffed behind me, and my legs were shackled. A chain linking them together pressed into my spine. I had been propped up in the corner of the room, clad in Mitcham's restraints. Gasping, I looked down. Blood and vomit. All over me.

"Are you uncomfortable there, Bobby boy?" Mitcham snickered. "I was worried you weren't going to wake up and miss all the fun."

My head felt as though it had been split like a melon. Pain coursed from my left temple across my skull and down to my toes. "You don't plan on . . ."

"Plan to get away with this?" He laughed. "Of course not. You and I are locked in the belly of the dragon. This is San Quentin, Bobby, your final resting place. But I do have a plan. I'm going to kill two birds with one stone."

I leaned my head against the wall and tried to gather my thoughts. There was no way out of this unless the guards crashed through the door. I listened for any sound coming from the corridor. Nothing.

My words were garbled as I spit out blood and tried to breathe. "The guards will be in here any minute. The sergeant is just outside the door. He had to have heard what was going on."

"Yeah, they'll come in eventually, because I'm going to let them in. But if I were you, I wouldn't plan on the cavalry storming through that door any time soon. We have a whole hour, Bobby, that's the rules."

"This isn't going to change anything. You're to be executed in less than twenty-four hours. What's the point of this?"

"The point?" Mitcham growled. "The point is retribution. It's a reckoning, Bobby boy. It's justice being served."

"You said that you were killing two birds with one stone. I assume killing me is one of them. What's the other?"

"You're going to die, and that's bird number one. Bird number two is the American justice system coming to life. You see, Bobby, killing you will require another trial, and you can't put a murderer on trial if you've already gone and murdered him."

I stared at him, trying to make sense of what he had said. He was right, his execution would be postponed to try him for the murder of a prison chaplain.

"You forgot where you are, Bobby? This is California. The court system here is so jammed up it's going to take years to get me back into the gas chamber. Besides, there's already talk that the bleeding hearts in the government are going to abolish capital punishment."

Standing, he pushed the chair away and stood over me. With a deep-throated giggle, he kicked me in the side. I doubled over and cried out. "It's a win-win, Bobby boy. You're going to save my life, and I'm going to take yours."

The world around me spun. My mind was filled with dark clouds, and all I wanted to do was sleep. Closing my eyes, I began to drift into a place of comfort and peace. There was no pain there, no fear. Then there was that voice again. "I want to talk to him."

The water was over my head; I had waded out too far. I kept jumping up to take a breath, but each time I got a little deeper. "Help, help," I screamed, but no one heard me, no one cared. The water was in my nose, in my mouth. I couldn't breathe. I panicked. I'm only ten, I didn't want to die.

"Wake up, Bobby." Mitcham poured water over my head. "You aren't going to sleep through this. Wake up."

I wasn't at the lake with my dad. I was in a holding cell with the devil. For a few terrifying moments I had returned to Lake Comanche where my stepfather had tossed me in. He believed that it was the only way I would learn how to swim. The fear that overwhelmed me in that lake was as tangible now as it was then.

But strangely, as my mind cleared and I took stock of my present situation, I realized that I had no fear. I should be as frightened as I was in that lake because I was facing death, but I wasn't, not really. I was in God's hands, not in Mitcham's grip, and I knew it with absolute certainty.

Taking as deep a breath as I could, I calmly said, "Curtis, I told you that I am sorry for offending you. I know that it was wrong and that it goes against the love that God wants me to have for you."

Stepping back, he glared at me. "Love? Give it a rest. I don't need to hear any of that crap. Don't forget, buddy, I'm the one that's going to kill ya."

"I know." I looked him in the eye. "God's been telling me that He wants to talk to you."

"Oh, really? I suppose He's going to tell me something from His book about how I should live." He laughed. "Does He want me to read 'His Word'?" He sneered and lifted up two fingers on each hand gesturing quotation marks.

"I don't know how He is going to talk to you. I just know He wants to."

Picking up the old, worn brown Bible that Sergeant Roman had brought in, Mitcham held it in front of my face.

"Is this the book God sent me? Is what I'm supposed to do in here?"

"I'm pretty sure it would be."

"Well, good, then let's just see what your God wants me to do." He snickered.

Pulling the chair up next to me, he sat and slowly opened the cover. "I don't see no instructions here. Let's just keep looking." He giggled and thumbed through a few more pages.

Sitting back, he crossed his legs, glared at me, and put the Bible on his lap. Rapidly flipping pages, he stopped and looked up at me, his eyes widened, and his mouth fell open. "Well, what do you know? I think I've just been told what to do."

Lifting the Bible up, he turned it around so I could see the pages. In the center a rectangular hole had been carved out and in it was a shiv. Slowly he took it out and examined it. "Mighty fine workmanship, even if I do say so myself."

He held up the six-inch dagger, with razor-sharp edges and a gray handle made of duct tape. "This had once been a soup can. Now it is a scalpel. How creative." He giggled.

He put the blade against my cheek and pressed it just hard enough to cut into my skin. Blood ran down the side of my face.

"Looks like God wants me to do a little carving on ya, Bobby boy."

"Curtis, I want you to know something, and I want to say it while I still can. I forgive you for what you're about to do. I don't know what brought you to this place in your life, but I'm not going to leave this life with hatred in my heart. I forgive you."

Rage flashed across his face. "Forgive me! Who the hell are you to forgive me!" he screamed, and slashed at my face, opening a gash just below my right ear. Blood splattered in every direction. He backed away with a sardonic smile and watched me wince.

"Still forgive me now?" he snarled.

I looked up at him and knew that what I was about to say wasn't me, "Yes, I forgive you. There is nothing you will do to me that was not done to Jesus. He was tortured and died for you too."

He tossed the chair out of his way, rushed toward me, and put the knife to my throat. "You're going to die now, Richards!" he shouted.

Looking up at him, I said gently, "I know."

Staring down at me with that evil grin, he didn't move. It was as if time had stood still. I looked into his eyes and waited to feel a sharp prick along my jugular vein, signaling the end of this life.

My mind was no longer racing, seeking a route of escape. I wasn't looking for a way out or listening for the sound of rescuers at the door. There was no fear, because I knew that my life was in God's hands, and for the first time in my life, I chose to totally and absolutely trust Him, and only Him. I was completely at peace.

I asked God to protect Rosie and the boys and prayed they wouldn't hate this man. Then I prayed for Curtis Mitcham because he had no idea what he was about to do.

He growled, "You ready to die, Bobby?"

In a low controlled tone, I said, "No, I'm not. I have a family, children, and grandchildren I haven't met yet. I don't want to die any more than you do. However, if this is the Lord's will for me, then I'm ready to meet Him."

I never paid much attention before, but his eyes were dark, like pools of ink. If they were the window to his soul, then his soul was a very dark place.

"Does your God have anything to say to me now before I send you to him?"

"Yes, He does, but are you willing to listen?"

"Sure." He smirked. "Go ahead, but make it quick, I have some carving to do before the Quentin boys come through that door."

"God knows the pain and the sorrow you have lived through, and He knows the destruction and grief you have caused. That's all done now, Curtis. Your life is coming to an end. No one on this earth will weep for you because of what you have done, but God will. He gave you life and you have squandered it. He has seen your tears and heard your cries, but when He reached out to you, you rejected Him."

Leaning so close our noses almost touched, he whispered, "That's enough."

"God is giving you a second chance."

"I said that's enough."

"There's a man in the Bible who was in prison for murder and was awaiting execution. He, like you, had but hours to live. There was a prisoner exchange, and he went free. In his place they executed an innocent man. The condemned prisoner's name was Barabbas."

Mitcham leaned back. "I've heard that name before, maybe when I was a kid. There was an old lady in one of the foster homes that made me go to Sunday school. What a waste of time."

"Was it?"

"You think you can talk your way out of this, do ya?"

"No, I don't. There's a part of me that relishes the idea of you strapped in that chair in the pale green octagon, as it fills with hydrogen cyanide. But there's a bigger part of me that I never knew existed until about six years ago."

"I suppose you're going to tell me it was Jesus that brought you this new enlightenment. Well, where's your Jesus now?" Curtis said in a mocking and condescending tone, "Things aren't looking too bright for you, Bobby boy."

"You're right. It was Jesus, and He's here with me now."

Jumping up, Mitcham looked around the room. "Where is He? I don't see Him. He must be hiding. I think I scared Him." Curtis laughed.

Softly, I said, "I think He's scaring you. I never knew what freedom was until I asked him to come into my life." A long silence fell over the room. "He loves you, too, and whatever you do to me doesn't matter. He still loves you."

He turned away, and after several minutes when he looked back, I could see the fury in his eyes had faded slightly, and his face had softened.

"Do you think he could forgive a guy like me?" He chuckled. "I doubt it."

"He loved Barabbas, and He gave His life for him. He loves you, Curtis, and two thousand years ago He died on a cross so you could be set free. He saw you then and He sees you now. He wept for you then and He weeps for you now."

Taking the chair, he pulled it next to me and sat. He still gripped the knife tightly in his hand. "What am I supposed to do?"

"God has given us the greatest gift, and the most dangerous. It is free will, the right to choose. Jesus won't come into your heart without an invitation. Acknowledge that you're a sinner, as we all are, and ask Him for forgiveness."

Sitting back, he tilted his head inquisitively. "That's it? There's nothing more I have to do to get this freedom?"

"That's it. Jesus has already done the heavy lifting by dying on the cross as the sacrifice for your sins. All you need to do is believe it and commit your life to him. Although He is already Lord, now you must make Him Lord of your life. Do you want me to pray for you?"

"Yeah," he said quietly, bowing his head. A tear ran down his face. And mine.

We prayed for several minutes, asking the Lord for forgiveness and to come into our lives and take control. When I said "amen" the knife fell to the floor at his side.

He pushed the chair back, dropped to his knees with his face in his hands, and wept. God was talking to him, face-to-face.

I sat quietly waiting to see what God would do next. It wasn't a time for conversation but for reconciliation. The devil was no longer in the room.

The door swung open, and one of the guards who had brought Curtis down and put him into the interview room stepped in. He looked around the room and hit a red button on the wall near the door. Sirens went off outside, and a mechanical-sounding voice squawked, "Code red, Adjustment Center. Code red, Adjustment Center."

Moving quickly, he seized Mitcham, pushed him face down on the floor, and handcuffed him without resistance.

"What the hell is going on in here?" the guard said.

"Hell doesn't have anything to do with it anymore."

The guard's attention turned to me. "Okay, sir, take it easy." He gently pulled me away from the wall and unlocked my restraints.

He opened a pouch on his belt, removed a medical face-mask, folded it so the soft side was exposed, and gently placed it over the gash on my face. "Put a little pressure on that to stop the bleeding. The medical team is on the way, and we'll get you to the hospital."

The second guard who had escorted Mitcham appeared at the door out of breath. "What happened in here? Where's Sergeant Roman? He was supposed to be outside monitoring this."

"I don't know. Wherever he is, his butt's in a sling," the first guard said and lifted me to my feet. "Medical should be showing up any time now. Walk the chaplain down to Roman's office. They'll meet you there. I'll take care of Mitcham."

"Sir, can I talk to him for just a moment, please?"

The guards looked at each other and at me as though I had lost my mind. "Sure, why not," one said.

I walked over, slowly knelt, and leaned to Curtis's face. "Curtis, you have heard from God. Put your life in his hands, and he will walk with you now. It's His peace you are feeling. You are in his presence. Regardless of what lies ahead, you belong to Him now."

Mitcham twisted around so he could look up at me. He shifted and stretched his arms as far as he could so his hands could touch mine. Without a word he smiled at me. It wasn't the smirk of contempt that I had always seen on him before, but a real smile, a smile of hope, maybe for the first time in his life.

I reached down and touched his hand and noticed something I had never paid much attention to before. On the flat surface between his knuckle and the first joint of each finger was a small letter tattooed in old style script: *MISÓ*. The Greek word for "hate."

CHAPTER THIRTY-THREE

"Curtis," one of the guards said, "I need to know, is Sergeant Roman a member of the Savages? He's the one who unshackled you, isn't he?"

Mitcham closed his eyes and nodded. I looked back at the guards. "Did you get that?"

"Yes, sir, we did."

Several more guards rushed in, lifted Mitcham to his feet, and ushered him out.

"Take it easy with him, okay. He's got enough to face tomorrow."

I spent the night in the hospital getting stitched up and checked out. I had a slight concussion, but nothing traumatic, a broken nose, and two broken ribs. The doctor said they would heal, but my Greek profile might be a bit flawed. A plastic surgeon was called in who added eighteen stiches to my face. He told me I would look like Al Capone's doppelganger for a while, but in time it would fade. I think it will add a little character.

Rosie stayed with me most of the night, but I sent her home at 4:00 a.m. when she woke up in pain trying to sleep in a wooden chair.

At 6:00 a.m., breakfast was served, and I had the luxury of sucking mine through a straw. When breakfast showed up, so did Warden Kilpatrick.

"Chaplain Richards, may I come in?"

"Yes, sir."

"I understand you will pull through well and will be discharged this afternoon."

"Yes, I've been in good hands. As always, the Lord has been watching over me."

"I wanted to come and tell you personally what's been going on. A lot has happened in the last eleven hours. It appears that Sergeant Roman is the one who released Mitcham from his restraints just before you were taken into the interview room. He dismissed the guards and said he would take the responsibility of monitoring you during your time with Mitcham. He is also responsible for arming Mitcham with a knife he had stolen from the evidence room. It was used in an inmate stabbing two months ago."

Pulling a chair up next to the bed, he went on, "His motive was his loyalty to the Savages motorcycle club. He is a committed charter member and one of its founders. He and Mitcham were placed in the same foster home when they were kids, along with five others. He sees Mitcham like a brother."

I took a sip of breakfast and grimaced.

Kilpatrick leaned in and lowered his voice. "The FBI has been called in to assist our investigation, and late last night they served a search warrant on Roman's home. We have evidence that Roman is the key player in a smuggling ring bringing drugs, weapons, and contraband into and out of the prison."

"Is he in custody?"

"No, he's in hiding. According to the guard at the main gate, he was seen driving away ten minutes before the Code Red alarm went off." Kilpatrick leaned back. "The Feds will catch up with him. They already have a few leads. Unfortunately, we believe when the dust settles, we may have as many as fifteen of our employees in custody."

"How about Mitcham's execution? It's set for tonight."

"The only word we got from the DA is it's still a go. It's being taken to the courts by a truckload of lawyers on both sides. The odds are nothing's going to change. Disruptions aren't uncommon before an execution."

"If that's the case, then I would like to see him."

He examined me intently. "I don't know, Richards. That didn't work out too well last time. I'm coming up for an annual review, and I sure don't need a lot of bad press if you were to get hurt again."

"It's different this time. Roman's not around and I believe the Mitcham we knew isn't there either. He's entitled to have spiritual support in his last hour. Ask him if he'll see me."

Kilpatrick stood and looked down at me. "I have to get back to work. Let me think about it a bit and I'll let you know."

At eight o'clock Rosie and my son Casey came to take me home. Dr. Charles Laporte gave me the once-over and cleared me to be released but was hesitant to allow me to return to work. I was about to put up an argument when Cadet James Kilpatrick appeared at the door.

After introductions, I said, "What can I do for you, Cadet?"

"Sir, I have been sent to inform you that condemned inmate Curtis Mitcham has requested you to be his spiritual advisor and that Warden Kilpatrick has approved his request and yours to speak with him before his execution."

"That's good news. Please thank the warden for me." I felt the nasty glares from Rosie and the doctor.

"I hope . . ." the cadet's voice trailed off when he saw the look on Rosie's face. "I hope you get better soon." He turned and disappeared out the door.

"You are not thinking of going to see that man again, are you?" Rosie crossed her arms.

Dr. Laporte frowned. "I don't advise you to do anything more than go home and get some rest. Your injuries aren't life threating, but they are serious."

"I will, I promise, but please hear me out. This man is going to be put to death at nine tonight and I believe something very special has happened."

For the next fifteen minutes, I shared what took place and how I believed God had intervened, not only to save my life but to change that of Curtis Mitcham. Reluctantly Dr. Laporte agreed so long as all I did was talk, and as little of that as possible. Rosie, on the other hand, wasn't as amenable.

"I understand, Bob, but you have to be out of your mind to get back into the ring with a bull that has already gored you." She kissed me on my good cheek. "First, we're going to take you home to get cleaned up. Then I'll take you to the prison. I'm going to wait for you in the parking lot. You come home with me tonight, Bobby, you promise me that."

"I promise, I'll come home with you tonight."

Mitcham had been moved to a holding cell about a hundred feet from the execution chamber. It was much larger than a standard cell to accommodate family members who came to visit with the condemned man. There was a small table with bottles of water on it, four chairs, and a leather sofa. Mitcham sat alone on the sofa.

"Curtis." I stood at the gate.

A tall, thin guard stepped to my side. Behind him stood two more guards. "Chaplain Richards, I recommend that he be cuffed and shackled, sir."

"No, that won't be necessary."

Looking at my bandages, the guard shook his head. "Okay, sir." He unlocked the gate.

I stepped inside, and a chill ran through my soul when I heard the gate shut and the lock click.

Mitcham rose slowly from the sofa, looked me over, and stepped toward me with his hand out. "You've got a lot of balls, Richards. Thank you for coming."

We shook hands and my mind flashed on holding A. J. in my arms as his life drifted away. The hand I held was the one that pulled the trigger. What am I doing here?

Letting go of my hand, Curtis walked over to the table. "Come and sit. What's your take on capital punishment, Bob. I'm just curious."

"Do I believe that there are men who deserve it? Yes, I do, but only those without sin should cast the first stone. Since none of us have been successful at avoiding sin, I suppose we might want to look for another alternative."

"So, you don't believe in it?"

"I didn't say that."

"Well, it certainly stops a killer from killing again, doesn't it?" Mitcham chuckled.

"Yeah, but beyond that it's not much of a deterrent. While you're being put to death, someone out there is being killed by someone who isn't taking the consequences of their actions into account."

Lowering his head, he folded his hands on the top of the table. "I need to do something, something I did once when I was a kid, but never since. Saw no point in it until now."

Lifting his eyes, he looked at me with an expression of true sorrow. "I'm sorry, Richards, I'm sorry for what I have done to you and your family. I'm sorry for killing that cop, and for all the crap I have done to hurt so many." Tears ran down his cheeks. "I'm so sorry. I'm sorry."

I said nothing because it wasn't a time for words. I sat there while he wept with his head buried in his arms. His body convulsed as though he was in extreme pain. He just kept repeating, "I'm sorry, so very sorry," over and over.

After several minutes, he regained his composure, and we talked about his family who had abandoned him at an early age, a wife who had run away because of his abuse, and children he had never seen. Then we talked about God.

At 8:45 p.m., Warden Kilpatrick, Chaplain Hays, and three guards appeared at the gate.

"It's time, Curtis," Warden Kilpatrick said as the gate opened.

We stood. "Do you want me to go with you?"

"Yes, please," Curtis said.

Our procession was short and quick. I stood by the door of the chamber as Mitcham was ushered in. They strapped him into the chair, attached electrodes to his chest, and

Warden Kilpatrick read the death warrant while Chaplain Hays prayed.

"Curtis James Mitcham, do you have any last words to say?"

Looking out though the glass at the spectators, none of whom he knew, he said, "I'm sorry for what I have done to you and to those you loved."

Turning back to the open door of the chamber, he stretched to look around the warden who quickly stepped aside. "Richards, thank you. For the first time in my life, I'm going home. Thank you."

A guard moved to his side with a black hood. Curtis shook his head. "No, no, don't cover my head, please. I've always been afraid of the dark."

The guard looked to Warden Kilpatrick, who nodded.

The chamber was sealed, and I moved around to an observation window. Mitcham spotted me and gave me a thumbs-up. Everyone sat quietly waiting for the anticipated ringing of the red phone on the wall that would postpone Curtis's execution. It did not come.

Warden Kilpatrick turned to someone we could not see behind the chamber and nodded. The room went silent, and only the sound of a sharp click could be heard as a bag of sodium cyanide dropped into a pail of sulfuric acid below the chair.

Curtis stiffened and took a deep breath. A light blue-green mist rose from the floor around Curtis's feet and filled the chamber. His hands clutched into fists, then he looked out at me and gave me another thumbs-up. Exhaling, he smiled, closed his eyes, and inhaled deeply. His body tightened and jerked violently. After several seconds he slowly relaxed and went limp. The prison doctor standing just outside the chamber monitored the reading of the electrocardiogram.

At 9:11 p.m., Curtis was pronounced dead. Curtis James Mitcham had finally gone home.

In the cool night breeze, I repeated a ritual I performed each time I entered and left the formidable walls of San Quentin prison. At the water's edge I took a deep breath of salt air, looked toward heaven, and asked God for wisdom, words, and protection.

Tonight, I stood in awe of God's grace, knowing that there was no one out of His reach or unworthy of His love. No sin, no matter how great, could dwarf the compassion of God's heart for each of His creation. Nor could our conduct overshadow how far He would go to retrieve those He loves.

Rosie told me that she sat quietly praying, waiting for me to return. She had been there for nearly four hours, sitting in the dark talking to God. At the bottom of the steps to the parking lot I could see her silhouette through the side windows.

Walking to the car, I heard the chants and shouts of the demonstrators at the main gate. Their presence was expected. They rolled out every time there was an execution. Both sides of the death penalty issue were well represented, and their voices were heard. Neither side actually won any points because neither side could be understood through the screams and shouts.

Behind me was the constant thunder of voices echoing off the concrete walls of the cell blocks. In front of me was the hysterical banter of opposing views battling for supremacy through screeching bullhorns.

I opened the door and slid into the seat next to Rosie. When the door closed, a welcome stillness took over. We sat silently in the darkness. There was an awareness that took place between my wife and me. There were times we just knew that there was nothing to say, not then, maybe later. Now was a time to just be in each other's presence. Having her at my side made all the difference in the world. Tomorrow would be another day.

Sliding next to me, Rosie slipped her left arm under mine and took my hand. Putting her head on my shoulder, we sat and allowed the oneness of our lives to settle in around us. We remained in the dark for nearly half an hour listening to the muffled sounds of protest in the distance.

"Are you ready to go, Bobby?" Rosie whispered.

"Yeah, I guess it's time."

I started the car as Rosie took her shirtsleeve and wiped away a tear that had run down my cheek.

Turning to her, I said, "Can you believe it, I'm crying over a man who was my enemy. I should be pleased with what happened today, but I'm not. I'm just sad."

She said nothing. She didn't need to. Leaning over she wiped away another tear and kissed my cheek.

We drove out of the parking lot slowly and through the main gate, being quickly surrounded by a horde of demonstrators yelling and holding up signs. On one side were those who vehemently condemned Mitcham's execution, demanding that the death penalty be abolished. On the other side were those celebrating Mitcham's death, shouting that more condemned inmates needed to be put to death. Scattered throughout the crowd on both sides were small groups with their heads bowed, holding hands and praying.

Once we cleared the crowd and were a block away, I pulled over to the side of the road and watched the mob in my rearview mirror. They chanted their tirades and waved their elaborate posters high above their heads as if their challenging words and actions would sway the position of their respective opposition.

As I watched them silently, I wondered what side of the street would I be standing on? I believe I know the answer to that question, but there are others like it, that I still need to work out. I'm confident that the Lord is not finished with me yet, and no matter what life brings my way, I will choose to trust Him.

I felt Rosie's soft, gentle hand on mine as she leaned over and again kissed my cheek. Then putting her head on my shoulder, she whispered, "Bobby, let's go home."